YOUR PRESENCE IS REQUESTED.

BY MICHAEL WOJOWNIK

Acknowledgements

I would like to thank my family and friends for all the support they've given me in the creation of this book. They've kept me sane and focused throughout the journey of putting my thoughts to paper. I'd like to thank my coaches and therapists who have helped me personally and professionally and who have stayed by my side through thick and thin. Now it's my turn to shine a light on those who are struggling that no one knows about or what they can't talk about.

I'd also like to thank Tristan specifically for his help with this book and for outlining the story. The meetings at the coffee shops and local breweries and his advice to me were invaluable.

TABLE OF CONTENTS:

PREFACE

As many citizens have identified, the criminal justice system within the United States and beyond is broken, and I agree. This is an issue important to me, and I will donate part of the proceeds of this book to causes that help revamp the Criminal Justice System and help those affected by the system get back on their feet.

I'm a first-generation Immigrant who has found his way to Park City, UT. I love the mountains and the endless skiing, snowboarding, and hiking that are so accessible from my backyard, not to mention the international community that descends here throughout the year, adding to the culture.

I've traveled all over the United States and the World. With over a decade of experience in sales and a decade of bartending, I've pulled from life experiences to write this compelling thriller with slivers of truth.

18th September, 2024

Park City, UT

Michael Wojownik

PROLOGUE

"Writing a book is an adventure. To begin with, it is a toy and an amusement. Then it becomes a mistress, then it becomes a master, then it becomes a tyrant. The last phase is that just as you are about to be reconciled to your servitude, you kill the monster and fling him to the public."

-   Winston Churchill

I entered the Beer Crew Pub on a snowy day in February. I'd just sped down the off-ramp in a rush. I was late; it was cold, and I was panicking. I'd hastily thrown on a snow cap and a winter coat I had in my car just so I could make it to the other side of the street. I was sprinting across from where I'd parked – there was ice on the roads, but I'd take the risk today.

The pub was tall and thin, an older piece of architecture sitting right in the heart of Salt Lake City next to a bunch of modern apartment buildings. Non-locals might have scoffed at their attempts to bring a pub to the most infamously dry state in the U.S., but if they'd seen the crowd that night, they'd reconsider. I looked around the room – I didn't see Hal.

Dan's eyes turned from the bar to me as the door creaked shut. I had known him for years as the owner of the pub, and we'd shared plenty of drinks together in the long, wintry Utah months. He was a good, jovial, brown-bearded, gray-haired hipster guy, crazy about beer, and the kind of guy that wore hiking shoes, Levis, and a beer t-shirt no matter the weather. At 5'11", he was tall enough to see me over his customer base. He gave me a quick wave and ushered me in over the commotion of his customers and televisions.

"Hey Edward, stop letting in the cold air! It's gonna freeze in here!"

I shuffled in, head hunched over my body from the cold and from the news I'd received that day. Dan's friendly demeanor towards me turned to concern when he saw the panic in my eyes and my less-than-cheerful entrance. My face must've looked extra pale that day.

"Hey, what's going on? You look like a shit-storm hit you."

I took off my cap and attempted to warm my beard. I wish I had time to talk with him today, but I couldn't beat around the bush. Any other day, maybe, but not today. I took off my cap and leaned on the bar. "Dan, I need your help. You got somewhere private Hal and I can talk, like downstairs? I really need the privacy."

Dan looked shocked. "Well, um, sure," he stuttered. "Are you sure you can't just use a booth?"

I looked around. I didn't want Dan to be suspicious of me, but I couldn't tell him or the bar patrons what was going on. Dan and I had built up camaraderie, but he'd already noticed that I wasn't feeling like myself. I knew it was a bit too much to ask for during the post-work rush. Whatever a booth would have to do.

"Sure. Fine, uhh, Hal!" I waved across the bar, still desperately looking for Hal among the faces along the crowded bar. Suddenly, a hand shot up, and a head poked out that I recognized.

Hal smiled warmly. "Hey, Edward! You're late!"

Hal was an old friend from the time when I was working at Samurai Brewing. We'd never known each other particularly well when I worked for him – his territory was San Francisco, and mine varied from week to week. He technically worked for me, but it never felt like it. I didn't have to keep tabs on him, but we were always busy when we were out in the market. After leaving the brewery I'd reconnected with him, at least to watch sports and chat every once in a while. The Beer Crew Pub was our usual stomping grounds as well, giving me no excuse as to why I was late that day.

Hal's brown hair was thinning, but he had a good face. He wore a beard sometimes and not others, looked Irish although he was German, and had an ear-to-ear grin that always greeted me whenever I entered the bar. The years had been nice to our friendship. I was worried today would change everything.

I pushed myself off the bar and walked over to where Hal was sitting. He was drinking a Templin Family Brewing Ferda today, a local double IPA that hit long and hard. He was always drinking IPAs. I didn't take my own seat as I approached him. "Hey, uh, listen. Can we move to the booth? I need to talk about something with you."

Much like Dan, Hal looked concerned and confused. I guess I was just that bad at hiding my panic. I wasn't scared, but I needed someone to talk to, someone I could trust.

Hal stuttered a second. "No, uh… no, sure. That's fine. After you."

As we walked towards the booth, the conversations at the bar faded into the background. Still loud, mind you, but just quiet enough that Hal and I could talk so we could hear each other, and nobody would hear us.

"Yeah, man, you look terrible. What's going on?"

"Tell me about your day first. I need to hear some good news."

"Well, I don't know. Still looking out for my kids. Max is doing hockey every week. Still trying to get my brewpub up and running. Haven't had a ton of time to relax or explore the outdoors, hit the slopes, you know how it is, right?"

"Yeah, yeah, I get that. That's perfect."

An awkward silence. I needed to just tell him. God damn it.

I put my cap on the table and started spewing information. "Some investigators for the Utah police have been hounding me for weeks now, and I didn't know what it was about, right? They were being shifty, and they wouldn't be straight, and they told me that I needed to confess information to them and that I called them when they called me, and so after, I got a call from Mantiss, right? And they tell me"

"Alright, alright, slow down. Slow down. What did they want? It might have just been someone you know in trouble. Do you know that it's about you?"

"Hal…" I paused, looking for any other way to phrase what I was about to say. "I'm under employment investigation. Mantiss Analytics is investigating me for sexual assault."

Fuck. Hal looked at me like I'd just told him there was a bomb in the pub. I felt sick even telling someone. I hadn't even told him that I'd just gotten the call from Mantiss's offices to grab my shit and leave. There was so much neither of us knew at the time.

I felt the uphill battle being laid out before me just from Hal's reactions, and I couldn't blame him. I don't know how I'd have reacted to the situation either, and I could barely keep myself together in the moment. I didn't know how long the investigation would last, and I didn't know what tribulations awaited me. All I could do was sit at this booth and wait to see if Hal would stand up and walk out of the pub right then and there or if he would help me at that moment. I don't know which option I would have chosen.

CHAPTER 1

New Year's Eve, several years ago, was when I probably should have figured something was wrong. I still don't think anybody would have known what would happen. I didn't even have a job at Mantiss yet, for Christ's sake.

I stood outside Thomas' condo in much the same style of getup as I did for Beer Crew, bundled head to toe in three layers. Even though the condo was warm on the inside, the pathway to it was entirely outdoors. I was freezing. Thomas had told me to dress for the occasion so I had a sports coat on underneath as well. I didn't usually put anything in my hair, but I'd tried to make the natural black stand out today. Despite all this, I was still feeling the temperature.

I knocked. "One sec!" I heard from the inside.

Figured. Nobody knows how long a second is. I braced for the cold.

Thomas had been trying to hire me at his tech startup, Mantiss Analytics, for about six months at this point. I'd been doing sales at Samurai Brewing for several years, working myself to the bone, flying to multiple states each week. I'd been living out of my suitcase and was pretty much at my wit's end. It had been lucrative but horrifically rough. Last month, I'd finally caved and agreed to do an interview with Mantiss to escape my manic schedule. He'd heard me brag about how well my sales team was doing, and it was obvious he wanted me on his team instead.

He was trying to be sneaky about dropping hints. We'd be carpooling to an event or sitting down at a bar, not worried about work at all, and he'd bring up his jacket or something similar. He'd tell me that he's "Making three-quarters of a billion dollars tripping on his dick while Cary," his business partner and co-CEO, "had already made one billion." I'd noticed that he was bragging about his wealth and the "opportunities" at Mantiss a lot more in the past four months than he ever did before he saw me as a possible recruit.

Thomas had excitedly told me that before the interview, he'd want me to meet everyone I'd be working with at Mantiss's annual New Year's Party. I wasn't sure if I wanted to even show up – I'd still basically be a black sheep at the place. Even though it was just a startup, Thomas was already in the money from a previous venture he'd cooked up with Cary. Everybody at the party was going to be tech-bros and tech-lasses that were hired from their friend group and that tech company they'd sold for billions of dollars. But I didn't have anything planned and I did want the job, so I agreed. If it ended up being me just sitting in the corner getting drunk by myself, I could handle that.

CHAPTER 2

He said we'd meet at his condo near City Creek. The party was at Cary's house, but we'd be pregaming at his pad, then heading to Beer Crew with one of the heads of sales at Mantiss Analytics. After that, we'd go to the party, have a few drinks, and then crash at our respective homes. We'd planned this, I was on time, and yet here I was, being punished for being punctual.

Finally, Thomas opened the door. "Edward! How are you doing?"

"Great, man. How are you holding up?"

"Better! Better. Come on, get on in here. It must be freezing out there."

"Don't have to tell me twice, Jesus."

I scrambled into his condo and took off my snow cap. I hadn't been in his condo too many times, but of course, it was nice and upscale, with marble on the fireplace and an open floor plan – he was a tech co-CEO. Nothing these guys owned was modest.

Thomas was already dressed up for the occasion – a sports coat as well, slacks, and some shoes I'm sure he'd tell you all about if you asked him. He was always a tad overweight – 200 pounds at 5'5", and usually wore something a lot more casual, but the sports coat was hiding it all well. He had his black hair slicked back for the occasion that matched his beard. It was an open secret that both were dyed. His piercing blue eyes always immediately grabbed your attention. He immediately ran to the kitchen-bar separator and started pulling out drinks. "Vodka Soda, Ed?"

"Nah, I'm good, man."

Thomas immediately started shaking up a vodka soda for himself. No quip, like "more for me," he just started making it. I guess that's what it took to be a billionaire in the tech world.

"I'm really glad you decided to come to the party tonight."

"Oh, no problem, no problem. Excited to see what all this tech hubbub is all about."

That wasn't strictly a lie. Another strange element that was occurring in Utah counterculture was the rise of a bunch of modern tech companies. The sell-off of Thomas' previous company had brought a bunch of big names from the tech world to the barren, religious deserts of Utah – perfect in both looks and price to create a new Silicon Valley for a fraction of the cost. It was impossible to read local news and not hear about the unfathomable amounts of money that was pouring into the Mormon parts of town from California and

New York. Even if I didn't get the job I did want to see what that publicity had bought Thomas and his friends.

Thomas laughed at my comment. "Hubbub? Yeah, I guess you could call it that."

"What, is it worse? Better than that?"

"I don't know, you know, it's just business, always a shit show. I see everything from the inside. Everybody's got their eye on us, everybody's competing over the same clients, it's a tough time out there right now. You gotta keep everything under control, you know?"

"Well, you know, sounds crazy, but it is what it is."

Thomas downed some more Vodka Soda. "It's stressful, is what it is. But that's why we're scouting out people like you. People with skill, with results."

"No, yeah. I know you want me to do sales, and I'm down to. Anything'd be better than what Samurai's doing to me."

Thomas leaned over the bar separating us. "Listen, it's important, but this isn't something you're doing for me. You've already been a great friend, more than I could ever ask for. You've helped me through dark times, man, and I want to pay you back. You've done the hard work at Samurai, you're quick on your feet, and you even got us into the Beer Crew tonight. All of this partying and shadowing stuff –

don't worry about the crowd. Think of it more like meeting my friends. I can look out for the people who've helped me. Let me do that."

I backed away a bit, simply wanting some space. "But you're sure it'll be different?"

He smirked. "It'll be easier, I promise."

I'd only known Thomas from after he'd started Mantiss – we were mostly drinking friends beforehand, but he'd always been one of the elites. He'd talked about his upbringing and how proud he was of going from welfare to a billionaire plenty of times, and while I wasn't exactly in the same situation, I could sympathize. I'd worked my way from the poor kid in England to a busy but stable salesman, and I'd talked about it plenty of times, too.

Thomas pushed himself off the table and took another sip of alcohol. "Alright, enough of that," he said, "You ready to go?"

"Sure, you're driving, right?"

Thomas smirked again and pulled out the keys to his Tesla.

CHAPTER 3

The air outside hit my face fast as we stepped out of the car and entered the Beer Crew. Dan was there, tending the bar as always, but he greeted us with purpose today.

"Hey, Edward! Thomas, I presume?"

"Yeah!" Thomas went over and gave Dan a gripping handshake. Dan returned in kind.

Thomas gestured to a blond man dressed in a blazer and slacks drinking a julep at the bar. He was of average build, similar to Thomas in weight, probably 6 inches taller than him, but his wavy hair was slicked back, and he had a fairly distinct jawline despite everything. You could tell he worked out a bit more than Thomas just from his attire. He couldn't have been older than 40. "That's Terrance over there. He's our Chief Revenue Officer. If you get the position, he'll be your boss. Worked for us since the olden days."

"The last company?"

"Yeah, Protract."

Oh, I was meeting my future manager. And he'd been working for Thomas since the Protract days. All my nightmares were coming true at once.

Thomas then looked at me and started to roll his hand, darting his eyes in Terrance's direction. He wanted *me* to greet him? I looked over at Terrance. He hadn't even noticed us yet. Okay, I guess if Thomas *wanted* me to.

I walked up and stood up straight, trying to look my best. "Are you Terrance?

Terrance looked back up at me with brown and bright eyes and immediately lit up. I guess Thomas had told him about me.

"Uhh, nice to meet you, man! I'm Edward, with Thomas tonight?"

"Oh, yeah! Nice to meet you, man. Bitch of a day outside, right?"

Ah, okay. I'd been around executives and CEOs before, so this wasn't new, but it was a relief. My previous boss at Samurai, Hal, was totally this kind of guy too. They all want to be the "Cool" guys at the party, given that they feel like they're rapidly losing it due to their seriousness and age. I didn't mind. It took a load off of me.

I pushed my way back to Dan and Thomas with Terrance in tow behind me. I yelled to try to get Dan's attention. "HEY!"

Dan looked over. I smiled. "You ready to head downstairs?"

"Yeah, yeah! Glad to have the stars of the show here tonight. Hopefully, everything's fancy enough for you."

Dan kept a treasure trove down in the basement – a real classy man cave decorated to the brim with glass and wood. Along with some plush leather armchairs and a pool table, Dan had a collection of some of the nicest bourbons and cigars you could find anywhere in the world. As we descended, I heard Thomas and Terrance's awestruck voices.

Thomas noticed the collection first. "Is that a Hirsch from… 1974? No shit!"

Dan always loved talking about his travels and how high-class his collection was, but you could tell from the way they talked and dressed that these tech guys already knew. We poured ourselves some drinks, grabbed some cigars, and took seats in the chairs Dan had picked out for the room.

Terrance lifted a glass of Blanton's and swirled it around. He turned to me. "So, you used to work here, huh?"

I leaned back in my chair. "Yeah, as a bartender before I worked at Samurai. You think Dan would have let us in if I were a stranger?"

Dan chimed in. "We'd go down there and swap stories all the time when we were, what, five years younger? Six?"

"Yeah, crazy to think how short it's been."

"It's felt like an eternity for me, but Edward here's been working his ass off, climbing his way up. Probably completely forgot about this room, huh?"

I laughed. "How the fuck would I have forgotten?"

Thomas sunk back into his chair and was obviously taken by the room and the establishment Dan had created. "Well, it's a nice place, great area. Not a lot of crime around here?"

"Nah. We've got security, but we haven't had an altercation in probably months."

Terrance took a puff of his cigar and looked over at Dan. "Yeah, I don't think I'd ever be caught dead working here, even if you *do* have some great stuff down here."

Thomas huffed out a laugh. Dan wasn't usually taken back by statements like that, not that anyone had put him down before, but I could tell from the nod he gave us that he'd noted the comment and wasn't too happy about Terrance's attitude.

"And how are things with the wife, Terrance?"

"Oh, you know. Rrrrrrrrrrgh!" Terrance made a choking motion with his neck and began to feign strangling himself. "Nah, things are fine. She's doing a lot of Tai Chi recently, actually, so she's been calmer."

"How about you, Thomas? Are you getting married to that girl? I can't remember."

"Ah, no. Not yet. She's a wild one, Edward will tell you. But not too much, alright!" And then Thomas burst out laughing.

Dan leaned in. "This that same girl you were dating, Ed?"

Oh, yeah. I'd met a real estate agent around town while selling beer. We'd gone to events together but couldn't make it work, mostly because of our schedules. She started dating Thomas shortly after. It's how we first met, actually. I'd told Dan the story multiple times already.

I responded, "Oh, nah. Nah. Someone else."

"But you know the new girl?"

"Yeah, yeah. I do."

I knew more than I probably should about Thomas's current girlfriend. I wasn't at liberty to tell anyone, though. And so we drank and smoked, recounting our stories of business and sales to each other for a few hours, with Dan and Thomas swapping ownership stories between the tech world and the beer world. By the time 7:30 rolled around, we decided that we were ready to head to the party, so we bid our farewells to Dan and headed upstairs.

CHAPTER 4

The house we were headed towards was up in Cottonwood Heights – far enough away from the city to live quietly, behind gates, within striking distance of four ski resorts. The Utahn's dream, I supposed. Judging by the sports cars that were there it looked like I was going to be among guests very similar to Thomas, meaning they were all living the dream in some respects.

As Thomas, Terrance, and I pulled up to the house where the party was being held, I noticed it wasn't a house at all – this was a mansion. Oh, this wasn't going to be casual at all. It wasn't going to be like anything I'd been to Thomas with. We'd mostly been hitting up bars and would close down with it, typically shit-faced by that hour. Or, at least, *I* was. Once again, I knew this world, but I didn't know if I wanted to spend New Year here.

Thomas walked up to the door and we could already hear the commotion from inside. The party was packed. Chatter and jazz filled the rooms. Everyone was dressed to be there. The inside of the house was staggering – chandeliers, marble all over the floor, and enough room in the foyer to fit 20 guests. I might've expected something a bit more modern to be honest, square rooms and open space everywhere, but it was surprisingly old-fashioned for someone making their money in tech.

Thomas ushered both me and Terrance in. Terrance tapped my shoulder and said, "I'll meet up with you two in a few," and then ran off. Thomas and I stepped into the living room and got a good view of the whole party from where we were standing. It was rowdy; there was lots of noise, but nobody was acting crazy or out of line. It felt like any other upscale party I'd attended, to be perfectly honest, just that the amount of people here and the scale of the party was a lot larger than I expected. Not that that bothered me, but I did feel like I was going to get lost in a wave of strangers.

I looked towards Thomas. "So, are all these people Mormon?"

Thomas chuckled to himself. "Nahhh. I mean, not all of them. You'll find plenty of people like me and you. Most of these people are either friends of Cary or me tonight, so they're all Mormon, but there's plenty of worker bees though that you'll meet that aren't."

"I still don't get how you run a tech company in rural Utah, but I got it."

Thomas shot me a smile. "Tech isn't all about the technology, Edward." He then eyed the charcuterie board in the living room and motioned his elbow towards it. I nodded. Time to go in.

Thomas immediately started spreading some cheese on crackers as I looked at the wine selection. A blond woman about my height, five 11, probably, wearing a white dress, walked up next to me and took a bottle of champagne. I could see it in her face. She looked Mormon, from the looks of it. Rosy cheeks and a full smile. Long hair done up in a bun, just for the occasion. I'd see her without it shortly. It felt like every single person at this party was Mormon and blond. As she poured, her eyes darted over to me a few times like I had something on my shirt. When she was done topping off her drink, she turned to face me. "I don't think I've seen you around before."

I turned around with a piece of cheese in my mouth. "Oh! Uh, no. You haven't."

"Yeah, Mantiss Analytics is a pretty tight-knit community. Nice to meet you, I'm Laurie. I'm an Enterprise Account Executive around here."

"No, yeah. I'm Edward. Nice to meet you. I'm with Thomas."

"Oh, you're the new recruit, huh?"

Before I had a chance to respond, Thomas looked over and jumped into the conversation. "Well, not yet – he's just shadowing for now, interviewing, so it's still up in the air."

Laurie gave Thomas an eye roll and a sly smile. "Shadowing, interviewing, right? Right. What do you do right now?"

"Oh, beer sales."

"Sales, really? In Utah? With who?"

"The new guys, Samurai."

"Ah, yes. The bad boys of Utah beer, as they say."

"Yeah, dry state no longer." I looked at Thomas. "Good for us, you know?"

Thomas laughed. Laurie smiled. "Well, I hope you get the position. You'll fit right in with the sales crew. If you're friends with Thomas, I'll see you around either way."

Laurie immediately walked away like she had other business to attend to. I started to pour myself some red wine and turned once again to Thomas. "She's Mormon?"

"Yep, she's one of 'em."

CHAPTER 5

Huh. She knew about Samurai, and after chatting with her for five minutes, she definitely didn't strike me as a Mormon woman. Couldn't judge any of these books by their covers.

The night dragged on with a continuous cycle of me drinking and attempting to make connections with various Mantiss employees. This must've happened about five times before it became obvious to me that I was drunk. I wasn't too worried about my alcohol intake that night – it was New Year's. A bunch of people flew by me, asking questions about how I knew Thomas and if I'd met Cary yet. I got told, "You *gotta* meet Cary. He's such a swell guy," and "He's a genius!" and "He brought tech to Utah!" multiple times over the course of the night, so much that it was eventually drilled into my half-inebriated brain that I should talk to the guy.

I don't remember exactly how I got back to where Terrance was standing, but he was acting jovially and talking directly at me. A woman was next to him and I think he had told me her name was Merideth or Mary or something. I noticed that Terrance had his arm around her waist. I don't *think* Terrance had told me his wife's name yet.

The night had turned from a business party to a New Year's party for sure, but we weren't quite going to give up the veil of this being a Mantiss event. And it seemed like Terrance was trying to help us continue that trend. He might've also just wanted to brag. "So you've heard about Cary, right?"

It took me a second to think about it in my inebriated state, but I did remember Cary's name. "From Thomas, a little bit. We don't talk about work much. Why, what's up with him?"

"Aw man, the guy's a *legend*, dude! So, he sells Protract to this *huge* tech conglomerate, right? And then he comes up with the idea for a data analytics system that uses cloud computing, which is *sort of* what the other company was doing."

Mary rolled her eyes and put her hand on Terrence's shoulder. "Oh, come on. Everybody already knows this story, Terrance!"

Terrance took his hand, put it on Mary's, and leaned in drunkenly. "Nah, nah, Mary! We gotta let the new guy in! We have to let him know!

Thomas butted in, laughing as he said – "He's shadowing!"

Terrance butted right back. "So anyways, he wants to try to double-dip! You only sell one company in the tech universe. Cary went for *two!* And he –"Terrance hiccupped, "— excuse me, he decided that he wants to take employees from that tech company he's now hired at and recruit 'em for this new company. The conglomerate gets pissed, of course, but they can't do anything about it, so he just takes their employees and leaves and gets a *bunch* of investors to sign up for it! For the second time in a *row!* God, the guy knows his shit, and that's why we're all here!"

Funnily enough, I hadn't even met Cary yet. I knew what he looked like from news articles, but I hadn't seen him around the party and all, despite this being his house. Thomas didn't really hang out with Cary before, and I'd never been introduced. And now it seemed like he was some sort of wunderkind in the tech space, so I'm not sure how much I'd even have in common with him.

"God, it's going to be a big year, Ed. We're going to shoot the fucking moon!" Terrance clinked his glass against Mary's, and they laughed for a while. Their laughs started to sound blurry – I was losing consciousness. The bourbon from earlier was mixing with the wines I'd been given, and a familiar feeling started to fall over me. Terrance and Mary disappeared from my view, and I was left to fend for myself against my need to pass out.

What felt like seconds later, I came to the Tesla, hot air blasting on my face from the vents. Thomas was driving in the cold Salt Lake darkness with no expression on his face. I wiped the sweat I had on my face off and suddenly froze in panic. I didn't remember the end of the party or the ball dropping or anything.

"Hey, what happened?"

Thomas glanced over before returning his focus to the road. "Oh, Edward, you're back. Don't worry. You didn't do anything bad or something. You just conked out, is all."

I sighed. Thank God.

He returned his focus to me, but his blank expression didn't change. "So… what do you think of Terrance?"

"What do you mean? If I think he's cool? Seems like a nice guy."

"Yeah, anything else?"

Anything else? I mean, I'd noticed that he was particularly close with that girl. Mary was her name…? Other than the conversation we'd had at the Beer Crew, that was the only thing I remembered. Was that relevant? It didn't feel like it. Plus, he was going to be my boss if I got hired.

"…Not really, I guess."

"Nothing with Mary and him? You think there's something about them going on?"

Oh. Shit.

"I mean, I don't know. Not really. I don't really know either of them well enough to tell."

"Alright. Good. Glad you had fun." Thomas said softly, returning his eyes to the road once more.

I was given a moment to wake myself and attempt to sit up straight in the Tesla. It must've been past midnight as I could hear faint fireworks in the distance. At the stoplight to get on the 15, Thomas pulled to a complete stop and looked at me. "Well, other than blacking out, you made a pretty good impression. I think as long as you ace the interview, you'll be golden."

I yawned. "That's great. I'm looking forward to taking it easier."

"It'll be easier."

I didn't see Thomas' reaction as he spoke. Really, looking back on it makes me think he would have said just about anything to get me on the team. And looking back I also think he might have been testing me. Thomas always knew what he wanted and always tried to tease out whether other people were on his side. I didn't know what was in store for me at Mantiss Analytics, but Thomas had promised me that night that it would be easier. He'd said it twice. Whatever motive he had in mind, whatever he'd been referring to, be it business or the culture, all I know is that he'd lied to me.

CHAPTER 6

Hal obviously needed a second to pull himself together. I wasn't in the best of states either. He took a few deep breaths on the table and then downed some more of his drink.

"So, when did they fire you?"

"Today. Sorry, no, they didn't fire me. I've been placed on temporary leave, but I found out today. HR just called me and told me I needed to clean out my office, so that's why I was late."

"And who is it? That's accusing you, you know. Do you know?"

"Laurie. It took a while to get it out of him, but I got the name. All over the past two hours."

"Holy shit," Hal said, pausing to think before speaking again. "So you haven't had time to tell anyone else then."

"No. I rushed here. I haven't even been able to think straight."

"So you gotta call your lawyer then, right? These are really serious allegations, man. This isn't – it's –"

And as Hal fell silent, I knew he was right. I hadn't had time to think about the weight of the situation, but as I started to explain it, it hit me like a truck. The police had already called me about a criminal investigation, and Mantiss had already been informed for who knows how long. Both had tried to get me to confess to something. I had no idea at the time what they wanted, but I had the foresight to keep to myself.

"I know I must look crazy for just coming out and telling you I'm under investigation, but I need your help, Hal. I came to you because I trust you. I didn't do it. I think someone's setting me up, and I don't know why."

The color on Hal's face had nearly drained, and we were both already a bit drunk. He put his hand to his head. "I'm going to withhold my judgment until we figure out what's going on. I'm – I'm not sure I know how to help you other than that. You should call your lawyer, Ed."

"Okay. You've already helped. I'll do that."

Hal tried to smile but he was struggling hard.

"I can only wish you the best. Good luck."

I nodded. This was going to be a nightmare.

I excused myself from the booth we were in silently and stepped out of the pub, still feeling flustered. Still, I knew what I had to do. The first step was to call Grant. He'd been my lawyer for over a decade, having only ever helped me with a DUI while I was still bartending. In the industry I was in, it was natural to go to bars and buy people drinks to get acquainted with people, so that's what I did, and we've been friends ever since. He had a disarming personality around anyone he was friends with, and he looked like a professional. He just wore his brown hair brushed up – he didn't need gel to intimidate, and he had well-proportioned facial features, conventionally attractive. Just the type of charismatic guy you wanted to be your lawyer.

I jogged through the snow over to my car and dialed Grant's number into my phone. It rang a few times before going to voicemail. Shit. I knew he was busy, but I rang him again anyway. Voicemail again. Over the next ten minutes, I must have rang him a dozen times. Whatever he was doing, he was busy. I was going to have to do some digging myself. I thought for a moment and then realized there was another option. Call Terrance. If anyone was going to know anyone who might be involved with my investigation, it was him.

"Hey, Ed, what's up?"

I filled him in on what was happening when it came to the employment and criminal investigation. Terrance sounded surprised.

"Holy shit, this is going to get crazy then! I bet Cary already knows about this…"

"So you didn't know?"

"No, I had no idea. I haven't heard anything from anybody."

Fuck. If he didn't know, nobody except Laurie's in-group would know.

"Alright," Terrance said, "I imagine that there's going to be a meeting with the Chief Legal Officer and Human Resources. Did they ask for one today?"

'Yes, they told me they wanted one."

"Do not go into that fucking meeting. They're going to get information out of you without you even knowing. They'll try to pin you. Trust me, man. I've dealt with these fuckers before, and I'm telling you from experience."

"Okay. Got it. I left, like, two things at the office. Can you get them for me?"

"Fuck, yeah. Okay. We'll meet up somewhere in Salt Lake, but it's gotta be away from where the Mantiss crew usually hangs out."

"Got it. I've still got places in mind. Does Dala work downtown?"

"Yeah, um, sounds good, but… listen," Terrance paused. "Watch your back. Thomas and Cary aren't the same as they were back in the day. They are a lot more about money than they used to."

"I figured. Gotcha."

"Listen, everyone's going to be at the Annual User's Conference, so I won't be able to talk this week, but keep me informed, alright?"

Right. The Annual User's Conference. Three days of fun. Mantiss ran its own Apple Keynote-style press conferences but with a budget that'd rival the big names in the Bay Area. All the employees got to go and loved going, which was surprising for what amounted to an annual press conference. Despite selling cloud technology, Mantiss would bring in musical acts and guests from the entertainment industry to perform and promote their brand. As I'm describing it, it sounds kind of indulgent, but that's because it absolutely was. As I worked at the company, I saw the event grow from its not-so-modest roots to doing crazy things like getting Drake and The Chainsmokers to perform at this event.

Despite it being in the center of downtown, the locals had no idea these kinds of events existed and honestly didn't even know what Mantiss did. There'd been plenty of news stories that would come out proclaiming Utah as the next Silicon Valley, even ones that had direct lines to Thomas and Cary, but none of them were very adept at explaining what we'd actually sold. This event was for prospective software buyers. They were taking hundreds of thousands of dollars and sending their customers to Alta and Snowbasin to try to get them to move to their cloud computing service.

And with all of this mess with the employment investigation, all this meant was that Terrance wasn't going to be able to help me. Or he wasn't going to help me enough to clear my name.

"I've got you, okay?" Terrance attempted to assure me. "For the meeting this week. I'll get your stuff. It'll be good to see you."

"Thank you so much, man."

And Terrance hung up. The Annual User's Conference was in a week and I knew that I couldn't get in to try and scout for more information. Not without help, at the very least. I needed to think about how to either get in or talk to people outside the event. I might be able to confront them and start to finally understand what was going on.

CHAPTER 7

And then Grant finally called me back. I snatched up my phone again.

"Hey Edward, what's going on? I was just finishing up some work on-"

"Grant, I just got called by Mantiss's Chief Legal Officer. They received a complaint about me, and now I'm under employment investigation. I think I'm also under criminal investigation – I think Laurie's husband went to see Thomas and the CLO and-"

"Edward, Edward, stop, okay? Are you asking me for help?"

"Yeah."

"Listen, I can't deal with this right now. I'm prepping for a trial with someone looking at life in prison. Whatever you do, you do not say shit to anybody, alright?"

"Well, I —"

"Well, you what, Ed? Keep it quick, please."

"I called Terrance and told a friend of mine. I'm trying to figure out how this happened! Who's involved, what's going on? Terrance is giving me info."

Grant's sigh over the phone was deafening. "That's gotta stop. The more you talk, the more you're going to slip up and say things you're not supposed to."

"All right, didn't mean to put you out, but that's all I needed to know. Thanks!"

"Okay, adios. Talk soon."

Click. God, damn it! I needed more help than that. I knew that Grant had worked on high-profile cases before this, so I knew he was holding back, but he was busy. I needed more info. I mean, I knew where they were all gathering. I know I couldn't show up to the conference itself, but I knew where they were going to be after. I trusted Grant, but he needed my help. I knew I had mine in. The ability to interview, to research, to get insider info on what this investigation was about. I still couldn't put my plan into action. They'd have to wait for now, but I needed to strike fast when the time was right.

CHAPTER 8

Laying low for now meant that I needed to find a new spot to drink. Dan and I looked out for each other, but I didn't want to drag him into this by having the police bust down his door or whatever. I had tried to visit different bars around Salt Lake just to keep my experiences new but it felt more important than ever to lay low and drink around town. The first part of the plan was to make sure I didn't get arrested or noticed by anyone at Mantiss.

The day after I talked with Grant, I woke up and remembered that I didn't need to go to work. The day was slow, comparatively. I scouted out a few areas and remembered Boarder's Company, a place downtown that was a bit smaller than Beer Crew and wouldn't attract attention. It was still trendy and wasn't sketchy by any means, but not as many people knew about it.

I drove to Boarder's Company just as the sky was turning dark. I walked past the patio and into the mixed modern and rustic interior decorations. I pulled up a leather bar chair and signaled for the bartender to give me something hard. I took another look around – this would do nicely.

The night went on for about an hour and a half with nothing out of the ordinary. I must've downed around three drinks and sat at the bar, rubbing my temples from stress every ten minutes over so. I didn't know the owner like I did Dan, so I simply sat in silence at the bar. I didn't want anyone to notice I was there, and I just wanted to blend in with the atmosphere.

"Hey, man, how's it going?"

Hmm? Guys sat next to other guys all the time and ordered beers without ever talking to each other. But when I looked in the direction of the guy's voice, he was simply staring into his beer. Without looking at me, his voice upbeat, he said, "How are you holding up this winter, mate?"

I glanced towards him. The guy looked five years younger than me, but he wore a snow cap and a sweater, just like me. It was obviously cold out; it was February, but something about the way he presented himself made me feel like it was his sense of fashion. Still, this guy was massive. It was hard to tell how tall he was, as he was sitting on a barstool, but he was taller than me sitting down. Probably 6'3", maybe 4". I prided myself on staying in shape, but this guy looked like he could stand toe to toe with me and bench more than 400. Honestly, after all that was going on with the two separate investigations, I couldn't tell if I had met him before and we were old friends or something. I had forgotten a lot of people from before I worked at Samurai. I tried to put his face to a name, but it evaded me. Something felt like it was up with this guy.

I raised my eyebrow, but I guess it was more likely he was friendly than hostile. Beer people in Utah tended to stick together.

"Uh, fine, I guess. Sorta."

"Yeah, same here, man. Days go by." And then he reached out and patted me on the back. I recoiled, but it was already too late. He'd invaded my personal space. As he stepped away from me he leaned up against the bar and posed me another question. "So, what's up with your life? Tell me what's going on that's making it, 'fine, I guess.'"

I was thoroughly confused at this point. Nothing was ringing a bell. This guy was acting like he knew me, and I had no idea who the hell he was.

"Sorry, what's your name?"

"Elliot, man. Elliot."

I mean, it felt like he was trying to jog my memory, but nothing was coming up. Still, I'd met so many contacts around Salt Lake that it was hard for me to remember. Fine, I'd just nip this in the bud.

"Do we know each other?"

Elliot laughed. "I mean, you look familiar, but I can't quite put my finger on it either. Whatever, if I did, it's nice to be reacquainted."

Okay, something was up. I mean, I was in a bar. Something was always up.

"So, you haven't told me where you're from?"

"England. I know. How did I end up in Utah, right?"

"That's the question on everyone's mind, right?"

"You?"

"Oh, Iowa. How did I end up in Utah, I guess, am I right?"

I chuckled. At least Elliot had a sense of humor, even if it was a basic one, and I still wasn't sure about the guy. "Here," he laughed to himself, "On me." And then he pointed to the bartender and called for a refill.

Once the drink was poured, Elliot slid it over to me. "So, what are you up to this weekend? You got any plans?"

"I guess I'm going for a ski trip with Jason – I mean, some friends from out of town."

"Oh! Nice, nice. Hey, maybe I'll see you round? Are you coming to this place often these days?"

I thought about it for a second. I mean, I wasn't doing anything else except the trip. I had kind of planned to hit a few different bars to avoid the spotlight.

"I might not be around here until after the weekend's over, but I can hang out."

CHAPTER 9

Two days later, the trip with Jason officially started. I hadn't lied to the guy. Jason Morgan used to work with us as the Vice President of sales at a beer distributor in Washington, D.C. In my travels across the country, I'd met him, gotten him to deliver Samurai's product, and come to know him as a friend. He'd invited me for a ski trip up at Alta Ski Resort and I'd accepted weeks ago. This was before the police had started hounding me over the phone, so I didn't know that my life was going to turn into hell.

Jason loved skiing inherently and had explored the East Coast looking for powder, unlike a lot of the businesspeople who would visit Utah just to explore Park City. He was still a rich kid, going to Brown, and his father working for the government, but he knew his way around a slope and was a fuckton more adventurous than the average sales manager. He wasn't built, but he was tall, and he always looked in shape. Dark hair still somehow looked a little like a greaser despite growing up with money. Jason was about my height and looked fairly fit, especially given his background in beer.

He loved Alta because it was a skiers-only resort, meaning that snowboarders weren't carving out huge chunks of the runs for themselves. I was a pretty good skier myself, having known my old boss at Samurai Brewing, Hal, who was a friend for backcountry forest runs. Jason was bringing about ten-plus guys for an annual trip, and I was always down to keep up with them.

I drove myself up that day with the intention of maybe driving home that night. As I pulled up with my skis to the slope, Jason was already there and chipper, ready to tackle the slopes. I couldn't have been farther from ready. I was keeping warm and doing well on the mountain, but the thought of Mantiss and what I had to do weighed on my mind. Grant hadn't called me back since the first phone call we'd had, so I hadn't been able to get help processing the situation. It wasn't obvious with my ski mask on that I was struggling emotionally that day. I tried to lay it bare by spraying snow on the slopes, but there's only so much skiing that can help a situation like this.

Afterward, we trekked with Jason's entourage to The Peruvian Bar at the Alta Resort. Given the area and the people I was with you might expect the same style of classy establishment that Mantiss would be proud of going to. In reality, the place felt straight out of the eighties, with wood beams and a rowdy atmosphere that matched the demeanor of the crew I was a part of. We'd go there and be raucous as hell, eat steak and drink beer, and then pass out in our cabins, ready for tomorrow. This trip was no different.

But as everyone walked through the double doors, I suddenly felt a bit sick. I hadn't been able to get my mind off of the investigations. While everyone flooded into the bar and started talking about how their lives were going, I went over to the bartender and ordered a whiskey.

Jason talked with friends while I sat in distress. I wasn't mad at him, and I just wouldn't have been much for conversation. But as he turned to try and find where I was, the excitement on his face melted off, just like Dan before him. It felt like I'd brought a lot of people down with me these days.

Jason patted his friend on the shoulder and headed towards the bar. "Hey, what are you doing over here?" he said, slamming his ski clothes on the seat.

I felt like shit, and I didn't know if I looked like it. "I'm going through it, you know?"

Jason took a seat and motioned for the bartender. "Just the IPA, please." He put his arms on the bar and looked over towards me. "What's on your mind, Ed?"

"I don't want to talk about it."

"Come on, it'll make you feel better, telling an old friend."

I scoffed and gave him a side-eye. "Nothing. I'm just on company leave right now."

"Oh, no shit. What's going on?"

I took a moment. I genuinely don't know why I'd told him the truth. It's not like I wanted to talk about what was going on. But I guess I didn't want to keep him completely in the dark. So I sighed. "Personal issues," I told him.

"Ah, I see. Something serious going on with your family?"

I took a drink of the lager I had in my hand. I wasn't about to burden someone else with this. "Yeah. Family."

"Sorry to hear that. I don't know if the crew will be there for you when ya most need it; they're a bit rowdy, but I'll always be here."

"Thanks, but this is something I have to solve by myself."

"Ah, okay. Are you sure you don't want to, like, head back to the cabin I got for the night? You'll fucking love these guys. I swear."

I set down my drink and then shook my head. I don't think my heart would have been in it. Jason was a good friend, but I wouldn't want to make him feel uncomfortable or let him down by being a spoilsport.

Jason leaned in. "We're going to have drinks. Take whatever you're dealing with of your mind."

I sighed. I know he meant the best.

Jason and I trekked across the resort grounds back to the cabin that he'd bought for the night. It was true – everyone we'd been skiing with was there. It was still spacious; there was probably room enough for, like, seven of us in the house at a time, but there were probably about twelve people all trying to fit in. Still, once we were all situated and started drinking, it didn't feel like a tight fit at all. The cabin had about the same interior as The Peruvian, just with a bed instead of a bar. Logs all over and straight out of the Hot Tub Time Machine. Jason grabbed some craft beer from the trunk of his SUV and busted down the door, yelling, "DRINKING HOUR, JACKASSES!" and slamming down a cooler full of craft six packs. The other eight guys flooded in and started grabbing cans and getting drunk.

I started with another lager from the chest, drinking and talking with the guys from D.C. God. They were insightful. They were really smart guys, just like I remembered. Dry wit, much like you'd hear on the East Coast. As the night went on, I took some more beers out of the cooler and started chugging to forget and have fun.

And the next thing I remember was Jason sitting in a loafer, looking at me with shot eyes like I had just hit a deer in the road. Ah, fuck. I'd told him already. I tried to make out his reaction. He was at a loss for words. At least he didn't immediately leave the room, I suppose.

Jason stuttered a bit before exclaiming, "Holy fuck, dude!" so the whole room could hear. His friends had heard, too. I didn't know them as well as Jason. I had no idea what they'd even think. I hadn't even gotten information from Mantiss yet, and I was already spilling the beans.

Some guy I didn't remember the name of was in the corner of the cabin and butted into the conversation. "Listen, I don't know what you're talking about, but it's obviously serious. Be like a typical politician in D.C! Deny! Deny! Deny, and then Deny some fucking more."

I looked back at him as he tried to fix the situation from the wall he was leaning on. "I don't know, doesn't that make me look guilty?"

"You can't worry about that right now. Everybody's going to think you're guilty or innocent or whatever. You can't change that. That's not your business. Your business is in denial!" And then he walked away yelling "Deny! Deny! Deny!" a few more times, just to make sure it got drilled into my head. Hadn't even asked if I'd done it. I guess he told me not to worry about that, but still…

Jason paused. He stuttered and then said, "Holy shit, I can't believe it." It was the end of the night, and the party was winding down. Some of the guys had already gone to bed, so there was enough room for me to hear Jason's silence. He put his shoulder on mine and said, "Listen. Stay the night. Crash on this couch and go skiing tomorrow with us as well. We can keep all your stuff here."

I tried to make out words with my lips. "No, I couldn't. It's your weekend, not mine."

"But you need this! And you're not imposing on us at all by doing this. Please."

I sighed and rolled my eyes. If I had been in any position to drive down the canyon, I'd have done it, but I knew somewhere within myself that I shouldn't be driving down a snowy canyon while drunk. Whether I liked it or not, I was going to have to stay locked up in this cabin for the night.

"Alright, I suppose. Thanks, Jason."

Jason nodded and smiled. At the end of the day, I knew he was just looking out for me.

CHAPTER 10

"He who poses as a fool is not a fool" - Robert Greene, The 48 Laws of Power

The next day was mostly the same. I woke up with the same feeling I had the night before. We got a late start as about half of our squad was recovering from the night before. Our next stop was Snowbird. Same canyon, same crew, different resort. The air was a lot clearer, with less snow on the mountaintops, so that was nice.

I decided to spend about a half-day on the slopes before calling it quits. Today was better, knowing I had friends there to help me out, but it still wasn't enough. The entire weekend felt like it had been shot.

I holed up in the cafeteria, taking a seat next to the window. No bar, just a shitty table with a four-pronged leg. I pulled out my phone and scrolled through my notifications mindlessly.

At some point, I remember Jason entering the building, but I don't remember exactly how much later. After he picked up a coffee from the cafeteria line and saw me, he walked over, pulled out a chair, and threw himself down into it, tossing his helmet and goggles on the table. He took a breath and settled down. I could tell he wanted to talk about the incident more.

"So who is it? Someone I know?"

I sighed. "Laurie. Account Exec at some tech conglomerate now."

Jason blinked. "Oh. I guess I didn't really know anybody you worked for. Don't know why I asked. Sorry."

I tried to hold back from rolling my eyes. Just from frustration. "Nah. You're fine, man."

"She Mormon? I just know you worked with a lot of 'em, so I want to know."

"Yeah, she was. Her husband is, too."

Jason took a sip of his beverage and sighed like the weight of the world was on his shoulders instead of mine.

"Fuck, man. I wouldn't know how to deal with it. I can't imagine."

I continued scrolling through notifications. A bunch of e-mails I would never read, a bunch of stuff that didn't apply to me because I was on leave from Mantiss, and a notification from LinkedIn. Wait, LinkedIn?

Someone had viewed my profile. From the profile picture, it looked like just some average guy in a suit. It was true that I was on employment leave, but I wasn't looking for another job in particular right now. Nor did I think anyone had any interest in hiring me. I did some digging, tapping on the guy's profile. It was… a director of global security.

"What the fuck?" I said to myself. I turned to Jason with the screen. "Hey, Jason. Look at this."

Jason looked down at the phone screen and then at me with confusion. "What about it?"

"I got my profile viewed on LinkedIn today by the head of global security by that tech conglomerate Laurie works for."

"Oh, what the fuck?"

Jason looked at the phone again and gave me a concerned look.

"Do you think it's her?"

Oh. He was right. Oh my god, what was Laurie doing? Was she dragging Mantiss into this? Fuck, I absolutely knew why.

I threw my hands down on the table, sending my phone to the floor. "Fuck, that's what they're doing. Holy shit."

"Alright, calm down, man. Calm down. This isn't the world's biggest deal. I can't imagine it being related to anything else, but what are they doing? Why do they care?"

"No, this is – this is bad, man. I know what they're trying to do. They're all trying to tackle me at once. Laurie went to fucking everyone, dude. I don't know who else she called. But everyone's going to be out to fucking get me, dude! I know that if this – if this gets out, they can try to take down the company. I think that's what they're after. And I know that there's bad blood, and I know that if there's a chance to bury Mantiss, they'll take any fucking opportunity to do it, and they're going to use me as the pawn to do it –"

"Hey, man, HEY!" Jason stood up and put out his hands. He wasn't about to grab me; he wasn't that kind of person, but he was panicking. He shook his hands a few times, motioning for me to take a few breaths.

"You're still in public, man. Are you sure you want to be talking about this matter in the company of others?"

I looked around. It was loud in the cafeteria, so nobody had really paid attention, but I knew he was right, even just for my safety.

Jason put his hands down. "Edward, man. You have to take things one step at a time. This is another problem to add to the pile. Sure. I can give you that. But if things are going to get out of control, you can only start from where you are."

"I can promise you, Jason. There are a lot more people that are going to come after me if the tech conglomerate gets involved. They're all going to take me down. Mantiss, the police, everyone."

"They've got a leg up. It's true. But don't jump to conclusions yet."

I shook my head and buried my head in my phone. I opened Instagram furiously and started making a story. I knew whoever was tailing me was going to be following me on there. I didn't care anymore. The stewing in my head was driving me insane. It was ruining my fucking life. I wanted to find out who was going to get pissed off.

"I'm rockin' my peers, putting suckers in fear, makin' the tears rain down like a monsoon." – LL Cool J.

I wanted to set a trap. Something that would put those fuckers if they got offended. All the fucking executives at Mantiss and that tech company were going to know what that was about. And I'd figure out who'd really been truthful to me for all those years. I didn't know if anyone would respond. But if they did, I could give them hell, and I knew that. Jason sighed and sunk into his chair again.

I took my leave from Snowbird shortly after. I said my goodbyes to Jason.

Jason shook my hand. "Hey, to next year not being the world's biggest shit-show, right?"

"Fucking cheers to that, man. See you around."

And their flight back to D.C. left that night. I traveled down the canyon in silence with my thoughts. I didn't have a lot of support in Salt Lake other than Hal. The weekend had been a shit-show. Jason had been right about that. But it felt good to be able to get it all out. I knew they would carry the story to D.C., and I sort of wished I could take it somewhere far away from Utah as well. Either way, Jason had the privilege of forgetting about it. If just for the car ride, I tried to gain that solace, too.

CHAPTER 11

I resumed hitting random bars across Salt Lake and going to different places for dinner when I got back home. At the very least, my paid leave was giving me an opportunity to explore the city. I leveraged some relationships with people I'd sold beer to and got into some nice places pretty consistently. One of those places was Masuri, a Japanese restaurant for lunch by myself that week. The fact that we'd gotten beer in here was nothing short of a miracle – Masuri was probably the most respected Japanese place in town.

I took a seat at the bar and ordered a sake from their specials.

"Hey. Good choice."

Not again. I just wanted a nice meal for myself. I looked, and it was a guy dressed to the nines, sitting by himself with an empty seat between us. "Thanks, man."

"You know a lot about this stuff?"

"Yeah, I used to do sales for Samurai Brewing. Not the same…"

"Yeah, no, shit, man, that's cool. What do you do for a living now?"

"I work for Mantiss. On the sales team as well."

He took a sip of sake and smiled. "Small company, huh?"

I laughed. "Ah, yeah, you know. Not Bay Area massive by any stretch of the imagination, at least."

"I'm an investor. I know how big you guys are. I just funded them recently."

"How much, if you don't mind me asking?"

He waved his hand and then stood up and straightened himself a bit. He was a little flush in the cheeks.

"150 million."

Oh my god. The irony hit me like a fucking brick. I couldn't bring myself to do anything but just put my head in my hand and laugh.

The guy looked around as I laughed and tried to chuckle along. "What, you know something I don't?"

Oh shit. I would talk to Jason, I'd talk to Hal, but not this guy. "Oh! No, no. Small world is all. I know they're going public shortly. That's what it is. Hopefully, you all make a return."

The guy smiled assuredly. "That's why we invested. It's amazing what you're doing."

I mean, what could you even say in a situation like that? I just nodded and tried to take my leave as soon as possible. I bolted out of the back door of the restaurant without saying another word to the guy. What a circus.

I walked out into the cold back street where the parking lot was. I caught the chirping of a car lock system about three cars down from me. I turned around just to look and was shocked to realize… I recognized the guy.

"Edward, are you following me?" It was Grant. Holy hell.

"What the fuck, man!" I said, smiling at the sheer coincidence. I took his hand and gave him a hard handshake. "Fucking hardly, mate. What are you doing here in town? Where are you coming from that you parked here?"

"Oh, just finished a meeting, that's all. Don't want to bump into anyone, you know?"

"Me neither, I guess!"

We both laughed. "So. Day off?" Grant asked.

Huh. Strange. I'd told him, right? "No… I got put on leave because of the employment investigation, remember?"

"Ah, alright. That's what you called me the other week. Okay, catch me up on the latest."

As I explained the situation to Grant, his face got more and more classic for him to do so, but it started making me nervous that I was in a deeper hole than I might have even realized. After I finished, Grant took a notepad and a pen out of his coat pocket and started writing. The first thing he did was crack-wise. "When you called, I one-hundred percent thought that it was that FBI agent you dated that did this."

"Oh, her? Nah. New person. Laurie. When I called the detective, they told me over the phone."

"Alright. No worries. It all makes sense. I need to formulate my plan for taking this, but I'll handle Mantiss and run interference there for now." He waved his pen. "Good on refusing to go in for the interview. The last thing we need is these guys fucking with you and causing you problems. You said a detective's been bugging you? I'll try to drop him a line as well. Figure out what's going on for myself."

As I saw everything Grant was saying, the whole thing laid out, I got a little queasy again. "Are you sure there's no chance of this blowing over? The crime they're investigating was years ago. I'm worried because they're after me, but I don't see how they could even charge me."

Grant clicked his pen. "You'd be surprised, man. Once they wrap up their investigation, that's when they decide if they'll end it or send the investigation to the district attorney's office to be screened for charges. All these types of cases are getting sent to them right now." He reached out for another handshake, and I obliged. "I will see you around. Keep laying low. I got you on this one. You're doing great."

I opened my car door and then did a double take back to Grant.

"Is it possible to keep me updated once you call the detective?"

"Yeah, I can do that for you."

I slammed the door shut. Okay. Grant was on my side. It was a long road ahead, but I had him. One step at a time.

CHAPTER 12

The next step for me was to meet up with Terrance at Dala to collect my things from the office. I arrived about five minutes late from traffic. I stepped inside. Dala was fancy and large for a Utah bar, with a huge selection carved into the entirety of the back wall. This was probably Terrance's favorite place to hang out. I found Terrance at the bar and sat down. He immediately summoned the bartender and put some money down for my drink.

"For you. It's fuckin' unfair, so this is the least I could do," Terrance said, motioning with his hand in sympathy.

As the bartender handed me a pint, I just shook my head. "It's been a mess, man. Laurie's company is after me, and I'm bouncing all around town trying to avoid Mantiss and the cops, I can't deal with this shit."

"Yeah, and all this as Mantiss's going public, too."

"Fuck, that's right. I forgot all about that." I groaned and took my first sip of the lager Terrance had bought me. Terrance didn't even look at me. He just kept his eyes down, maybe remorseful or at least trying to comprehend what I was going through. He finally brought himself to look at me for a second.

"Hey, here. I got an idea. Tomorrow's the last day of the conference. You remember that?"

I chuckled. "I mean, it's not like I was invited this year. You think I give a shit about when you're in-party is after all this?"

Terrance lifted his hands. "All right! All right. Well, we're all holding an after-party near the convention center. You are invited. By me."

Huh. Strange. Really? Me, invited? "Where is it?" I asked.

"Oh, another bar across town. You know, MEND?"

"Sure, I remember that place."

"Everyone from Manhattan'll be there. Did you want to go with me?"

"Um..." Not really. Laurie worked at the tech conglomerate at this point, so I knew she wasn't going to be there, but I didn't know what I was going to say to anyone else. I hadn't seen them in weeks, much less in a state of calm or cheer. Mantiss was going public, as Terrance had said, and everyone had been busy closing up accounts. Or at least that's what they had been doing before Mantiss sicced their legal department on me.

Terrance set his drink down on the bar side. "You should come. They all want to see you. We're all on your side."

I mean, I knew there was also the possibility that one of my co-workers from Manhattan would know what Laurie was up to, but I wasn't sure if they'd even want to help me.

I sat for a few minutes, contemplating my choices. I knew Terrance wasn't lying about my friends wanting to see me. There wasn't bad blood between any of us, as far as I remembered. But did any of that change this? Were they hiding things from me as well? I didn't know. But regardless of everything, I just needed to see if they knew. The procedure alone justified my going to the party. I had my concerns, but this was the only way that I was going to make progress on the case myself.

I looked stoically at Terrance. "Alright. I'll be there."

"Great, man. Really happy about it. Starts at six."

Terrance and I both had a few more drinks before heading out of the bar and towards Terrance's SUV. He opened his trunk and as I looked inside, I heaved a sigh. A ton of shit I needed to take, and it was all just papers and computer parts. I took my leave from the parking lot with about seven different boxes in tow. When I got to my apartment, I lugged the boxes in one at a time and then passed out on my couch. What a fucking week.

I spent the next morning and afternoon attempting to mentally prepare for my meeting with my co-workers. I didn't know what they were going to ask me, and I didn't even know if I was ready to say anything. I spent my time in the morning unpacking all my papers from the boxes and just trying to stay calm. Tonight was going to be difficult, but spending time putting stuff away would help me relax.

CHAPTER 13

"Lord, protect me from my friends; I can take care of my enemies." Voltaire showed up that evening at MEND late to the party. Organizing shit all day had taken a lot out of me, but I had taken a breather. I parked my car outside, inhaled, exhaled, and then walked in.

When I pushed the double doors open, I saw Terrance standing with the other people I'd worked with up until two weeks ago. Everyone seemed in high spirits. I assume the conference had gone well. Some people looked at me with concern, but most of them were focused on the party. I didn't think too much of it.

From the looks of it, there was a healthy mix of clients and account executives, meaning I only knew about one-tenth of the people here. Of the people I did know, most of them stared at me with confusion. I knew they hadn't seen me in a while, but I also didn't know who knew what. Everyone was treating me the same, cordial but distant, but it all felt obnoxiously uncomfortable at the same time. I could feel it from everyone else as well. In their eyes, I wasn't supposed to be there.

Terrance was right; there were some people from Manhattan here, but there were also a few people missing. I didn't see Christa anywhere, for starters. She was one of Thomas' assistants and was friends with Laurie and her husband while I was there. I walked up to them and tried to stay pleasant.

I got a lot of "Hey Edward? How have you been?" that night, with a majority of the people who I knew were friends with Terrance just not even asking about why I was gone or what was happening with the investigation. I expected them to know, especially because they were part of the inner circle of the executive who'd invited me to the party. My conversations didn't garner much information. I think everybody was sort of tired from the Annual User's Conference at this point.

And that's when I met eyes with a guy who seemed to know me better than I knew him. And he wasn't afraid of me at all. He seemed surprised to see me and ran over me, blocking my path to the people I actually worked with. "Edward? Look who it fucking is!"

It was some guy from, I want to say, the Chicago team. Sean, I think, was his name. It had been a while since I'd talked to anyone outside of the Manhattan crew I worked with, but I remembered this guy's face. I don't know what he wanted to talk to me about, but I don't remember a ton of our conversations being cordial. From what I remember, of which there was very little, he didn't have a girlfriend or a wife or anything. You could tell the guy worked out, or at least tried to work out on a regular basis.

He outstretched an arm and waved me down. At the top of his lungs, he shouted, "The prodigal son returns!"

I rolled my eyes and shook my head. "What the fuck is that supposed to mean?"

"Oh, I meant that there's trouble right now."

"Look who's fucking talking. Drama queen."

"Me? A drama queen? Never?"

I laughed to myself, trying to hold my annoyance in. Guy had just called me the fucking prodigal son. "Yeah. Right."

Sean put his hand on my shoulder, invading my personal space. "What the hell are you even doing here right now? There are rumors around the office. You're supposed to be suspended, right?"

"I… don't know who told you that, but I'm dealing with family issues. I'm here with Terrance and the Manhattan crew. Not like I needed permission to be here."

"Right… right. The in-crowd. Right. Whatever." He leaned in, nearly whispering in my ear. "So, I heard that there's some crazy shit. Related to that, maybe. You doin' alright?"

God damn it. "Oh, really? Enlighten me. What have you heard, Sean?"

Sean caught my combative tone. "Oh, man. I can't say. But you know?"

I narrowed my eyes. "Yeah, Sean. I fucking know. And you're not supposed to know. So, how did that happen? Did one of the execs tell you something?"

"Oh, I… Uh…" Sean stuttered.

As if on cue to save him, Terrance stepped up out of nowhere and tapped me on the shoulder. "Hey Ed," he said, "let's go downstairs and get a drink. I have some clients I want you to meet." I side-eyed Sean, still waiting for an answer, but he'd retreated. He was silent.

I walked downstairs, but Sean unfortunately stuck in my mind. He knew. I expected my friends to know, but the gossip was spreading fast. None of those guys would be good allies if they'd already been briefed on the situation by Thomas, Cary, or whatever executive told them.

There were even more account execs and clients downstairs. This being the last day of the conference made sense – this was the last time this year that any of these people were going to be in Utah, and it was the account execs' final chance to make progress on deals before the conference was deemed a win or a loss.

Terrance laughed and introduced me to the entire swarm of businesspeople as I entered the lounge room. "Hey everyone, this is my good friend Edward! Mantiss' employee. He is great at his job. Say hi to him when you get the chance!"

One of the clients closest to me reached for a handshake. "Pleasure," he said as he squinted. "Have we met before?"

Terrance answered, "No. But remember I was talking about the guy that was the Peaky Blinders guy, Thomas Shelby? This is him."

The client looked stunned. He staggered back. "Whoa. Fucking hell of an introduction."

All this talk confused me pretty greatly. I chimed in myself. "Uh, what's Peaky Blinders?"

The client looked at me in shock. "You've never seen Peaky Blinders? Holy shit, man. Terrance has been talking you up for months using Thomas Shelby as a reference. Mostly 'cause you're British."

Terrance laughed and raised his glass to me. "You don't take shit from nobody, man. It's a compliment, trust me."

I smiled. "Well, sounds like I gotta watch it now."

Terrance smiled. "You should! It's a masterpiece in my book. Besides, Thomas and Cary are crazy about it, too."

God. Those names. "Well," I started, "If these motherfuckers at Mantiss know what's going on and they keep talking, then I guess I'm gonna have to fuck some shit up." I punched through my hand. The whole crowd of clients around me laughed out loud.

Another friend of Terrance's chimed in from the back. "You got some drama going on right now?"

"Yeah, listen, he's under investigation right now. We gotta keep fucking quiet about this shit!" Terrance said, yelling at the entire room and laughing.

The room went silent. I turned my head and widened my eyes. Was Terrance fucking serious? Hearing Terrance say that, I looked at his glass. He'd been drinking since before I showed up. Fuck, that made sense. I looked back at his face. I certainly wasn't about to explain the situation for a fifth fucking time. Terrance' eyes perked up, and he suddenly noticed his mistake. "Oh! Sorry. No. I mean, just by the company."

"What's going on?"

Terrance, now overcorrecting, took over the conversation. "Nothing! Nothing. Listen, nothing's happened. I don't believe for a second that Edward's done anything wrong. But yeah, he's on company leave."

I gave Terrance more looks of disdain, but everyone else seemed content with that answer. Fine. I moved away from him and spoke to the crowd. "Alright, where's the drinks, everyone?"

The night was simple. I drank with a ton of clients that I'd known in the past but hadn't caught up with, talked some shit with some of the account executives across America, and leaned on the bar countertop relaying stories of sales past. Honestly, in those moments, it felt like nothing had changed. We were all still selling cloud services to a bunch of VPs in suits, just like in the old days.

A few drinks in, and I found myself upstairs, standing next to Sean. I'd already done the rounds, dodging questions about my employment investigation left and right. I'd been able to evade a lot of tough conversations despite Terrance's slip-up. Or maybe because of it. But Sean had caught up to me as I was heading out of the restroom and had trapped me in a conversation. Most of what he said went right through me, with me nodding along, until Sean dropped a bomb.

"So yeah, there's another after-party after the annual user's conference. Different convention hall, different people, everything."

"Oh, huh," I said. Sean was already some drinks ahead of me, which was a feat in and of itself. "Where is it?" I asked.

"Oh, like, Sugarhouse. 1300 East... I can't remember the South. Let me pull it up." He dug his phone out and flashed me the address. "And yeah, that one's mostly just for employees and high-level clients. Can't fucking wait to take a load off. I'm not taking anyone."

CHAPTER 14

Damn. There was a possibility that Terrance was there. Or Cary, even. I didn't even know if Sean was supposed to tell me about it. I thought about it for a second. Even if they wouldn't or couldn't tell anyone, after all this hiding, I wasn't just going to sit the fuck around on this information. That after-party was the perfect opportunity to start figuring this fucking mess out. Or at least let them know I wasn't scared of them. They should have known better. Loose lips sink ships.

"So, you want to go to the next after-party?" I asked him.

"What? No, you're not fucking going there."

I scoffed. "You just told me where it is, Sean. I'm going, and it's just about whether or not we're sharing the Uber."

Sean took a minute to self-reflect and see if he'd told me where the party was. He had. His hand met his face. "Fuck. FUCK! God, no. You're not going. You're not invited to this one."

"That's why you're gonna help me. If anybody asks, you're going to tell everyone that I'm a client, alright? I know how these events work. You can bring clients. Say that I'm digital marketing at, I dunno, Delta. You work in Atlanta, and it makes sense."

Another minute. Sean needed to think. "Alright, whatever. Did you get me for half the Uber? And you got a plan? I'll take you. If it's gonna be a shit show, it'll be a hell of a shit show. I'm willing to wreak some fucking havoc with you. You ready right now?"

I grinned. I wanted to see how they'd react. Those assholes at Mantiss wouldn't even know what hit 'em. "Let's go."

Sean called the Uber, and we stepped into the car for a five-minute drive. He didn't even look at me as we took the drive. I just buried myself in my phone. I was ready to take them all on. I tapped my keyboard and posted again to my Instagram story.

"Goliath never had a chance to be like David. 100"

My heart was beating, but I was ready to come in swinging. As we walked into the venue, Sean donned his lanyard into the event and walked closer to me, visibly nervous. I nudged him, trying to get him to relax. He straightened up, but nothing about his concerned demeanor changed.

There was a security guard at the main entrance and one of those metal detector things that you walk through blocking our path. The security guard at the event checked me over, eyes darting between Sean's lanyard and my lack of identification, and turned to address Sean.

"Who's this?"

"A client from Delta."

"Alright, right this way."

You could hear the bass from the DJ's sound setup from the entrance. Down the hall was a few sets of double doors that Sean pushed open for me. Inside was a smorgasbord of sound, color, and Mantiss branding.

The after-party was being held in the main ballroom of the event space – looked like the space was planned for wedding parties. Columns on the side, Mantiss banners everywhere, and a pop-up bar that pretty much everyone was hovering around.

Sean left me to fend for myself pretty early, so I sauntered in. That was when I saw Christa. She was about a hundred or so feet from where I was standing, but the minute I saw her eyes, she looked like she'd seen the Grim Reaper. She knew. Of course, Laurie's gossip crew knew about the allegations. I just smiled and started laughing. If every fucking executive got to blab about my investigation to literally everyone at Mantiss, I was allowed to show up to this party and let them know I wasn't scared of them, no matter how much they talked.

I looked around for anyone else. However, some people from the team were there, mostly Maurice, Christa, and Yanni, people I worked with closely to close sales. Thomas was nowhere to be seen. Neither was his wife. Someone must've told them I was here. Eh, whatever. I knew where probably 98 percent of the skeletons in this company were buried anyway. If he wasn't going to show up to try and defend himself, those skeletons were about to receive their skeletons very shortly. No one at the time knew it.

But someone else was there. Someone I'd only met a scarce few times before. Cary. Right there in the middle of the room. A red carpet was rolled right up to the guy. His Mormon blond hair and blue eyes stared into the eyes of his co-workers as he told his stories. His stance was poised and prepared, standing just below me at six feet flat, fully engrossed in conversation. There was a crowd of people around, mostly salesmen from what I could make out, trying to talk to Cary directly about business analytics or tech or whatever the hell. I barreled through the crowd. He was right there. I stepped onto the red carpet with zero fear in my body. Nobody else was there on that carpet except me and Cary. When he finally acknowledged me, he didn't even flinch. Neither would I.

I reached him and looked for another handshake. "Hey, Cary! Good to see you! How's the week been with the Annual User's Conference?"

Cary just talked right back to me. Nothing. No fear, just classic fucking professionalism. "Great so far! Great. But you know how these events are, non-stop talking for days."

"Yeah! No…" I looked back to catch a glance at Christa. She still looked like I'd knocked over a beehive right next to her. Petrified of the consequences.

There was no way this guy didn't know. I continued. "Actually, this is the first one I've missed since you started doing these. And, um, congratulations on finally setting your wedding date! That's exciting."

Cary didn't even skip a beat. "Thanks, bro! Couldn't be happier." His smile may have been genuine looking, but I couldn't tell what was actually going on with him. I didn't know if he recognized me. He didn't even say my name.

My adrenaline couldn't be any higher. I wanted to confront him on so many things but as he stood there, looking straight at me, I didn't know what I'd even say. Anything that would help me anyway. Even if he did know who I was, the person who made the first move and spoke up about what they knew would lose this battle. And I knew no matter what I said, Cary wasn't going to budge right now. Not in front of everyone. He was smarter than that.

"I'll let you go. Great catching up." I said as I turned around and walked away, back into the crowd. Maybe some of them would talk to me like they knew me.

Suddenly, a group of women approached me. It took me a few seconds before I realized they weren't approaching me maliciously or anything like that. They all looked relatively calm and happy, which surprised me. Some of the women that I recognized were acquaintances of Cary in some way. His fiancée, one of the Enterprise Account Executives she was friends with – Emily, I remembered, and another one of her friends, but some of them were people I'd never even met.

Emily looked like a soccer mom and played the part – she had short, curly blonde hair and a shorter stature, probably about four inches shorter than I was. She lived in the suburbs and had been a stay-at-home mother, but she did numbers regardless. An absolute bombshell for someone living out in Atlanta, too. She was forward, and she spoke first. "Edward! We're so sorry you're going through this. I can't believe this is happening to you of all people…"

I couldn't tell their intentions. All I knew was that everyone inside Mantiss knew, apparently. "Well, it is happening," I responded, furiously trying to mellow myself out.

"How are you holding up?"

"Still need to find a stable job but doing okay."

"Okay, good, good. Stay safe, alright?"

The group of women bid me farewell and disappeared into the crowd of Mantiss elites. Yanni appeared shortly after, approaching me with concern and worry on his face. Yanni was a tall guy, 6 foot, brown curly hair, darker skin, about as young as I was. He'd told me his story before. He'd been with Mantiss since the beginning, having known Cary at the right time. He'd worked his way up to Strategic Enterprise Account Executive.

"Hey, Edward."

I sighed. "Hey, Yanni."

He cut straight to the point. "This is fucking bullshit. Let me tell you. We all know you didn't rape that bitch."

That caught my attention. I hadn't heard that term used to describe my allegations yet. The confidence with which he said it was… well, he'd made a statement.

"I – I mean, thanks, man. Doesn't make it a nightmare. You never know what's going to happen in these situations."

"Yeah, glad I could help." Yanni then stared off into the party, taking his attention away from me. "Fuck, I mean, to call the cops, then have her new husband come into Mantiss years after the party she's claiming you raped her at and accuse you. It's fucking absurd. She divorced her last husband, and she can get Mantiss to fold in on the pressure right now… they couldn't have timed this better if they tried. It's about money in my mind."

I needed to get out sooner rather than later. I'd done what I came here to do, and Yanni'd been fine but wasn't adding anything at this point that I didn't already know. But I couldn't just leave him in the middle of the conversation. "Yeah, I could only guess that's the case…" I started, "But me and my lawyer… we think there might be something else going on as well. Laurie and her husband are trying to bury me criminally, too, but dragging Mantiss into this… they've been planning this for a while. There's something else."

"I know you, man. They shouldn't have fucked up your life. I've never seen you out of line. Every time we've traveled, you've been nothing but nice. There's a million people that work for this company that should've gotten the cops on 'em instead of you."

Yanni's confidence wasn't misplaced, but it was strange to hear someone so assured of my innocence and this direct about it. Not that I didn't appreciate it, but it was just such a departure from everyone else who'd voiced their support.

"You on your feet right now?" Yanni asked.

"I'm working on it. I've got a few bartending gigs lined up."

"It's fucked up, man. Listen, I gotta go and schmooze for a bit, but if you ever need anything, call me. Great catching up with you. Crazy that you're here."

"Yeah, same to you."

And then he was off. I looked around. I didn't want to talk to a single other person in this room. I'd made my statement. I just called an Uber and went home early. No use if Thomas wasn't there. Especially if I couldn't relay anything to him off the record or off the grid.

CHAPTER 15

The next day, I had a migraine, so I picked up a coffee, and headed to The Beer Crew early to talk with Dan about a bartending gig. My phone buzzed in my pocket on the way. I answered.

"Edward? Grant here. How's it going?"

"Good! Good. Just trying to figure all this out, you know?"

"Yeah. About that. I just got a call from Mantiss, and they said you showed up at one of their parties last night. Their Chief Legal Officer just called me. Is this true?"

"Yeah, yeah. I was over at an after-party for the Annual User's Conference. You know about that, right? Yeah, I tried to figure some stuff out."

"Curious Edward, cool, couldn't fucking stop you if I tried." There was silence on the other end for a second. Then Grant continued. "You need to stop. I told you not to do this and Mantiss is fucking furious at you. They called me and said to 'stop poking the bear.' Their words, not mine, although that is also my request."

"Dude, that's fucking funny. I haven't even started to 'poke the bear' or whatever if that's what they think is going on."

"Alright. I'm just relaying the message. They asked me to get you in line. That's what I'm doing."

"Okay, they want me to stop poking the bear? Can you tell them to shut their fucking mouths? I was informed by you and Mantiss not to tell anyone anything-"

"Ed-"

"No, let me finish. I'd only told one person at Mantiss. Terrance. He's getting info for me. Thomas or Cary or someone there, probably all those fucking execs, told everyone at Mantiss because every single person at that fucking party knew what was going on, okay?"

Silence on the line again. Grant spoke first. "Alright. Present moment. I won't call Mantiss and make threats, Ed, okay?"

"Well, if they hadn't opened their big fucking mouths and had every legal official spying on me on social media, I probably wouldn't have shown up."

"Okay! Okay. But you did, right? You did show up and it's exactly like I said. Whatever you're going to figure out is less important than making sure you don't talk to anybody to make sure you're safe, got it? I get it, but god, you're a stubborn fucking Englishman. Just leave them alone, okay? You don't want to jeopardize your job over this. Plus, they could take away your leave if you're not careful."

"I'm getting fifty percent, and I don't get commissions. I'm hurting, Grant. Or I'm about to."

"This is Utah. You can get fired for anything, and it's an At-Will state. Be thankful and find another gig."

"Come on, Grant. You think I don't know that they're keeping me on just to make sure I don't sue them back?"

"Yeah! Be grateful, Edward! That's what I said."

"Well, here's what I'm saying. Tell them to shut their fucking mouths, or I will come after them. I will go nuclear."

"Okay, I'll be clearer. I cannot make threats to Mantiss. What they're doing is reckless, but that's our advantage if we use it, and in order to use it, we have to keep our cool. I'm not going to tell you what you can and can't do anymore because that hasn't worked. But we should not, and will not, squander our advantage by threatening them in any way right now. We'll just take the case all the way. That's our retribution. If the criminal investigation passes, you can go back to work with no problem. In the meantime, find a job. I'm sure a bar or two would love to hire you."

"I don't even know if I want to go back to Mantiss."

"Fair enough. I've got another case on the line right now. I'll call you later. Stay safe."

And with that, he clicked the phone. I sighed. Grant was a killer. He knew the game. Fuck. I would need to stay safe. Fuck!

All those assholes at Mantiss didn't deserve for this to be swept under the rug, for it to just be a court case nobody except my co-workers knew anything about. And for all that time that they were talking shit about me, they didn't expect any consequences. They could just bury me under another investigation, pretend they never knew me, and just throw me under the bus. I wasn't going to let that happen, even if everyone told me it was better this way.

Whatever. I needed to keep Grant on my side. He was key to winning this. I couldn't face this alone. They didn't know I had my ace in the hole. The superstar attorney working on the hardest cases in the valley. The way to make him happy was to stop. So, I would until the time was right.

CHAPTER 16

"Fucking insane that you did all that," Hal said, swirling his glass of beer on the booth's table. I'd asked him to come down to the Beer Crew to catch up. He hadn't been busy this week, so I thought it'd be the perfect time to fill him in. He'd agreed.

"Yeah, it's been a pretty fucking god-awful week so far," I responded, "I got chewed out by Mantiss for a second time and had to talk to Grant about it."

"Going straight up to Cary and telling him to his face… sounds like something you'd do, all right. I just couldn't even imagine wanting to talk to the guy, let alone confront him about a sexual assault case."

"I had to. These guys have it so easy, and they thought they could just throw me out and not have to deal with me. With the case as they're going public? Fuck that. They know what they're doing. That other company Laurie is working for is on my case too. If they're gonna dogpile me, I have to let them know I'm not going to take it sitting down."

Dan then grabbed me on the shoulder, startling me a bit. He grinned. "Hey man, sorry about the lack of job availability around here. Haven't seen you around since we talked. Everything okay?"

I nodded and remembered what Grant had said. "Just some trouble with Mantiss."

"Is it okay if I take a seat?"

Hal was the first person to respond. "No worries, man, yeah. We can talk for a little bit."

And so Dan took a seat across from me in the booth. I'd need to pump the brakes on the conversation. I tried to motion to Hal to keep our conversation under wraps, but it was a tough message to try to communicate with just hand gestures.

Dan shook his head. "Sheesh. I'll fuckin tell you, man. Never never-ending drama over there. Is it Terrance?"

"It's all of them."

"God. If they're all like that, I'm surprised anybody works for them. I haven't liked Terrance since I met him in person."

"…In person?"

"Yeah. His family's old money. Old as the mountains. I've heard of them through some Utah contacts. He's got more money than Thomas and Cary combined, but you'd never know it. He doesn't really act like them, but you can tell something was going on with him."

"Trust fund, kid?"

"Who fuckin' knows? I guess. I mean, he acted like it."

"Yeah. He's helping me with some stuff right now, but…"

"Yeah. I don't know." Dan laid his arm on the table. "You gotta do what you gotta do, but I wouldn't trust a tech CEO west of the Atlantic Ocean." He laughed. Hal responded with a laugh as well.

Dan was acting cool, but I know he only knew all this because he came from old money. Older than the mountains themselves, and you'd never know it either. He was one of the co-founders of the first breweries in Utah, but he'd had some help. It was the 90s, and he'd had the dream to bring beer to the driest state in the Union, so he bought an old warehouse with his family's money and a friend of his and turned it into a small-scale brewery. Even though he had to abide by their nearly draconian liquor laws he was able to put out quality products and rule the industry.

Later, Dan decided that he'd rather work locally and on a smaller scale, so he sold his fifty percent stake to an outside partner and founded the Beer Crew. There was some in-drama that I was aware of between him and his former business partner due to the sale, but whatever. He'd wiped his hands of the event and ran one of the best bars in the state. He was his family's golden child, even if his successes were smaller than his ancestors. Or that's what he said. He knew money got to people.

He saw it in others, too. It was what Mac was trying to do for himself, trying to start a bar. And while Dan would never crush Mac's ambitions, not at all, I knew he knew more than he was letting on.

Having been a businessman, he knew all the personality types and wasn't particularly fond of venture capitalists and other CEOs. He'd been a disruptor in his industry, even *with* his father's money. He'd brought beer to Utah and watched as businesses around him sold out and lost their soul. You could tell he wasn't too happy to see the same thing happen to the tech industry. I think he saw all the money being thrown around and compared it to his own experience. He'd seen how antsy and obnoxious these guys got when talking about company sales but was content being an observer this time around.

"You haven't heard from Thomas about any of this?" Dan asked.

"No. He didn't even show up to the party." It was strange that he hadn't, actually. It was also sort of strange that he didn't reach out to me. I made a mental note to call him later and finished my drink.

"So, how serious is it?" I saw the concern on Dan's face. He'd seen me three times this week, and all three times, I'd been concerned.

"It's bad, man."

Dan shook his head. "Sorry to hear that."

I just shrugged and pushed my mouth to the side. There's not a lot Dan could do right now to help. He then slapped his hand on the table. "Once again, anything for an old employee. Just give me a ring, and I'll make myself available. Whatever it is, give 'em hell."

"Grant and I are working on that. I'm actually going over to his office after this to talk with him. How we're going to approach this, and all that."

Hal smirked. "The unstoppable team!" he said, throwing up his hands.

I laughed. "Maybe," I said, "But Mantiss's looking like the immovable object right now. They may be jackasses, but they're stubborn as shit."

God, it was good to still have friends here, even if they couldn't know everything. I bid my farewells and headed out for the afternoon. It was time to talk to Grant.

CHAPTER 17

I walked into Grant's office. Plain, decorated with accomplishments, mostly business, except for a picture of him and his wife. He greeted me with a laugh, still sitting down at his desk. "Good to see you again, mate! Take a seat." He looked more stressed than usual, but I'd noticed that he was more like this when he was working on cases.

"Good to see you too," I said, sitting down in the chair across from him, "How's everything going?"

"Ah, you know. Never ends. Working on cases, being in court, seeing clients in jail, etcetera. Just took a trip to the court today, actually."

I leaned back in the chair. He'd gotten a nice one for the office. "That's the life of a hotshot lawyer, I guess."

Grant just scoff-laughed and started scrolling through his computer for files. "Yeah, yeah. Anyways, let's get down to business. I got to the detective, mostly the reason why I called you down here. Looks like the 15-minute call you made won't cost you your freedom for the rest of your life."

Holy shit, thank God. "Well, that's a fucking relief."

"And it was Laurie that put the allegations out."

"Okay, at least we both know now."

Grant gave me a look but returned his eyes to his computer screen immediately. "Alright. Can't tell you exactly what he said, but I can say that he barely knows anything about you. So… nice work on that. You had me worried there for a second."

"Yeah, dodged, deflected. Like a Samurai, you know." I made a sword-slashing movement with my hands towards Grant. Grant laughed hard at that one, putting his arm on the desk and taking a second to compose himself. "Yeah, you're right about that," he said through a red face.

"So what's next?" I said, chuckling as well.

"Well, the guy hasn't wrapped up yet, and it sounds like he hasn't found much merit in the case so far."

"Awesome. So, we're in the clear, right? Or at least once he's done with the investigation?"

Grant shook his head. "I fucking wish. I mean, you know there's a ton of cases like these out there right now. 'Especially in all these high-brow industries. They're all getting screened for charges. We're not gonna be out of the woods for weeks, probably months."

"So, wait, it's still gonna get screened? What the fuck, man?"

Grant put up a hand in frustration. "It's not my fault, and they're just dragging all of these out right now. CYA mate. Cover your ass and pass the liability on."

"So, they're still gonna screen it. Fuck! Of course, of all times, they choose this one. So what, I just get to play Russian Roulette."

"All I could do right now is update you. It's gonna be fine. You still on paid leave?"

"Yeah."

"And you know that these are two separate investigations, right? We've got your criminal investigation and your employment investigation."

"Yeah. A criminal investigation is with the detective, and an employment investigation is with Mantiss. Right. We're working on my criminal investigation first."

"Right. Your criminal case is going to trump employment laws, so if you do get charged, we should be able to get the information we need to tackle the employment investigation… unless they've handed everything off to their attorneys."

Huh. That didn't sound great. "What does that mean?"

"Shouldn't have said that. Sorry. They've definitely done that already. Every single one of these companies has lawyers out the ass. Outside law firms. They're going to hide everything behind attorney-client privilege so we don't get any information."

I breathed out. "So… Mantiss could hand off anything that they deem sensitive to their lawyers to hide it. So, like my employment file."

"Mm-hmm."

"So they could put whatever they want into the file? I guess… depending on how they want to defend themselves, it could be a loaded deck for us or a pot of gold."

"You got it. Our job is to wait for Mantiss to make the first move and then figure out what they know for themselves. Keep laying low. We have to see if the criminal case goes any further and what Mantiss plans on doing with it." Grant leaned back in his chair. "God, I need a drink. It's been a long fucking day." He pushed off the ground and rolled in his chair to a closed cabinet. He pulled out two crystal glasses and a bottle of Buffalo Trace Bourbon. Slamming both down on the table, he tipped the bottle and poured one of the stiffer pours I'd seen in a while.

"Cheers. It's not your fault I'm like this, by the way. It's good to see you. Just wish it wasn't under these circumstances."

"Likewise! Thanks for all your help on this."

We clinked glasses. Grant took the larger sip of the two of us. I continued. "And the rest of the boys at the office are doing well?"

"Ah, yeah. Tom and Hayes they're doing good. Working around the clock like me, you know?" Grant answered, taking another long sip. "Early mornings, late nights between jail visits, being in court non-stop, office work…it's work, man."

"I don't know how you all do it," I said. "From the outside, you all make it look like you're Casanovas at work."

Grant just laughed heartily again, probably a little influenced by the bourbon we were both drinking.

"Don't make me fucking piss, man. We all have your back as much as we can. Obviously, I'm the one representing you, but you know."

"Cheers, man. Can't thank you enough." And then we clinked our glasses and went on our ways. I walked out the door, and Grant went back to work.

CHAPTER 18

"It is far better to be alone than to be in bad company."
- George Washington.

I spent the next night drinking at Boarder's Company again. Between bar jumping, the conversation with Grant, and a lack of time in between interviews, I hadn't been there in a while. I hadn't heard from Elliot, but I'd called him just to have a drinking buddy around.

"So, what's been going on with you lately? I haven't seen you around." Elliot placed his hand on my shoulder, but it felt different from Dan's, firmer, like he had to put in effort to be my friend.

"Life's kicked me in the ass. With work and everything."

"What are you doing for work right now?"

Shit. I didn't know how to answer. "I'm on temporary leave."

"Shit, for what?"

Fuck… whatever. He could know what was public information. "Employment investigation."

"Holy hell, that's not fucking good, man! What are you going to do?"

"I was fucking tired of the job anyways. They're paying me fifty percent of my income to stay away, and I'm fine with that, to be honest. They're all snakes over there."

"So wait, are you under criminal investigation as well?"

I raised an eyebrow. "No comment on that one."

"Jesus, the two for one, man. That has to suck. What did they think you did?"

"I'm not talking about it. Can't. Only with my lawyer." The stiff answer that I hadn't been able to give came easily when I was talking to Elliot.

"You've got a lawyer, though? That's good."

"Yeah, running interference with both the detective and the employer right now. Don't know what I'd do without him."

"Who is it? Anyone I'd know?"

"Grant Harland."

"Oh, what the fuck? Grant Harland? What kind of fucking trouble are you in?"

"Not any type of trouble I'm willing to talk about."

"It's just a fight with your employer, right? You don't need some sort of badass super lawyer like Grant for all of this."

"I'm in deeper shit than you think. If this goes all the way, Grant's the only person that can fix this. He's a friend. He can help."

"Hey, I've got a friend that's a lawyer too, someone you can trust. His name's Gordon Weller. He's gotta cost a tenth, and he'll get you out of this. Even if you're guilty."

Alright, what the hell was this guy on about? I'd told him I already had a lawyer. This was getting real fucking pushy for someone I didn't know two weeks ago. "Fuck off, man! I'm innocent and I've already got Grant. We have got a plan."

"But he's expensive! And you were saying that you're only making fifty percent of your income right now?"

"I'm looking for bartending gigs right now. I used to work for a few bars back in the day. Nobody's bitten yet but it's only a matter of time. I'm overqualified to shit, you know?"

"Yeah! Yeah. All that still sucks, man. It really sucks. I'm just trying to help. That's all."

Elliot leaned back into his chair.

"Hey, listen. Does this whole… thing mean you have a criminal record now?"

I gave him another side-eye. "No, actually. Why?"

"Oh, that's great! The cleaner you are, the better."

Oh, God. "For… what?"

He threw his head forward and started speaking in a quieter tone. "I have connections for drug running. Not slinging, like, actually transporting. Cars, trucks, all across the Western United States."

I didn't respond even though my mind was racing a million miles an hour. Holy shit, is *this* why the guy was talking to me? Because he was looking for candidates for mules? Was this how it worked? Elliot would just go up to guys at bars and try to get them to ship narcotics. I mean… was it worth doing at this point? Could I afford to be running drugs when I was already under criminal investigation?

Elliot continued. "You'll get 25 thousand per run, and your clean record would probably qualify you to do two runs a week. Fifty K. One week. Pretty good deal, five figures towards Grant. If you want to use him."

I rubbed my face and, at first, just contemplated how I got here. I'd been a salesman for the majority of my adult life at this point. Mantiss may have been a cesspool, but it was *secretly* a cesspool. The fact I'd even be offered to do this and that I was seriously considering it was… completely different. Not bad. Different.

From the way I talked and the employment investigation I was under, Elliot must've thought I was a bad boy. Maybe he'd scouted me or something. I don't know how, but there must've been some miscommunication. I wasn't about to take shit from anyone, but I'd never worked for anybody illicitly before. It'd be different, but I wouldn't be disappointing anyone or anything like that.

Elliot still didn't know what my job was or where I came from, but it didn't matter. Grant wasn't cheap. If he was serious – and who the hell knew if he was, I might have been interested.

I just started simply – "That's a lot of money per hour," I said, "Are you trying to fuck with me?"

"Well, the runs aren't straight shots. You've gotta take back roads and follow speed limits so you can tell if you're being followed."

"Jesus Christ. Have you done this before?"

"I did, but I'm an organizer now. Good money but rough running. If anything turns shit, you're dead and your family's probably dead too."

Elliot's words hit me like an electric shock. Was this guy out of his fucking mind? "Fuck! What the fuck are you talking about then? Why are you offering me this?"

"Because! We're always looking for fearless, no-nonsense guys who will execute, and from everything you've said tonight, you fit the bill. Don't take shit from anyone, right?"

I sighed. Could I do this? Just based on my previous experience, no, but I was about to go ballistic on Mantiss. And it wasn't like my childhood (and adulthood) wasn't filled with fights with men bigger than me. I could hold my own. "Alright. I can take the pressure. I'm sure of that. Highjackers, grifters, ringleaders, I can run 'em all over if I need to. But let's say I did one to two. Or even enough for a year and make… 2.5 million–"

"Oh, yeah. Once you're in, there's no out."

"Dude–" I led off with, slamming my drink on the bar, "that doesn't make any sense! How are you getting people with clean records if you can't get out?"

"It's just not how it works, and they understand that, Edward! Once you're in, you're in for life. But it's the money you need."

"Okay, elaborate. Once I'm in, who the hell am I with for life?"

"Can't tell you."

I rolled my eyes, and Elliot finally caught on. He grabbed my shoulder and said, "No, no! You're the perfect fit! You're white, and you're from England. No police officer would ever suspect you."

My mind was swimming from the absurdity of the conversation as well as the alcohol that night, so I wanted to get home and stop thinking about this. "I don't know if I'm down to commit to a life of crime *right* now. Can we pick this up another night? I'd need a lot more information before I'd agree to this."

"I don't know what else you'd need. I've basically told you what you need to know."

"Mm. Okay, well, I still need time. I'm getting fucking tired. Life is already complicated as it is."

"No problem. It's always on the table."

I bet. There probably weren't a ton of people busting down their door to become drug runners. I shook Elliot's hand, but this whole conversation felt like a fever dream. I walked out, warm from the alcohol, and quickly drove home to go to bed.

The conversation had come out of nowhere, but Elliot was right, and I guess I couldn't hold that against him. I wasn't going to take shit from anybody. That's what Elliot said, and it's what Terrance had said. But I was willing to stick it out. I wanted to see where that strategy would actually take me.

I was just sitting in my apartment, watching television and trying to unwind, when I remembered what Dan had asked. Why hadn't Thomas called me? It's not like before this, we were on bad terms, and I seriously needed his help more than anyone's. I'd talk to him even just to know whether or not he was on my side with this. It might be dangerous to talk to him, but he might have connections, or funds, or anything. I sunk into my couch and pulled out my phone. For the first time since the investigation started, I dialed Thomas.

My heart rate went up as it rang. "*Hello, this is Thomas Jameson with Mantiss Analytics. Please leave –,*" And then I hung up. Playing phone tag with seven separate people this week hadn't been fun. I don't even know what I was expecting. How the hell was he going to pick up the phone for me after everything I'd already done?

I called again. Help was the most valuable resource I could ask for. "*Hello, this is Thomas–*" and then I hung up again. I called again. "*Hello–*"

I threw my phone on my table. Thomas was one of the only people I had fully trusted at Mantiss, and now he'd gone radio silent on me. I didn't work directly with him on, like, a day-to-day basis, but he'd been a true friend. Someone I thought I could rely on.

CHAPTER 19

We'd met as he was dating my roommate (and my ex-girlfriend) about... a year or so before he recruited me to Mantiss, and we'd hit it off immediately. With him being a beer enthusiast and me working for the most popular up-and-coming brewery in Utah, it was pretty obvious we'd be friends. At the very least. By the time I'd gone to the New Year's Eve party, we'd both been wingmen for each other, we'd both bought drinks for the other, and we'd both pulled each other out of bars before things got nasty. And he'd offered me a nicer job when I was working myself to the bone.

About a week after the party, I received a call from corporate. It wasn't Thomas, and it was someone else asking me when I wanted to set up dates to shadow. I'd said anytime I was free that week, and so they told me to show up on Thursday with a signed non-disclosure agreement that they'd send me through my e-mail.

I pulled in on shadowing day and saw a lot of the same cars I'd seen on New Year's Eve – BMWs, Porsches, some of the most expensive-looking sports cars and electric cars I'd ever seen. The building was a classic campus – brick on the outside, renovated modern office on the inside. Marble, wood, and open spaces as far as the eye could see. There was more glass and windows than I'd ever seen in any building I'd been in before. It was like a super-charged Apple Store, which is what I assumed they were trying to convince people Mantiss was. Compared to Samurai Brewing, the office was absolutely massive – even from the reception area, you could see the multiple floors of the building they owned and operated from.

It was the first day I'd formally met Yanni. He was supposed to be my guide for the day. He walked in quickly from behind the receptionist's desk and met me at the front door. He greeted me with a firm hand wave.

"Cheers, man. Edward, right?"

"Yeah, same."

"I'm Yanni, and I'm an Account Executive for Manhattan. Only heard and seen good things about you so far, from what Laurie and Thomas have said."

"Yeah, well. I'm no pushover. I'm here to try and make a killing." I laughed.

Yanni responded well, laughing along with me. "Well, it sounds like you've got the drive. That's what Cary's looking for. Follow me."

Yanni and I walked down the hall toward the sales department, the walls turning from modern, bright concrete to bright yellow as we came closer. A mural was painted, covering the walls and ceiling of the hallway, with the words "LIGHTNING NEVER STRIKES TWICE" written in big golden letters.

Yanni must've caught me staring at the ceiling. "Oh, yeah," he said, pointing at the mural. "That's a reference to Protract."

"A… reference? Like, a positive reference?"

"I think it's supposed to be motivating. Like, this isn't gonna get done by itself."

"Seems like tempting fate to me."

"Eh, it's art. I don't know what they meant."

Pfft. Whatever. It was just art on the wall. And the ceiling.

"So," Yanni told me, "You're going to be shadowing the Enterprise Business Development Team today. The biggest accounts. That's why you had to sign that NDA. Real high-profile stuff, like J.P. Morgan, Anthem, eBay, companies you've *heard* of before."

"Are you kidding me? A tech company in Utah doing all that stuff?"

"Yeah, crazy stuff. You prepared?"

"Fuck yeah, why would I not be? Just surprising. Never thought I'd be here."

"For sure, for sure. If I had to guess, someone's got big plans for you."

I hit the sales office and immediately felt thrust into a completely different world. The few days I got to be in Salt Lake City when I worked at Samurai Brewing, everyone was relatively laid back, even if they were focused on work. The workspace they had here blew me the hell away – I'd never seen anything like it, save maybe in a few television shows I'd seen recently. No cubicles, just tables set up like dining hall tables up and down the massive room. Chrome white leather couches were set up in odd positions all around the tables.

Everyone was dressed business casual, but many of them were having conversations with each other, walking freely around the office, making calls, and typing furiously on their phones. They were busy, but they were all different types of busy.

"You haven't seen an open floor plan yet?"

"No…No. I haven't."

"More crazy stuff, right? You see the inside of Google or Airbnb; their offices look like this. We just copied them, honestly. They haven't told me what area you'll be working in yet if you're hired, but this is where you'll be when you're back in Utah."

I still could barely fathom the scale of the operation. I knew they were successful, but I hadn't even thought about what their success might look like. "All these people are doing sales?"

"Yeah, some less than others. We're always looking for profit wherever we can, but some companies are just more important than others."

I thought back to Samurai Brewing and the sheer force of will it took to keep that ship afloat. I couldn't even fathom a work environment where people could slack off and still make money. I turned to Yanni. "Hal would have killed us if we ran Samurai Brewing like this."

"Samurai Brewing isn't big enough to have excess workers. Our contracts can dwarf an entire state's worth of profit."

I looked back at the crowd. Thinking back, most of those guys' work wouldn't end up contributing to twenty percent of Mantiss's gross sales for the year. "Jesus," I said, "I guess this is what the big time looks like."

Yanni just continued giving his spiel, still fully in tour guide mode. "Yeah, so how hard you're going to have to work will be completely dependent on the territory you're working. You get Middle America, and you'll be living the easy life. You get California or New York; you'll be working till your ass falls off."

"I was a traveler at Samurai Brewing. As long as I *have* a territory, it'll be easier than this."

Yanni chuckled. "We'll see about that."

After the tour of the sales office, Yanni showed me his personal work area. He took a seat, looked around for another, and couldn't find one. He looked back at me with a pursed mouth. I waved him off. "It's fine. I'll stand."

He pulled his bag out from under his portion of the table and unzipped it. "Pardon me, I haven't eaten yet this morning. Is that all right?"

"Yeah, go for it. I guess."

Yanni pulled a sandwich from his bag, leaving the bag open for me to see. Looking out of the corner of my eye, I saw the top of a Ziploc bag that caught my eye. There was definitely something white, but I didn't want to draw conclusions *just* then.

Yanni unwrapped his sandwich and started taking a few bites out of the most high-society Banh Mi I'd ever seen. Artisan bread and the pork looked like they cost thirty dollars on their own. The wrapper was way too fancy to be related to the plastic baggie I'd just seen. I hardened my stance, pretending I didn't see anything.

It was ten in the morning. Was he already going to do it? It's not like the beer industry was a clean industry, either. I'd been across the United States, and wherever I went, I had to deal with a bunch of boozeheads up and down the chain of command of every business I worked with. But alcoholism and weed addiction felt different from straight-up cocaine. I didn't know what to think – was Yanni the only one here that did that? Was it really like Wolf of Wall Street or some shit? Or did they steal this lifestyle from the old tech executives as well?

"You have done cold calls and e-mail campaigns?" he said through food still in his mouth.

"Uh, yeah. A fair amount."

"All right. You're going to meet some of the Mantiss executives and watch them close some sales in a conference call, but for now, I'm here to teach you about prospecting."

And so I watched as Yanni took the phone, introduced himself to assistants, and sent out massive amounts of e-mails to managers and executives. You always had to be forward as a salesman. Yanni already looked like a pro. He was working fast, too. I didn't wonder why.

I leaned in and took a look at the e-mails. Pretty standard business stuff, just talking up Mantiss as "Innovative" and "groundbreaking cloud technology." Cloud technology. I mean, I knew what iCloud was, but that was the extent of my knowledge. "Hey," I said to Yanni, "Thomas was never able to actually explain to me what cloud technology or data analytics actually *is*. I feel like that's important, you know what I mean?" Yanni just shook his head and took another bite out of his sandwich. "You know Excel?"

"Yeah, I know Excel."

"If you know what Excel is, you know what data analytics is. It's a visual platform that lets people view… all their market research that they've done and all the math they've done to get there, let's say."

"So you sell Excel."

"You say that like it's a bad thing. Microsoft sells Excel and it makes them billions of dollars a year. Plus, it's got cloud integration. You know how you have to file quarterly reports, and if your boss asks you for a change on the sheet, it's a huge fucking pain in the ass? You have to alter the data, and then you have to re-send the e-mail, and then merge changes with his version of the document? That's what Mantiss solves, and it just updates everyone automatically. That's what we're selling."

"That still sounds like it's pretty much Excel but slightly better."

Yanni saluted me. "Exactly. It's better."

He looked back at his computer, thinking of other tips to give me. "In terms of prospecting, you'll be in charge of finding leads on big-name companies that look like they have a lot of lower-level employees. You're going to be selling to managers and executives. Some of them will know how to implement the tech, and some of them won't. You're not looking to sell to the people who are going to use the platform; and you're looking to sell to their team leaders. The bigger the team, the more software sales we make. So don't worry about knowing all the ins and outs of the software. Our IT guys are the best in the world, and they can barely keep this whole labyrinthine system running. It's always on the verge of an update, so just sell them those."

"Well… what should I be figuring out?"

"No matter where you work, Mantiss is all about giving out samples. So, you know how you'd go and push beer on the front lines? Grocery stores, breweries, all that, and try to convince customers to try the product?"

"Yeah."

"Mantiss is all about that, except not like free trials or anything. We're generous with our gifts. You're going to be buttering a lot of people up before selling them the product."

"Oh, huh. How does that work?"

"Once again, not something you need to worry about until you get hired. You good with that?"

I nodded, although I was confused. Sounded like we hired escorts or something, but I didn't push Yanni about it. It wasn't the time nor the place. Not yet.

CHAPTER 20

After my morning, I was shown the food hall (as they called it), and I was offered a free lunch, which I was pretty stoked about. Even the food they had for their employees was high-end, like quinoa salads and stuff like that. I sat down with my lunch across from Yanni and looked at him as he inhaled his salad.

"So, did you work somewhere before this?" I asked.

Through food in his mouth once again, Yanni answered. "Oh, uh, Adidas, actually. In sales. I was a friend of Cary's in college, but it was mostly the Adidas stuff that got me here."

"*Whaaaaat?* Are you serious?"

"Yeah, just a shoe salesman, you know. Humble beginnings, but Thomas and Cary saw the work that I did and wanted me on the team. They actually poached me as well, if you can believe that."

"Hell, you must've been doing pretty well."

"Yeah, you know. I was talking to executives at Shoe Palace, and Foot Locker, and I was reaching out for sports sponsorships and whatnot. I was fucking killing it, dude. And the craziest thing is that it's not even that different from what I do here."

"So, is everyone like that?"

"You'll hear all sorts of stories once you're hired. I don't have time to tell you about *everyone's* backstory. Some of them are pretty wacky. There's a guy here that's a CrossFit junkie that I'm pretty sure used to work for Bernie Madoff's investment firm. Or you know," he said, making air quotes, "'investment firm'. And I'm assuming you've heard the Cary and Thomas anecdote?"

"Plenty of times."

"Mm. Fair enough. But yeah. If you dig deep enough here, you'll meet some strange souls. These walls are all smooth, but behind them are some real fucked up woodwork."

I finished my lunch soon after, and Yanni invited me into a hall and showed me to a conference room filled with executives. "So, these are the Executives and Enterprise Account Executives. You start the sale, and then they close it. All those insurance and finance CEOs want nothing to do with us. They want to talk to Cary, Thomas, and the rest of the executives right below them. But it's important to know what they're knocking down so you can set them up. I'll come to lead you out after. You good?"

I nodded and walked into the conference room. Everyone was wearing designer clothes that must've cost a fortune. More brands than I'd ever seen in one place before

– Prada, Tom Ford, Gucci, Dior, Louis Vuitton, High Tops, fucking everything. Maybe not my style personally. I was more of a G-star guy myself, but different strokes, I guess.

The guys were all huddled around a projector that had another man wearing an expensive suit on it as well. Couldn't tell what it was through the picture quality. My suit wasn't a pushover, either. They must've spent at least eight thousand more dollars than I did. One of the executives came up to me.

"You're Edward?"

"Yes. Am I good to shadow this still?"

"Yeah, yeah! Just stand in that corner over there… we just don't want the client to be distracted."

"Sure, sure." Awkwardly, there wasn't a chair in the corner.

"So, we think that you could probably sign up for our mid-size package and have great results with your team."

"Yeah!" The man on screen said, "I think this is a great opportunity, and I'd love to work with Mantiss, just on brand recognition alone."

One of the executives hit the stop camera and mute button. The executives all looked at each other and snickered. I didn't understand what about. When they turned the camera back on they acted like nothing had happened.

"Alright then," the executive continued, "we're excited to work with you! Can you put

They exited the call, and then one of the execs slammed the laptop shut, nearly breaking it and my ears. "YES!"

"That's what I'm talking about, five hundred K, baby!"

Five hundred *thousand* dollars? No fucking way they were talking about this much money with me in the room.

I met Yanni back near the front of the building. He looked ready to leave. I was also ready to turn in, so we headed towards the exit.

"I hope I get hired. Knowing Thomas only took me so far."

"Yeah, I hope you get hired too. I feel like you're a pretty good guy. Direct."

I gave him a cordial smile back. "Same. Back to you."

"Hey, I've got some cocaine in my bag. Did you want to do a quick sesh?"

Oh. Oh my god. "Heh," I laughed nervously. "Good one. Good one. No, I'm good."

"No, no! I can show it to you. I'm not kidding." He started pulling out his bag. "We can just go to my office and make it quick. Keep it on the down low."

"Uh, no, no. I'm just not a cocaine guy, you know? Never tried it."

"I mean, the perfect time to try if you ask me. I promise it's nothing I wouldn't take. And I'll be there for you if you need help. Listen, everybody does something here. Maurice, you'll meet him later. Up-tight young Mormon, right? Xanax. All the time. Says it helps him deal with the stress. Of everything. Home life, Mormonism, being perfect, all that."

I'd never met someone so intent on getting me to try cocaine. How could I get this guy off of my case? "Listen, honestly, I don't think I need it right now. My life is hectic enough as it is. I don't need cocaine making me loopy or anything."

Yanni shrugged. "Alright, man. Whatever you say."

Well, I guess at the very least, I could rest assured that Yanni liked me enough to offer to do drugs with me. Maybe that'd help in the interview, and maybe it wouldn't. But if anybody could help me get in, it'd be this guy.

I showed up to the interview next Thursday with full-fledged confidence. I had the backing of Thomas, I had the shadowing experience, and I had a perfect sales record to boot. I wasn't even worried about being a beer guy. Sure, it was maybe going to be a culture shock to the Mormons I knew worked here, but Yanni had made it clear that you didn't need tech success to make it around here.

The interview was going well, but the man interviewing me was slow as all hell. I heard his pen click in the back of my mind. Over and over again. I wasn't nervous. I'd splurged on a Giorgio Armani suit to impress them or at least fit in. I had money from working at Samurai Brewing, and I wanted to use it to give myself a better opportunity.

I twiddled my thumbs, waiting for a response from the interviewer. I had places I wanted to go that night.

"So, you worked at Samurai Brewing, huh?"

"Yeah, for four years. Salesperson."

"Gotcha, gotcha. I know them. I don't drink, but I know them."

Trying to be as professional as possible, I launched myself into the story. "Well, yeah. Me and my sales team basically had to build the company from the ground up. I started months after the first brewery opened, and I worked with Hal and his business partner directly to get into bars and pubs across Utah. For the optics, you know."

The interviewer nodded. It seemed like it was going well. I continued. "We got a lot of good press and everything because of the high-alcohol percentage and all that, but everything after that was product quality and sales. We're nationally distributed, and I worked on that."

His eyebrows raised. "Huh."

He went back to his pen, clicking and started thumbing through my resume again. I was qualified. I don't know what this guy was doing looking over my resume for the fifth time. I'd only been hired for sales once before, but I knew it wasn't supposed to take this long.

"I'm honestly surprised. You're not really what I envisioned when I saw your resume for the first time. Mostly someone less lean, if you catch my drift."

"Ah, the beer thing? Yeah, no. I've got my life together." I smiled wryly. Everyone in the beer community knew the phrase, 'Never trust a skinny beer rep.' I'd bypassed the stereotype mostly by working out and being English. People trust your opinions on hard alcohol if you look European enough.

"No, your history with Samurai Brewing is something else. I was kind of set up to offer you a position as a Corporate Account Executive when you walked in, but…"

Fuck, *really?* "What's wrong?"

"Well, you don't have tech experience."

That was *important.* From what Yanni had been saying, it didn't sound like it was a problem at all. And now it was going to cost me my job?

"Um, I was told that would be alright. By Thomas and Yanni, you know."

"Oh, well, I was thinking. You have experience in sales, right? Pretty big ones, too."

"Yeah, national beverage distributors."

"Right. Do you think you could do research on companies like that? Make first contact?"

"Oh, yeah! That was my job beforehand."

"Great! I think you'd be perfect for this role if you were the traveler you put on your resume. I'll send you over to the Enterprise Business Development team. You'll have to re-interview, but I can't imagine that they wouldn't take you."

"…Does that still pay well?"

The interviewer nodded his head firmly. "Oh, yeah. You'll be fine. You'll get four to five weeks of holiday pay, and I can guarantee they'll pay you more than Samurai Brewing did."

"Alright," I shrugged, "sounds fine to me, I guess." As long as someone here wanted to hire me, I was prepared.

"Nice to meet you either way." The interviewer shook my hand out of respect and showed me out the door.

I'd only taken a week off from working at Samurai Brewing, so it was back to sales while I waited for the second interview. It was hard to have my heart in my work when Mantiss was stringing me along, but I didn't have another job yet. Hal hadn't sent me off on any business trips in the interim.

I walked into the conference room for a second time with even more confidence, but this time, I felt like it might not even matter. I threw open the door and saw three men waiting for me inside. It was Yanni and Terrance, and another guy that I hadn't met before. He was wearing a white button-down and a polo over. Our age, but didn't look like us three. He didn't *seem* like he did coke. I wasn't going to jump to conclusions, though.

"Hey, Edward!" Terrance rushed up and gave me a rough pat on the back.

Yanni looked cheery that day as well. "You met him already? This guy's a real one."

The other guy at the table looked much more calm and collected. He was surprisingly built, too. That guy was Mormon. For sure. Despite all that, or maybe because of that. Brown slicked hair, 6' 2", and I'd learn that basically every guy here was a gym rat. This guy was the same. Lean motherfucker. What they didn't know is that I worked out at one of the most hardcore gyms in America. While all these Mormons were mostly going to Utah gyms, I'd gone to one of the exclusive places with executive, semi-pro, and ex-pro athletes and the occasional ex-military badass you'd only ever hear about in books or see on the big screen; they'd also said they had ties with Hollywood. If you knew, you knew.

The Mormon guy, who I would learn was named Maurice, gestured towards an open seat and sat across from me with all the paperwork, flanked on both sides by Yanni and Terrance.

"So. You three know each other?"

Yanni jumped in. "Yeah. Terrance met him at the New Year's party. Thomas told me about him, did he tell you?"

My pulse raised. I didn't know what this guy was like, but I had seen Yanni be pushy.

Maurice gave me a nod. "No, he didn't, but I trust you three. Shall we get started?"

I exhaled. Remembering Yanni's… robust personality, I guess I was expecting his boss to be a bit harsher on him. Hal wouldn't have stood for that, although Hal couldn't stand much tomfoolery.

Maurice started to look through the papers. "You worked at Samurai Brewing?"

"My work precedes me, I guess."

"No, no. I was in the food and beverage industry as well around here. I worked at Talon Distribution up in Ogden?"

"Oh shit, no way! Small world. Did business up there all the time."

"I must have seen you around somewhere if you've worked for Samurai Brewing from the beginning. Can't drink the stuff myself, but my co-worker's endorsements speak volumes about you already." The guy then slammed down a stack of papers onto the table, causing it to wobble slightly. "Alright. Let's get this quiz over with, am I right?" Honestly, thank god these guys were all the laid-back type of professionals. Maybe less work for me, in that case.

The "quiz" the guy was talking about was some basic questions about sales and how to approach new clients, mostly stuff that both my experience at Samurai Brewing and my day with Yanni had taught me.

After the grilling, the guy tapped his papers and smiled. "No, yeah, these two were right. This is basically a done deal."

Yanni fist-pumped. Terrance grinned as well. "I can't believe you're going to be working with us, man!" he said. "Trust me, it's a lot more fun finding and selling to accounts than it is kissing their ass all day."

I shrugged. "Finding and selling accounts is what I know."

Yanni responded. "Fuckin' a man. That's what we need."

CHAPTER 21

It was about two or three days before the e-mail popped up in my inbox. Orientation was in two weeks, and I was told I had to show up at 8:30 sharp. I couldn't believe my eyes. I'd nailed the interview, but the e-mail still knocked me out. I immediately called Mac. I'd known him for a while, but he'd always worked in San Francisco and had only recently found his way back to Salt Lake City. When we hung out in the Bay Area, I'd found him to be a pretty calm and nice guy, so he was one of the first people I wanted to inform about my promotion.

"DUDE! I got the job!"

I could hear his surprised laughter over the phone. "Holy shit, man, holy shit, really?"

"Yeah! Starts in two weeks!"

"Oh my god, dude! Congratulations! What are you doing to celebrate?"

"Damn, yeah. We should, shouldn't we? I didn't even fucking think about that!"

"You were a beer seller, running yourself ragged, and now you've got a cushy job in tech! You did it, man. That's fucking worth celebrating. Listen, I've got some ideas. We'll go out and give you a real party. Maybe just at the Beer Crew? We can still ask Dan to break out the cigars again."

"Fuck yeah. On me, too. I'm getting out of here, and I got a pay raise!"

Mac huffed lightly. "Alright, don't get too crazy now, buddy. We've all got cash, I'm not letting you flex your wealth when you still need to figure out if you like the place."

I rolled my eyes. "We'll see how you feel when you're getting free drinks tonight."

The night before orientation was quiet, and so was the atmosphere around the Beer Crew. Still, Dan greeted me with a large yell of "EYYYYYYYYYYYY!" He ran past the bar to grab my hand.

"Congratulations, man."

I was just in a daze. It didn't feel real having people excited about a new job opportunity. "This all just feels like a prank, man. *Me,* selling software, like, how the hell did I end up here?"

"I'd be fucking asking the same question. The first drink is on me, but you have to buy every single one afterward."

It must've been me, Hal, Dan at the bar, and three other people sitting together in a booth. We spent the night breaking into Dan's collection of cigars and then traveling across Salt Lake City looking for parties happening at pubs once the Beer Crew closed for the night.

Hal must've told every person in Utah that I was hired at Mantiss, as everywhere we went, he screamed it at the top of his lungs. Some of the people he was screaming towards even knew what that was. I got a few free drinks and even got to talk to a few women who were very interested in my new position. Being the center of attention was fun for that moment, even if I had to go to work in the morning doing the same thing I'd been doing for Samurai Brewing. Except I'd be selling Excel.

Eventually, my notoriety wore off, and my memory started getting hazier and hazier. As I sat at the bar downing some whiskey, Dan came up to me and shouted at me over the noise of the bar. "This new tech world is crazy, man! Even crazier than beer. I know people who've lost their minds, man. The whole place is just flowing with a bunch of swelled heads."

"I'm tough as nails, Dan! None of them even seem that bad, honestly. And Thomas has my back! I've gotten into serious trouble on trips in the beer industry, I can handle some guys making money with 'cloud computing.'"

"Alright, whatever you say, man. Trust me, with my background, I know what these guys can be like. Just stay safe. You've got the wits. Just looking out."

I paused. "I appreciate it, Dan."

CHAPTER 22

And then everything went dark. I woke up with a pang in my head. I sat up in my bed, disoriented and close to throwing up. I knew I needed to get to work. I lifted my arm and moved towards my phone on my nightstand.

8:00. My sickness immediately turned to panic. It took 25 minutes to get to work, and I needed to clean up from yesterday night. There was no way I was going to make it. I threw on the Armani suit, quickly washed off, and barreled out of my apartment.

I curved my car into the parking lot and threw the door open, grabbing my bag on the way out. I checked my phone – 8:47. I burst through the doors and jammed towards the same conference room that I had entered the week before. Fuck. Yanni and Maurice were already there, waiting patiently for me. In business casual, as well. I was overdressed to shit.

"Edward, you're late."

I was out of breath and desperately needed a lie to cover up my mistake. "Yeah, sorry. I got caught up. I got hit with traffic."

Yanni looked at me and gave me a sly look. "Dude, you're fine. It's orientation, not doomsday."

I couldn't even muster enough breath to be grateful for the gesture. I just took my seat and

Maurice spoke first. "So! You'll be working under me. I don't think I properly introduced myself last week. I'm Maurice. Welcome to the team, I'll be your manager. I'm head of Business Development, you're going to be a Junior 'slash' Business Development Account Executive. I won't be your boss for the region where you'll be working, but you'll still be reporting to me when you're in Salt Lake City."

"And what region am I working?"

Yanni grinned ear to ear. "Manhattan."

"What, is that good? Do you work in that region, too?" I said, genuinely confused. Yanni looked ecstatic.

"Yes, and trust me, you want to work there."

I just shook my head in agreement and shrugged. I was getting good territory, I guess that was cool.

Yanni continued where Maurice left off. "So, you know Mantiss is growing way beyond its projections for last year, right?"

"No, but I could have guessed from the way Thomas was talking about it."

"Well, we've received huge buzz from news sites and getting positive reception from our clients. That's turning into venture capital that we've been using to expand our sales operations as well as our technological operations."

"Okay." Hal had always hated venture capital guys, he felt like they swung their dicks around and 'leeched off of small businesses' as he put it, but he'd always been in a more precarious position as a person starting a business from scratch with loans and debt and whatnot.

Yanni continued. "I'm sure you don't need to hear all this kind of stuff, though. It's only meant that we're popular and hip and we need to use that to our advantage."

Maurice butted in. "So, yeah. We're in an intense period of hiring and you're going to have to hit the ground running. Honestly, our sales projections are probably one hundred and seventy-five percent of what they were last year, and we're heavily supporting that with manpower to make it happen. You're not even the fifth to last orientation I have to do this week."

"One Seventy-Five? Are you fucking serious?" Oh. I turned to Maurice instinctually. "Sorry." I had Mormon parents. I didn't know what terms were acceptable.

Maurice laughed. "No worries, I couldn't stop Yanni."

Yanni smiled. "Yeah, stop fucking swearing, dude." I groaned. Hadn't heard *that* one before.

Yanni continued. "VC money, dude. These projections factor in the unfathomable amount of investment we've been seeing in the past six months and we've gotta show our investors that we're using the money wisely. Or, you know. Wisely enough." He winked.

Maurice looked at me with a glint in his eye. "Are you familiar with LinkedIn Sales Navigator?"

"Yes, but I didn't use it a ton at the brewery."

"Alright, let's start from there. We've got a lot of software to set up. We can talk about how much work you're going to have to do later. Let's just get some started."

And so Maurice pulled out his computer and started tapping away at the keyboard, pulling up Outreach so I could learn e-mail campaigns and DiscoverOrg so I could directly call executives instead of getting stuck with customer service representatives and whatnot. I also had to use Gong to track my sales calls and grade them by keywords and quality. I didn't know if I was ready to be recorded, but whatever, it was a tech company using other high-end tech. I was told that I'd need to learn all four of this software over the course of the week to succeed and that I was going to have to work on it in my free time. That was fine. No skin off my back at the moment.

Maurice leaned forward in his office chair and attempted to talk to me. "Okay, you're going to build a prospect list and you're going to have to use the Sales Navigator and DiscoverOrg to fill out the spreadsheets. Remember, this isn't practice, this is your first day. You're gonna be going up to American Express, Fox Broadcasting, and Pfizer and selling our software, put those kinds of accounts on the list. We can correct some mistakes, but we cannot babysit you, especially not when you're working in New York. We'll need this done in two weeks, just so you get some time to accustom yourself to the software. After that, we're going right into calls. Got it?"

"Yes, Maurice." No questions asked. This was all in my wheelhouse, I just hadn't worked with Pfizer.

From there I was ushered to about seven different people who were all tasked with showing me how a different software works. After setting up about four e-mails and creating thirteen different accounts with different software providers, Yanni took me to meet Calvin, our Strategic Enterprise Account Executive stationed in New York, over a video call.

Calvin lived in New York City and was a stereotypical New York Jewish man with a wife and kids. His hair was starting to gray and he was a bit less fit than Yanni and I.

Probably stayed away from drugs. From the video call, I could already tell he had his life together – he was surrounded by bookshelves and pictures of his children. He also looked worn to shit – bags under his brown eyes and just generally wasn't as charismatic as Yanni. He looked lazily at us. "All right. Glad to have another local on the team. I only know about Samurai Brewing from what I've been briefed on, but someone said that you did a two hundred fifty-thousand-dollar sale?"

Oh, they wanted to know about that. Well, I was in the mood to brag a bit. "In Dallas, yeah. And I had to work for it. It was with a distributor who I'd talked to in Vegas at a conference, and we'd chatted a bit but I knew he wasn't going to remember me. So I write him a letter."

Calvin squinted. "Like, an e-mail?"

I smiled with confidence. "No, like a handwritten letter. Two years ago, too. I had my phone back then." I picked up my phone to try and show him I wasn't kidding around.

Calvin's eyes went from narrow to wide in an instant. He nodded his head. "Wow, you're an old soul."

I scoffed but smiled. "Yeah, and the guy told me that the letter was the main reason he picked us up – that he wouldn't have even remembered the talk if I hadn't written him personally."

Calvin laughed. "Well, it's not out of the box thinking or anything, but that is the drive that we were looking for. Glad that we've got someone that knows what they're doing on our team, especially someone who already knows how to make sales."

"Well, thank you for the compliment." I thought about what he said, then responded. "So… do people not know how to make sales around here?"

"No, no. I'm just happy you're older than these Mormon kids. And you've definitely got years of experience on them. You're what, thirty-two? All these twenty-five-year-olds married with kids, it's nice to have someone devoted to work and partying. And you're single. All good things in my book, at least around here."

I breathed through my nose. "Well, I'm excited to party with you!"

Calvin replied plainly. "Do your work first. But afterward, we can talk about it for sure."

I was struck by his change in tone, but I nodded. "I understand."

Yanni and I left that conference with confidence in our steps. He looked particularly ecstatic, and not in, well, the way you would expect someone with cocaine in their possession to be ecstatic. "I cannot tell you how fucking excited I am to have you on my territory," he said, "I've got a cool guy generating sales leads on my team for once."

"Cool guy?"

"What, you don't think you are?"

"No, I do, it's just… is everyone else not?"

"You don't know what it's like working with a bunch of Mormons yet, right? Worked in the only business in Utah where you don't even meet 'em. Dude, when we go to New York City for events I'm finally going to be able to have a guy that goes out. You know, for like, drinks. Like a normal person. All these Mormon guys just go to their hotel rooms and talk to their *wives.* Like, listen. I've got a wife, no kids, but I'm not gonna go home and talk to my wife all fucking night long. Not in Manhattan, you know what I mean?"

I gave Yanni a knowing look. "Yeah, I gotcha."

"Dude, you're gonna love it. The women out there, whoo!" Yanni made a brow-cleaning motion with his hand, straight out of a cartoon. "Manhattan is the wildest territory in the United States, trust me. You're never going to want to go back to Samurai Brewing."

As we walked back past the mural with the phrase "LIGHTNING NEVER STRIKES TWICE" etched into the ceiling, I started to think that it wasn't the territory that mattered. Mantiss was just going to be wilder than any company I'd worked with before, and there was nothing I could do about it.

CHAPTER 23

The first Annual User's Conference (ever, actually) was the week after. I participated even though I didn't have clients yet, simply following Yanni and Maurice around and watching them try to scoop up sales. You might think that the first-ever convention for a startup might be a small affair, but no. This was exactly as bombastic as the years after, perhaps even more so. I felt a sense of urgency and concern as Yanni and Maurice talked to insurance executives like they really had to work to please these guys.

The after-party was no slouch either – I believe they'd gotten X Ambassadors to play that year and the atmosphere was rowdy. People were dancing in the center of the floor and some people were even getting close to the ground with some break-dancing moves. Felt like I was in Run DMC's It's Like That music video. I'd joined for a few minutes, but I was content to move my way through the crowd and hang near the bar as usual. I was about two drinks deep. Yanni was on the dance floor and Maurice was sitting at a table talking up some MetLife executives.

Out of nowhere, Calvin appeared behind me. He tapped me on the shoulder and I jumped.

"Hey, Edward?"

"Calvin? Oh my god, nice to meet you in person!"

Calvin looked the same as he did over the video call but with slightly more stubble and facial wear. On the one hand, he was drinking a mixed drink – looked rum-based, but I couldn't make it out. I shook his other hand firmly.

"Same, Ed, same. Is it okay if I call you Ed?"

"No worries. Crazy that you made it out here to Utah!"

"Yeah well, Mantiss flew me out and paid for my hotel, so as long as it's on them, right?"

I laughed. "I suppose! If this is gonna happen every year."

Calvin sighed pensively. "I mean, I'm grinding every other day of the year. I gotta keep up with New York, you know? Got my wife and two kids, a private school, and an apartment, so I never have time to get out. This is the only thing Mantiss'll subsidize besides sales meetings."

"I can only imagine. But you got all that going for you. I know you want to hang out when we're in Manhattan."

"Of course, I'd rather go out every night, and party on the salary Mantiss gives me, but I get to see my kids grow up without hardship and give my wife everything she wants. Or, most of what she wants." He jabbed me with his shoulder. "But unlike these other reps, I can't see you wasting your money. So that's why I have to tell you – remember to enjoy yourself, you're going to be taken care of here."

I lifted my glass to that. "Thanks for the tip." We clinked cups and then Calvin was off.

As I lazily eyed the dance hall, I caught a glimpse of Thomas's current girlfriend, Ashley. Slim and slender, with long brown hair and sharp green eyes. Drop-dead gorgeous. Just like Thomas liked them. I'd met her before, we were exes, but I hadn't seen her in a while. I mostly hung out with Thomas, not his significant other.

As I approached her, she noticed me and ran up to me instead. "Edward! How have you been?"

"Great! I work here now!" I said, a little sarcastically.

"Yeah! Yeah, glad you landed on your feet. Even if Thomas had to do it for you." She winked at me.

Ugh. I remembered part of the reason I broke up with her. I fired back. "Looks like he's both got us in his debt, doesn't he?"

Ashley gave me a more solemn laugh this time, but she kept herself together. "Yeah, he's not here right now, but it's good to see you. I'll tell him you're getting settled in."

"Yeah, cheers." I lifted my glass again, but only about half as high as I did with Calvin. My conversation was short, but I'd had enough for tonight.

I tried to make my way back through the crowd, bumping into quite a few people who gave me dirty looks. I didn't recognize anyone, but it felt like they were all looking at me.

As I tried to avoid everyone's gaze, I backed up directly into someone's drink. "Hey!"

"Sorry, sorry," I said with my eyes down. When I looked up, I saw a sweaty businessman who had obviously just gotten off the dance floor. I'd know him later as Sean, but for now, I had no idea who this guy was. Nor did he know who I was, or so I thought. "Oh, you're that new guy, right?" he said, still a bit out of breath.

"Yep, Edward, nice to meet you too."

"Yeah," Sean said curtly, a smile completely absent from his face. He then walked past me without acknowledging my presence. Huh. Most of these guys have been nice to me so far. Whatever, no skin on my back if the guy was an asshole.

I continued to make my way around the dance floor over to the bar, noticing quite a few more pairs of eyes headed in my direction. They *were* all looking at me. Some with disgust, some with intrigue. Most of them were looking at me with disgust.

I ran over to Yanni. He was chatting up a woman next to us, not looking at me at all. I had to tap his shoulder to get his attention. "Hey, why is everyone looking at me?"

"Um, what do you mean?"

"Well, I feel like half the people here are staring me down like I ran over a deer or something."

"You're just the new guy on campus. That and I saw you walked up to Thomas' girlfriend like you know her."

"I do know her..." I reminded him, "Thomas is the reason I got hired, remember? I'm friends with him..."

"Well, yeah, but I don't think any of them knew that. You're part of the clique now."

"The clique?"

"Yeah, the Manhattan clique! You're at the top of the heap, you know the owners, and you've got the best accounts right out of the gate! I wouldn't blame 'em for being jealous."

"Wait, you're telling me I have the best accounts? And now everybody hates me?"

"Not everybody. Just the other sales guys. Plus, you've got us. Don't worry about them, they're not doing any work."

"So, wait, are you saying that everybody that works in Manhattan knows the owners?"

"Yeah, pretty much. I'm an old friend from BYU, snuck my way in after working at Adidas, you know? Not a coincidence but I think everyone that works there has earned it."

I stared at the ground. Yanni had struck me as a guy who came from money, but I didn't know that I was going to be part of the elites. Or even the elites of the elites. The crazy thing about looking at a crowd full of Mormons is that they all dressed for the occasion, so I hadn't been able to tell which ones had been rich and which ones had been poor. But I guess we were all here now, apparently swimming in a pool of money fifty feet deep.

I left the party soon after. I started to feel my head spin from alcohol as well as the weight of responsibility. I had a bunch of thoughts racing around my mind, and none of those thoughts had answers. How was I going to keep up when I was working in Manhattan? What was Thomas' expectation for me at the company? I had to shake my head and take a few more sips when I got home to take the edge off. I climbed into bed. Everyone had said this job was going to be easier than Samurai Brewing, but I decided that night to work harder than I ever had. If I was getting paid the premium and everyone was jealous of me being at the top, I needed to earn it. Even if no one else was.

Orientation continued normally. I put my axe to the grindstone and started pushing through new accounts. Yanni and Maurice were there to boost me towards more and more customers with larger and larger brand recognition. The week after I started rolling calls. I rang up each executive with a strong resolve, ready to pester them with Mantiss's story if needed, but fortunately, pretty much all of them rescheduled on me or wanted to meet me in person. My schedule for when I traveled to Manhattan ballooned as I continued to ring up CEOs of all sorts of companies. I knew I was supposed to offer them "favors" but I wasn't privy to what those were yet.

CHAPTER 24

The next break I got was a company tailgate party two weeks later near the University of Utah. Every year the U of U would fight Brigham Young University in a single football match that the entire state would hype up. Given the whole "Brigham Young" background of BYU, it was a much bigger deal than anyone outside the state could comprehend. Even for a feature college football match, people acted a bit zealous. The posters around the office called it a "Holy War" football game, for god's sake. I liked college football well enough, but I wasn't a die-hard like these guys. I mostly still called it "handball" around the office as a joke. I could square off with the best of them when required, but real football used your feet. America's wasn't the best kind of football by a mile. I wasn't going to betray my English heritage for a game that only mattered to a bunch of Utahns.

Still, Terrance had roped me into going because the whole crew was going to be there. When I told Terrance all this information about my experience with handball he laughed. "Yeah, okay Englishman, let's ask The Hand of God himself what it's really called."

I smirked. "You act like you care about Argentinian football all of a sudden."

"Hey, it's what happened. And it's soccer to you."

When I drove up to the party I saw a bunch of barbecues and a buffet laid out in front of a giant soccer field. There had to be upwards of fifty to sixty people there, probably every single person who had been at the New Year's Eve party. Yanni, Maurice, Terrance, and Sean were all there, hooking up belts to their waists, ready to play flag football. And right amongst them, I saw Cary. The myth himself once again in the flesh. Cary looked fairly fit for his age, a bit shorter than the rest of the team, and you could tell he was trying to work on his fitness even more because of that. He was standing near a gazebo filled with food trucks hooking up the flag belts to his waist with Yanni and Terrance's company.

"Hey, can I join?" I yelled from across the parking lot.

Terrance noticed me first. "Yeah, yeah! You can fill in for blue."

Cary looked at me and he immediately smiled. "You're Edward, right?"

I grabbed a flag and said, "Yeah, you've heard of me now?"

Cary squinted. "Ehhh, sorta? All that matters right now is what side you're on today."

"Oh, me? I don't have a horse in this race."

"Come on, you're a Utahn! It's mandatory to have an opinion."

"I mean, I'll support BYU if that's what you guys want."

Cary laughed. "Alright then, fence sitter over here, everyone!"

I narrowed my eyes but smiled. "Don't think I won't kick your ass on the field if you talk to me that!"

Cary's eyebrows raised. He looked at me and laughed me off once again. "Alright, we got a fighter here then!"

The match wasn't really that tense overall. I was on Yanni and Terrance's team and it seems like they had pre-gamed, so their motor skills when throwing the ball had deteriorated to the point where it was fairly easy to tackle them and rip their flags. Cary was quarterbacking for the other team, throwing out directions and orders like he was back at Mantiss. When he was in control of the ball, he could outmaneuver anybody.

About twenty minutes in, during a fourth down, Cary called for a hike and both teams collided with each other. I could see Cary's eyes darting back and forth – he was looking to make a pass. Sean was supposed to be open but he wasn't doing a very good job. There were a lot of burly, more built men working for Mantiss than you'd expect. Cary threw to center, hoping that someone would be there to pick up the slack. Eyeing the spot where it was going to land, I jammed myself toward the center of the field. Nobody was there. The ball started falling. I reached out and it practically landed in my arms.

As I ran towards the end zone, ball in hand, I saw someone clapping in our general direction. It was Christa, Thomas' executive assistant, standing next to two other women, one of them I didn't know, and one of them being Laurie. She was shorter than me, and it was hard to tell exactly how tall she was then, but she looked about 5'10" off the top of my head. She was thin but curvy, wearing a dark dress and an orange shirt that accentuated her and matched the sunset pretty well. Her hair was nearly black which really contrasted the bright orange and red colors she was wearing that day. Looked like all three of the women had been talking with each other during the football game. About what I could never guess.

Laurie was wearing her hair up today and had a much more casual shirt and jeans on, but it was definitely her. The minute I scored the touchdown, she saw me and gave a quick one-motion wave. I gave her a salute from where I was standing. Cary looked a little put out from the score I got on him, but it was just a game – nothing was really on the line except for bragging rights.

Terrance stood over his legs with absolutely no breath at all. Yanni called out, "Intermission!" and all ten of us took a walk to the gazebo. I peeled off from the group to go chat with Laurie and her friends, but Cary intercepted me on my way over. "Good job out there, man. You a linebacker in a past life?"

"Hey, thanks, and nah, man. I've just got stamina." I said, catching my breath.

He started with small talk. "Did you get a chance to try any of the food? Complementary, you know."

I looked over at the gazebo. I hadn't clocked that the food trucks looked like they'd be overpriced but they certainly weren't the type you'd just see on the side of the street downtown. "Ah, no. Not yet. I've got all night to snack on food." I said respectfully.

Cary nodded. "So, you're working sales, huh? That's what everybody's been telling me, that we've got an aces sales rep that used to work for Samurai Brewing."

I laughed. Glad he knew who I was. "That'd be me. I'm ready for Mantiss."

"Where's your accent from, by the way, just England?"

"I grew up about an hour outside London, but yeah. Still pretty thick."

"And you moved out here and became a beer salesman, huh? Crazy story man. Thanks for deciding to work with us."

"Yeah, crazy to work for you guys now, you and Thomas."

Cary's face suddenly dropped its cheerful demeanor. "Oh, uh, you know Thomas, huh?"

"Yeah, we've been friends for a long time. We actually met–"

"Gotcha. Hey, could you give me a second?"

"Uh, yeah. No problem."

And then Cary walked away quickly. The flags around his waist whipped around in the wind. Wow. Don't know why he suddenly had a stick up his ass. Was there something wrong about me mentioning Thomas?

It didn't matter. I continued my way towards Laurie and gave her a wave to get her attention. "HEY!" she yelled from the sidewalk near the parking lot.

As I walked up she jabbed me with her shoulder. "What's up, new kid?"

"Yeah, long time, no see. I couldn't find you while I was shadowing, but I remembered you from the party."

"Same, same. I heard you were shadowing that day too. Guess we just missed each other."

Laurie walked over to a streetlight and grabbed it like a character from a musical or something. She seemed tired.

"Alright. Proper introduction time. I'm Laurie, I'm an enterprise account executive."

I tipped my head a bit. "Nice to meet you…"

Laurie threw her head back a little and fell back onto a bench below her. "Man, it's good to get away like this for company retreats. Get a babysitter, hang out with the husband and your friends, you know."

"You got kids?"

"Four of 'em, yeah. Married early, you know how we Mormons were."

"And you're on the…"

"Enterprise team, yeah. I close leads, actually, unlike what Terrance told me you were doing."

"That's still a shit ton of work, you know? *And* you've got children?"

"It's not easy. That's for sure. Our kids are pretty high maintenance, but we're making enough to be able to afford a babysitter. They know it's the big game tonight. That's why we're out tonight."

"So you worked here a while?"

"Yeah, you know. I'm one of Cary's followers if you know what I mean. I and my husband both used to work at Protract and now we're here. He's treated us well."

"Yeah, yeah." Cary sure fucking seemed like the man around town, even if he'd blown me off earlier. I smiled wryly. "You know he's the only guy in Utah to try his hand at two tech companies?"

Laurie laughed. "You know we're supposed to tell that story to clients too, right?"

"Really? Like, just when we're hanging out or…"

"During the meetings. It's supposed to be one of the first five anecdotes we say or something like that. I'm not sure. Every executive's here at the party if you want to ask."

"You know, in beer, and I assume some other businesses as well, you're supposed to sell the product. You're definitely not supposed to talk about whatever the guy did previously. I thought we were supposed to be selling software, not Cary."

"We are. This is just how Cary sells. Me too, now, honestly."

I let out a puff of air. I wasn't about to try and upend company sales culture, especially if they had this much money to blow. Laurie noticed I had something on my mind and smiled at me. "Something wrong?"

"Nah, nah. Just always a lot to take in."

"Mantiss's a lot. No matter what it is, what we're selling, it'll always be a lot." She propped herself up off the streetlight and gave me a spirited look back. "I'll see you around."

I saluted her as she walked off. "Same to you, I assume."

I just stood still as she walked towards the gazebo, calling over to some women who had gathered around the poke bowl food truck. Yanni then grabbed me on my shoulder, giving me a jump scare. I took a second to catch my breath. "Fuck, man. Don't do that!"

"Chatting up Laurie, I see?"

"Nah. Just a familiar face, man. But you're *sure* that girl's Mormon."

"I'd swear on my life. Born and raised. Married, too."

"Damn, so off limits." I joked.

Yanni just kind of did a shrug, an eye roll, and motioned his hands, silently saying "Kinda, but…" I gave him an arched eyebrow but he wouldn't elaborate.

Cary's team had a few weak points so our team won the pickup flag football game. I don't even recall whether or not the University of Utah or BYU even won that week. When I got back to work it was like the game hadn't even happened.

Calvin just greeted me the day after with a nod and a look that told me to work on leads.

Even though we were prospecting for accounts like Goldman Sachs and Sony and stuff like that, we were kept far away from the Mantiss executives. I didn't see Thomas and Cary during (or after) work. My first meeting where I'd see Thomas again was on a conference call month away. And yet I kept hearing the stories – of Cary's master genius, how modest his upbringing was, and how he was bringing wealth, prosperity, and technology to the barren wastelands of the Utah desert.

The employees really wouldn't shut up about him. I also noticed they didn't talk about Thomas nearly as much. Even the executives when I did see them constantly boasted about their experiences with Cary, talking to him over expensive seafood dinners, going over to his house for the holidays. As I started to hear more and more about them from co-workers outside the Manhattan area all about Cary, I started to bury my head in my work more and more.

CHAPTER 25

The first few weekends the non-Mormon guys took me out on the town to celebrate the new hire. I knew Salt Lake better than these transfers and even some of the natives so I was able to get all these guys in without having to wait in line. No money, just connections. Some of the bartenders actually knew my story already and congratulated me with a few drinks on the house. Every single bar in Salt Lake was a target, and we'd hit multiple spots a night. These guys had expendable income to boot, so rounds were on them and they passed them to whoever walked in the door. I bought a lot of Old Fashions and shots of Alpine Bourbon that first weekend. They all rustled me up and talked me up to the bartenders around town.

Alcohol flowed the whole night, and nobody in our group was sober by the end of the tour. Yanni was the real big spender. Obviously, with him closing massive deals on the regular, he was able to throw cash around to reserve spots for 20 or so people at the best restaurants in town.

As the weeks went on, some of the women who were single and even some of the married ones would join us out for dinner. The married ones would bring their husbands and we'd all go out to party. Every weekend turned into a wild social mixer with enough drinks flowing to put the UK underwater. Everybody that went out with us had a story. None of them were from Utah, a ton of them had left their jobs at well-known companies to work for Mantiss, all of them said the pay was better and that Utah was "better than they'd expected it to be." It definitely added to the allure of Cary that he was able to find these many recruits out in the desert.

I knew Yanni and Terrance were both married at this point, but I constantly saw them having rapturous conversations with women. Their arms were always poised to make a move, their mouths always talking about how they were spending their time and money on rich people's things, like Pickleball, or Maseratis. Yanni was a pro at conversing – it always seemed like he knew exactly what to say to keep someone engaged with him. He was a real hit with the ladies from the office at every party he went to – on top of being able to pay for their dinners.

The third time I saw Yanni talking to a woman I decided to say something. I knew the guy was a loose cannon but I'd distinctly remembered him telling me he had a wife. I was a bit too drunk to be courteous. I walked up to Terrance and tried to shout in his ear. "So Yanni's a bit of a ladies' man, even now, huh?"

Terrance looked over at Yanni with his arm leaning on the booth's wall, keeping the girl in starry-eyed wonder, and just shook his head with a smile. "Hey, you know, he knows how to sell, he may as well sell himself."

"Easier to sell yourself when you've got cash, I guess."

Terrance wheezed. "Same principle, man! Same principle here." Terrance was also pretty red in the face by this point.

"So, he's like that while he's working, too?"

"Well, if you mean that he goes big, then sure."

"'Goes big?'"

"Yanni's a bit more of a 'whale hunter' when it comes to working."

"What the fuck does that mean?" I yelled over the noise of the bar.

"You'll see when you get to Manhattan, man! You'll see when you get to Manhattan."

I took a second. Why was I over here talking to Terrance again? Oh, "Right, hey, isn't he married?"

"Dude, lighten up! We're just talking! We're just talking. And if it goes any farther, that's a good thing for us, right?"

"No, no, yeah. Don't want to mess up what he's doing, just wondering, you know?"

"Yeah, gotcha. Gotcha. If I knew how to talk to women like him, damn, I'd be doing exactly the same thing."

"And there's no, like, rules about it?"

"Eh, what you can get away with, right? Everyone good at it does it here. You can too if you think you've got what it takes."

If I got what it takes. Funny turn of phrase, but I definitely felt like I 'got what it takes.' I just felt like I was stranded a million miles away from any other company I'd seen, let alone the ones I'd worked for. I stared at the party again. A mass of employees larger than any company party in the valley right now, most of them I'd never really even know. Half that I was allowed to hit on, half that was hitting on the others with reckless abandon.

Terrance looked at me one more time and grinned. "You're the star of the show right now! Don't know if you can stay that way, but don't fucking waste it, get out there!"

I guess he was right. Even if this was new, if it was reckless, maybe it was better to embrace it. Don't live for a long time, live for a good time and all that noise. Thomas had lived his life like that for the five years I'd known him, and now he'd given me that opportunity tonight as well. So, I took a step forward and pushed my way through the mass.

Christa was on the other side. I gave her a knowing nod and got to talking with her.

CHAPTER 26

"What doesn't kill us makes us stronger."

– Friedrich Nietzche

"Did you see that car right there? The Mini Cooper across the street?"

"I mean, I don't see it now… I kinda remember seeing one."

"That thing followed me here. I'm sure of it."

It was 5:13. I was having a few beers at Boarders Company to take the edge off. I still didn't have a gig to go to and I was holed up in my apartment in the mornings, save for when I went to the gym. I slept on most other days until about one in the afternoon. I was starting to feel completely isolated, cut off from everyone except my attorney. Hal and Dan could only help so much. I was still under employment investigation; I was just waiting to see how the fucking mess played out.

I put my arm on Elliot's shoulder and continued to tell him my story. "So, there's a vacant lot on the other side of my apartment, right? And I noticed that there was that same Mini Cooper sitting slap dab in the middle of the lot. I've never seen a car over there before, but there was a guy in there and he had binoculars sitting on the dash. I swear. He looked at me and I could see him squirm in his car. I pulled out of my car, and he was looking in his rearview mirror the whole time."

"Are you sure this all happened, man? I know something's going on, but I don't know if they're *that* on your ass."

"You don't know what these guys are capable of. Eu–" I caught myself. Couldn't trust Elliot with where I worked. Especially if he didn't trust me. "The company I work for – rich fucks. This is exactly the type of thing they'd do."

Elliot nodded and swirled his bourbon in his hand. "So have you been charged yet?"

"Yet? What do you mean by that?"

"Just asking, you said you were under employment investigation, man."

I had told him that I was under employment investigation, but something was always up about the way he talked to me.

"I was just making conversation, man. Didn't mean anything by it," he continued.

I raised my eyebrow. "Okay… cool. What are we drinking then?"

"Another Alpine Bourbon Old Fashion, please."

I threw some money down. "On me." The bartender signaled to me that he got my message. As he prepared the drink Elliot shot me another strange look. "You gave my offer any thought? About doing the runs for me?"

I shook my head, trying not to roll my eyes. "Not particularly. Still thinking this all through."

"No worries, always open. Take your time." Elliot seemed assured tonight, almost too assured. Like I didn't even have a say in the matter, like there wasn't any chance in the world, I'd say no to his offer. I stood up. I needed to get some air. I walked out into the cold and looked across the street. Nobody I could see seemed to be looking in my direction.

I didn't head for Elliot when I got back inside. It took about five hours for the bar to close, and I spent every one of them talking to other people in the bar. Conversations with other bar patrons could sometimes be exciting, but my story seemed to overshadow them all. I took several more drinks to prepare to deal with Elliot. As the bar started wrapping up for the last calls, Elliot showed up next to me out of thin air and tapped me on the shoulder.

"Hey, me and some people I'm hanging out with are going to an after-party. It's down the street, like, about three blocks away. Do you want to come along?"

I groaned softly. "I think I'm good for the night, man."

"Nah, listen. HEY!" Elliot signaled the bartender. "You got some food here at the bar, right?"

"Food? Here? I've been a regular, and–"

"No, yeah." The bartender said nonchalantly. "We've got some small plates, *tapas,* you know, that kind of stuff."

Elliot looked back at me smugly. "Yeah, so they've got some food, it'll keep you up and we can continue our journey." He winked.

The bartender walked into the kitchen and came out with some charcuterie boards filled with cheese, crackers, pate, and two different types of jams. Elliot took first dibs on the crackers and cheese and started to Halk them down before I even got my hands on them, even though I was the one he was trying to convince to stay.

"I had no fucking clue they served food here."

"Well, I know the bartenders pretty well, I always know what they've got."

"I guess…"

"So, are you sure you don't want to come hang out now?"

God, he kind of had me backed into a corner. I didn't know what to do, or what I would even say. Elliot just seemed like the master at getting you into conversations and situations that you couldn't easily back away from. I was shit-faced and I kind of knew it. So did he.

"Fine. I can hang for a few more hours, I guess."

"Awesome!" And then he dragged me out of the bar.

Elliot's big after-party was at one of those new modern townhomes that had been popping up all over Salt Lake City. Given the new renovations happening in the area, it stood out among the random gray and beige industrial buildings that littered downtown.

Elliot opened the door to the townhome and walked upstairs towards a music source I could barely hear from the ground floor. I followed after him, stumbling up the stairs a bit to the second floor, where the party was still running at full force.

Everyone was dancing and listening to club music. Nobody seemed to be in a bad mood. The room was nice, clean, and spacious, with lots of paintings on the wall – you could tell that the person who lived here had their life together. Someone had thrown up a disco ball and some basic decorations. It wasn't a fancy party by any stretch of the imagination, but they had a few nice couches and a vacuumed rug. Elliot and I immediately headed towards the kitchen to find some more food. Apparently, the charcuterie hadn't been enough for either of us. "Told you it'd be fun," Elliot said through a mouthful of pretzels.

I took a seat on the couch and stared into space. The disco ball's lights put me in a daze and reminded me a lot of when I was at work. The parties in Manhattan, the bars back here, The User's Conference…

Holy shit. I looked around the room, closer this time. The lights, the dancing, the floor, they were just like every party I'd ever been to at Mantiss. The reality slapped me in the face – hard. This was a fucking set-up.

My mind was jumping around the room. The dancers, the disco lights swirling around, lighting up the floor… this was just like the Annual User's Conference. I remembered that they'd hire staged dancers to make the party look like it was a lot crazier than it actually was. Whoever started this party knew the exact patterns of the swirling lights and the forced smiles on the faces of the dancers. I looked over at Elliot – there was no concern or doubt in his eyes. No fear. I can't believe I almost walked right into it.

"Elliot."

"Yeah?"

"Show me your ID."

"Uh, no? Why?"

"Just show me your ID right now. I need to see it."

"What, man? No, fuck off. I don't just give my ID out. You literally know me."

I took a standoff the couch to steady myself and looked straight at him. "All right, I'm not fucking around, are you fucking in on it?"

"What? Fuck you, man, in on what?"

I grabbed him tightly by his shirt and started to yell. "What the fuck do you know? If you don't show me that fucking ID right now, it's gonna be in my hand and you're gonna be on the fucking floor!"

Elliot wrestled himself away from my grasp and pushed me back. "Stop freaking out right now, man. You're drunk, you don't–"

"You're a fucking spy, aren't you?"

"What are you talking about? I'm not! Why would I be spying on you?"

"Why don't you tell me? You're nothing but a fucking stranger that's always acted fake as shit! Trying to recruit me for a drug run, are you fucking serious? And honestly, you've been fucking awful at hiding it! You're working for them or the police, it's fucking obvious!"

Around this time some of the patrons of the party began to notice that a fight was breaking out between two people on the couch. I pinned Elliot to the wall and knocked over a lampshade while doing so. A guy dressed in a plaid sweater came over and threw out his hands between us. "Hey, HEY! Not that kind of party, guys!"

I let go of Elliot's shirt. His face went stone cold then and there like he was almost a completely different person. "I don't know what the fuck you think this is because you haven't told me. If you think I'm part of your company or a cop or whatever, then you're being a fucking freak about it. I'm not. I just wanted to be friends."

"Sure. This from a guy that knows I'm about to be charged."

I didn't stay to hear Elliot's response. The guy in plaid immediately ushered me downstairs and slammed the door behind me. Christ. At least I was outside even if I was alone.

Not that I would have trusted him in the car with me after that debacle. There was no chance in hell. I wasn't about to let him bail on me at a traffic light and let him crash me into a car – make it somehow look like an accident. I'm glad I'd walked to the townhome, but it also meant my car was still at Boarder's Company a few blocks south.

Elliot then threw the doors to the townhome open, exited the building, and turned left. On seeing him, I turned in the opposite direction. At this point, I was heading away from my car, but I'd evaded Elliot. As I walked down the street, I saw a man with a beanie turn and start walking towards me. I glanced up at him and we locked eyes. From the minute I saw his concerned reaction I knew I was in trouble. I sprinted across the street, trying to make it look as unsuspicious as possible. But someone was after me, of that, I was sure.

I heard cars in the distance, but they couldn't have been more than a block away. The screeching sound of their tires hit my eardrums like Q-tips. I wasn't in the state of mind to be able to figure out exactly who it was, but screeching cars out this late at night in Salt Lake City meant that gangs and cops were on the prowl. And they absolutely knew my location now.

I couldn't just lead them back to my car or my apartment. I had to stay in the streets, but I'd have to stay hidden. But first – I needed to get away. I hopped the fence to a single-family home and took a dive behind the bushes, scraping my sweater sleeves on the ground in the process. It didn't matter. I needed to stay focused and stay as far away from these guys as possible. I peeked out from where I was sitting, bruises and dirt on my sleeves. My arm still hurt a little from the fall.

I checked probably five to seven times to see if the coast was clear. It looked safe to go. So, I started walking down the street, making a right at the crosswalk and another right.

I took a tour of the four-block area I was in, weaving in and out of the street, making figure-eight out of my path to throw any pursuers off my trail. There was no time to be scared. I was just cold, and it kept me awake and alert enough to focus on making it out of there alive.

SCREEEEECH! I heard another car rev past, and I jumped another fence. There weren't any bushes. I hid in the shadow of the house. I saw the car pass by me, it looked a lot more like a van, windowless and everything. Did they really put out a hit on me? The car drove probably about five miles under the speed limit as it passed right by me and sped off a little as it rounded the street corner.

I caught my breath. I couldn't fucking take it. Stress and adrenaline were still rushing through my system. I needed to find a safe place to relax. Maybe get a cigarette or some food or something. There was a 7-Eleven about five blocks down if anything. Maybe I could hide out there.

It took me about twenty minutes to walk to the 7-Eleven. I saw more and more people on my way to the store – gang members, for sure. I was still trying to cover myself so they didn't see me, but I could tell from the way they were surveying the street that they were looking for somebody. Had the cops really put the gangs out to get me? Could have probably guessed. These were the fucks that tried to force a confession out of me weeks before for something I didn't even fucking do. Something bigger must be going on for all of this to be happening.

I got there safely enough, still walking, cold as the Arctic. There was one car in the parking lot, probably the employees. I threw the door wide open. The guy at the counter didn't give me a second thought. I looked for some drinks in the back of the store first. Water, Mountain Dew, more beer, maybe a hot coffee or something, I wasn't sure.

DING! The electronic buzzer went off at the front of the store, and it felt like a fire alarm in my head. Five guys staggered in, a stocky one with a chain around his neck and a puffy jacket, the others with sweaters and ink covering themselves head to toe. The guy with the chain is an undercover cop, for sure. The rest were probably lower-level gang members.

I couldn't hide in this light. Fuck. The man with the chain walked towards the drink section. I couldn't make a run for it, and there was nowhere to go. He paced down the aisle towards me. He hadn't noticed me yet, and he was occupied looking at the chip bags available for purchase.

The guy was getting closer and closer to my position at the corner of the shop. I tried not to check in his direction, tried to focus on only looking at the drinks in front of me, and not draw attention to myself. Suddenly he stopped. He opened the fridge door three doors from where I was standing. He picked up a Starbucks Iced Coffee, looked at it like he was inspecting it for quality assurance, and then closed the door to take it to the counter.

I breathed out a little bit, then turned to grab a Rockstar when I saw another one of the thugs right beside me. I must've jumped back a bit because he turned back at me and looked me right in the eye. I got myself together and stood my ground. Stared at him right back.

He exhaled sharply. "Hell of a fucking night, eh man?"

I adjusted to his mood swings. "Yeah. Fucking A. You're telling me."

He grabbed a Rockstar as well and walked away. This guy must not have known who I was. Thank the fucking lord.

I waited for them to leave before grabbing my Rockstar and finally ditching the convenience store. By the time I left the 7-Eleven, I was completely sobered up, and the sun was out. I finally got to Boarder's Company around 6:30 and was able to pick up my car. They couldn't do jack shit while it was daytime.

I drove my car the five or so blocks from Boarder's Company back to my apartment and parked in the parking lot outside the structure. I'd had my lights in the living room of my apartment on all night like I did most nights these days. Nobody could tell if I was coming, going, or what was happening. I had just walked up the pathway to my apartment when I heard the loud engine of some big obnoxious pickup truck pull into a spot right next to the lot entrance. I'd seen it for a few months but it hadn't been there long. Never seen the guy who owned it – until now. He jumped out of the car and pulled out a handgun, already loaded, beelining it for the apartment complex. I was pretty far away from the action, but I either had an undercover cop living in my building or I had a gangbanger after me.

My head throbbed in pain. I kneeled on the ground behind my car and tried to stay hidden and nurse my temples. I was hungover. I couldn't fucking take this guy right now. I made a break for the entrance, all I knew was that I couldn't stay here, once a fucking gain. As I tried to take the side door out of the parking lot I saw two more black SUVs drive past my apartment, about as slowly as the van from the party.

I dug in my pocket for my phone and texted Hal. *"I'm either going out in a gunfight tonight, or I'm going to Prison."* I sent the message.

I knew I wasn't in any position to fight any of these guys. My only plan was outwitting them, but I was still going to be outnumbered if they caught me. Take their gun and start firing back. Best let that not happen.

I still had my hoodie on from the cold winter night, so I pulled it tight and ran towards the light rail station. Every second I was nearly dying for breath as I was still tired and hungry from staying up all night. I ran across crosswalks, keeping an eye out for the SUVs, but I needed to hurry. If hiding by myself wasn't going to work, maybe hiding in a public place would.

I ran up onto the light rail platform and took a seat on the bench next to some homeless people who were bundled up tightly. As I threw myself onto the bench, they both looked at me suspiciously, but I just didn't bother. I'd dated a lady a decade earlier whose ex-husband was a DEA agent. I knew what to do. I just zipped up my jacket further and tried to blend in.

Down the street, I saw a black SUV. I tried to hide behind the frosted glass of the train stop, but it didn't even look like I needed to. They just drove on by. And by the way, they sped up out of the stoplight, I could tell they were pissed and gone for the day, at least. The light rail train eventually showed up, and I got on as a precaution. I hadn't seen the other SUV and wanted to ensure they couldn't follow my trail. They couldn't take me out around this many people, not publicly. I sank into my seat, finally feeling true relief.

And finally, Hal called. I fished my phone out of my pocket once again.

"Hey, Hal."

"Dude, what the fuck are you talking about? Why did you text me that? Are you okay? You have to tell me if you're in trouble."

"Hal, Hal, it's okay, it's okay. I'm on my way towards Sandy right now."

"Sandy? What – why?"

"Give me a second, and let me fill you in."

By the time the sun was the highest in the sky, I'd told him everything. Hal just sat silent on the line for a second.

"Un-fucking-believable."

"Yeah, man. The gangs and the cops are after me for sure. I guess if I was charged it'd cause problems for more than just Mantiss."

"Well, if you need to, you can always hire an army of bodyguards if you want to, but I'm not sure you need one."

"What do you mean?"

"I mean… sounds like you did pretty well for yourself last night. It's just… the way you walk, the way you're out for blood. I don't know if they want to fuck with you. Thank god your night didn't end with anything you said in your text."

I laughed, albeit weakly. I just had barely any energy left. "They don't need to fear my English blood, it's my Polish blood they should be scared shitless about."

Hal laughed back. "Yeah, yeah. Exactly. Where are you now?"

"On the rail line back to my apartment."

"Alright man, stay safe. Call me when you get going."

I hung up. Jesus. I wasn't even going to unpack it any more than I already had. I was just going to sleep.

CHAPTER 27

The night after Elliot's charade, I went to Guarder's Company again. Elliot said he showed up there often, but honestly, I didn't believe him. I'd stood up to him. Even if he was going to get a drink, I doubt he'd show up around here.

The crowd was a bit larger than usual. The space was small, so there were five or maybe six newcomers, but four of them stood out immediately. Two large guys, one muscular and one a bit heavier set, sat next to two girls way out of their league. I took note of them. They looked out of place.

One was wearing a beanie, and the other was wearing an Under Armor baseball hat. Both were wearing t-shirts, one with sports memorabilia while the other was a basic brown exercise shirt. They really didn't fit the clothes they were wearing, neither physically nor personality-wise. I knew exactly what was going on. They were undercover cops. Under Armor was a dead giveaway, and so was the baseball cap. I'd dated a woman about ten years earlier, and she'd told me all about undercover cops and how they worked at both the city and the federal level. Her ex-husband had been a DEA agent.

The muscular one was chatting up the girl next to him, talking about the Denver Broncos from what I could gather. His eyes were constantly darting between the rest of the bar and the conversation he was having. He was looking for someone. They were almost guaranteed to be looking for me. Honestly, they didn't seem like city cops from the way they were acting, but I knew that they were still dangerous.

They tried to be friends with you. Give you a false sense of security. Set people up by getting them to admit to things they didn't even do. Then they trap you. Then fuck you over. That was it. I'd suspected that this was how the shakedowns worked, with normal clothes and fake smiles, but I didn't want to believe it because it was so fucked up.

I couldn't take both of them on at once; one was my height, and one was taller. Nor did I want to cause a scene. I decided to sit next to them, staying inconspicuous by sliding and staying silent. I signaled for the bartender to get me the regular. He nodded. I kept a close eye on both the cops and the countertop to see if I could get any information.

I watched them for ten minutes as they scouted the bar. I smiled and laughed. What a joke. They didn't even know who they were looking for or what they looked like. Crazy. They didn't know I held all the cards, especially since I knew now that people were hunting for me.

"What's up?"

I looked up. One of them was looking at me with a slight smile. "Me?" I said, "Yeah, just hanging out. Nothing much, you know."

"What are you drinking?"

"A Negroni. Can I get you one?"

"Damn, what's that?"

I laughed a little. "Oh, it's from Florence, originally. Campari, gin, and sweet vermouth, on the rocks. A bit of an acquired taste."

"Never seen it. I'll take your word for it. Hey Bartender!" He said, throwing his arm up. "Can I get a Guinness?"

The bartender nodded and grabbed a glass. I looked at the other guy. He was turned around in his seat as the girl next to him leaned on his shoulder. He turned his head left and right. He was totally still looking for me.

"So…" the marshal next to me continued, "Where are you from?"

"Utah."

He laughed and slapped his hand on the table, startling his friend and the girls they were with. "With that accent? Born and raised here? Originally, where are you from?"

I looked him up and down. Yeah, no. He asked twice. This guy wasn't getting anywhere with that question. "Sydney. Australia, mate."

The marshal's eyes widened. "No shit, really?"

"Yeah. My mother was Mormon."

The bartender slid a glass of Guinness to the marshal. He grabbed it and took a drink. "In Australia. That's wild," he said. "Didn't know they had that sort of influence out there."

I knew that whoever was looking for me would be looking for an Englishman, just from others' description of me. I could play an Australian; everybody thought I was one, given I could tan during the summer. I didn't know how much information they'd been given, but it seemed like they'd obviously forgotten or they were playing dumb. Either way, great for me. I could play their games.

"That's cool, man, that's cool. Haven't ever met an Aussie before. Crazy shit over there. Would love to go there and take a vacation. See the outback. What part of Sydney?"

"Not far from a gym called 98 Bondi Beach Gym, if you've heard of it."

The marshal's eyes lit up. I'd hit the bullseye. "Well," he said, "you've had some damn good training, then." He then signaled the bartender and said, "One for this guy, on me."

I shrugged. "Alright, thanks, mate!" The guy still had things to talk about, and I was willing to hear him out, especially for free drinks.

We chatted cordially enough for probably about an hour before

"World's fuckin' crazy these days."

"Pretty important to protect yourself these days."

"Yeah, I got protection." I fired back. I pulled the blade I'd brought to the bar that night, a 6" blade, and showed it to the marshal.

"Wow, hell of a knife." He responded.

"Yeah, gotta protect myself, you know?"

"Still a bit slow if something happens quickly and you're in a fight, but it's got power for sure," he said. And then he pulled a small Swiss army knife blade and flicked his finger, shooting the small 3" blade out of the holder. "You probably want a blade like this as well. Comes out at lightning speed and gives you the advantage to get the blade in the gut. Then you take care of business."

I was a bit impressed, and I still felt confident. His logic was solid, but with both our blades out I felt I could take him on in this situation. "Yeah, I mean, I like that knife and the strategy makes sense," I said. "I should probably pick one of those up myself. Thanks for the info."

"No problem! No problem."

"Next round's on me?" I said.

"I'm not gonna argue with that!" He said. And so I signaled the bartender.

The night continued with me buying two rounds for me and the two marshals. These guys were good with me, and I still had the upper hand. I decided to test them to see if they were even paying attention. I usually don't close my tab out, as I'll just run it all night long and let them take the 20 percent. Tonight, I closed the tab and put my card face up. I looked back at the marshals. They had their eyes on the women they were hanging out with. There was no sign that either of them was even interested in doing their jobs. The bartender grabbed the bill and they didn't even notice that. Missed opportunity on their part. I chuckled.

I decided to head out at closing, walking at the same pace as the marshals as we all strolled out onto the street. The one marshal with the baseball cap patted my shoulder twice and said, "Thanks for all the drinks and the talk, man. Appreciated."

He was thanking me. What a wild thing to have happened. I said, "Yeah, same to you, man. And then they just left in the other direction. As long as all the marshals were like this, I'd have no problem evading them, especially now.

I walked down the street before I passed someone with a recognizable beanie. I looked back around me and saw Elliot's build and the shirt he always wore to Guarder's company. Was he still hanging around here? "Hey!" I shouted. He turned around immediately, with eyes wide like a deer in headlights. I sprinted up to him, right into his personal space. "Pretty fucking low of you to come around after yesterday," I said bluntly.

He was by himself tonight. Nobody else around him. No party, no agents, no nothing. And I could tell he was scared. "I – listen, man. I didn't do anything last night."

"Where did you go after you left the party?"

"I just went home, man. That's all I did."

"I know you were involved, don't play fucking stupid with me. I smell bullshit, Elliot! And I know exactly how to deal with people who are trying to fuck with me."

He didn't even know how to react. He just backed away quickly and started running. Fucking coward. He had fear in his eyes as he looked back to see if I was following. Holy shit. I didn't want to chase him. I just wanted him and his posse to leave me alone. But if they were going to, I knew that I could handle them. I just needed to stay alert and ready for anyone. The cops were trying to set me up from any angle they could, and I wasn't going to let them trap me, no matter how hard they tried.

CHAPTER 28

Work started every day at 6 am. Manhattan was always two hours ahead of us, meaning I had to wake up at 4:45, grab a coffee, and start heading down the road towards the office. Possibly the only good thing about waking up this early was the fact that traffic was fine.

I'd pull up to the office, scan my office-appointed badge, and head straight to my desk. Everyone from the Manhattan crew was already there as well, looking much more awake and alert than I could muster. No wonder Yanni did coke.

Maurice greeted me with a fistful of coffee most mornings as well. "So you're ready for your first trip to Manhattan, Ed?"

I'd gotten into the swing of things at Mantiss, but I hadn't been to Manhattan yet. Cary and Thomas, still nowhere to be seen, hadn't even explained to me what I'd be doing. I was going to be briefed later that afternoon by Yanni on how to conduct myself in New York. I was hoping to get the "favors finally" we were supposed to be passing out explained to me.

But I grinned either way and tossed a joke at my boss. "In what aspect?"

Maurice chuckled. "Well, I mean work. Whatever else you need to prepare for is your business, not mine."

The minute I got on my computer, I checked my e-mail campaigns to make sure that I hadn't messed up the addresses or anything like that. After that, in the first two hours of the day, I focused on new leads because time was always of the essence. If we already got a nibble from our aggressive marketing campaigns or word of mouth, we needed to hook them as soon as possible. Mantiss spent money on these, and I was told they needed to see a return on their investment. So I'd call them. Specifically, call–e–mails got lost and sent out into the Aether. These guys remembered voices, not text. I tried to hit 100 successful calls a day – meaning I actually talked to the person I was supposed to.

The first obstacle you had to overcome was actually reaching the executives. You'd hit the receptionist or the assistant first, then they'd try to redirect you to some lower-level executives without the power to make decisions, both things you wanted to avoid. You gave it the old college try, and if you actually got through to these guys, you'd remind them of the campaign, you'd tell them what cloud services were, and then you'd tell them you'd be in Manhattan. Tell them in flaunty business terms that you'd give them a goodie bag. I *still* didn't know what was in the fucking things, but I was told to tell the executives that.

The second obstacle was actually flying out to New York City to meet these guys. They remembered voices, but they remembered faces and experiences better. Plus, we had some "aces up our sleeves" as Maurice had put it. That's why he, Yanni, Calvin, and I crowded into a room on voice call a few days before my first flight out and had a briefing. Usually, I'd be sitting in on demos around this time, but today we had to prepare for the trip.

Calvin gave me a nod as we started. "You settled in?"

"Settled ain't the word for it, but I know what I'm doing if that's what you're asking."

He smirked. "Alright. So everything you've been doing here so far you're going to have to do in Manhattan. You're going to cut through all the people that don't matter and talk to these high-level execs and explain as much about Mantiss as you possibly can. They can be intimidating, but mostly because they think they're hot shit."

"I've dealt with execs before. I know what they're like. Even knew Thomas, remember?"

"Alright, just making sure. So, the gifts. Here's what we have access to."

Calvin's mouse made a clicking sound on the other side of the screen and I suddenly saw a slideshow of sporting events. New York Knicks, MetLife Stadium, Brooklyn Nets games, everything. And these pictures were from the balconies. Tables catered from the top of the stadium, behind glass walls.

"So what, we give them front-row seats or something?"

"Nah, we have boxes reserved with the stadiums."

"Wait, we just have access to boxes. The boxes in the pictures. At Yankee Stadium."

Yanni just shrugged. "Yeah."

Maurice chimed in. "Front rows at Madison Square Garden, too."

I scoffed. Honestly, I kind of didn't believe them. I knew they had money but I didn't think they'd just give this stuff out. "And I'm allowed to be in the box with them." I tried to clarify.

Calvin shook his head. "Once a month. Everyone you've invited will be there." He then flipped to the next slide, showing off a bunch of upcoming concerts – OneRepublic, Billy Joel, Black Eyed Peas, absolutely massive acts that we apparently just had access to at the drop of a hat.

"How the fuck are we getting these tickets? Venture–" I shut up. Yanni eyed me and gave me a thumbs-up. I had answered my own question.

"We're all about getting the customer by any means necessary. And we have the cash to brute force our way in – don't just leave that on the table."

I just sat, stunned by the names I was hearing and the things I had to promise. Yanni picked up on my confusion and said, "Listen, this is what they expect, and this isn't the long-term plan. We're supposed to cut them off after the first big-ticket event and offer them dinners and modest nights out once they get to know us. It's all about playing the game, man."

I tapped my pen on the table and tried to contemplate just what the hell I was being shown. "Feels like a fucking timeshare meeting."

Yanni paused, then said, "That vigor, yeah for sure. You honestly probably want to use your English background to your advantage, talk up your humble beginnings, and make Mantiss seem a bit more worldly and for everyone. Obviously, use discretion, though."

I shook my head. "Gotcha."

Calvin slammed his hand on the desk. "But you *have* to make sure that the executives we're targeting get the perks.

We need to be talking to the people who have the power to get Mantiss's software inside. We're spending a lot of money to be in there, it *has* to be worth our time, and that means you have to kill it when you're explaining Mantiss at these events, got it?"

I nodded. Yanni leaned in. "Don't worry," he said, "enjoying the game is part of the sales pitch." I just gave him a concerned look back at him. Was selling Mantiss's software part of the sales pitch at this point?

CHAPTER 29

The first plane I boarded I got first class. After all the shit I'd been told, maybe standard for the company I was now working for that had cash to throw around for concerts and shit, but I always flew economy or comfort on my business trips for Samurai Brewing. Especially five-hour flights. I was used to sleeping on airplanes. Even in my newfound digs, that's what I did. I'd already had brutally early mornings working for Mantis, and I was going to need the energy in Manhattan.

As soon as I stepped off the plane at LaGuardia, I felt the energy change. Everybody moved like they had somewhere to be. It was like everyone worked for Mantiss here. The newness of being in Manhattan as a worker in the tech industry started to get to me. I was going to be pitching to some pretty fucking powerful people.

I claimed my bags and got to the passenger pickup. Calvin was there, driving a gray mid-size, waving furiously and shouting "HEY!" to get my attention. I gave him a firm handshake when I got to the car. He looked at the two bags I packed and scoffed. "Light traveler, eh?"

"I'm just good at packing. Five pairs of business clothes."

"Yeah, it ain't like the Utah offices out here. Gotta actually dress up out here in the business country."

Calvin drove into the city like a true New Yorker, quick and forceful, and let me right into the heart of the Financial District. I'd never been. I had to research the shit out of the area before coming, though. It felt like Calvin had built the place with the way he was navigating. I looked around and all I could see were the towering brown and gray marble buildings that you'd only really see in movies about Wall Street. I was going to have to figure out how to get a meeting set up with probably more than twenty high-level executives in these buildings. Like they didn't already have enough fucking going on.

He dropped me off at the Residence Inn and motioned for me to get my own bags out of the trunk. As I ran out and he got out of the car, I cracked a joke. "No Four Seasons?"

"Not yet," Calvin replied. "We still gotta get every single rep up here. Can't be spending on rooms for all of ya."

"Strange where you decide to spend your budget."

Calvin shrugged. "Not up for me to decide."

I tapped my card on the hotel room door and immediately flopped down on the bed. I needed a second. In a few moments, I'd need to sit up and prepare for my meeting in the morning, maybe finish a few more calls before calling it a night. But right now, I just needed a second to take in what was actually going on. I was in a cushy suite in the rich part of New York, on the other side of the country. My world was changing. All I had to do was convince these businessmen that their world would change too.

The first place I needed to go was a firm in the center of the financial district. I was pitching to them early in the morning. I'd already chummed the waters by offering some of the executives some Imagine Dragons tickets at Madison Square, but this was going to be my first job actually convincing them to buy the software. My other job was to make sure they didn't find out it was my first.

I was dressed to the nines in a thousand-dollar brown suit that Mantiss had paid for. This wouldn't even be the fanciest event I'd need to attend. I walked through a crowd of traders and CEOs on the streets and elbowed my way into the first of many brown and grey financial buildings I was visiting that day.

The lobby of the building was massive and would have been charmingly old-fashioned if not for the sheer scale of it all. Marble plastered all over the floor supports, and ceilings. The only modernization was television monitors showing the stock tips for the day. The world of high finance was investing in its own self-image.

Tenth floor. That's where I had to go. I jammed the up button. The elevator jolted and came down to the ground floor slowly. I was prepared. Nothing to worry about.

I stepped out of the elevator and into a hallway made of pure white. The wall past the reception was made out of some sort of oak wood. I greeted the woman at the desk, gave her my information, and then took my seat in the bright-lit room.

A man whose hair was silvering suddenly appeared past the wooden wall. "Edward?"

"That's me."

"Cheers, then. Great to meet you." He stepped towards me and gave me a nod. The guy had a tough demeanor. Grey suit. Black tie. All business. He motioned down the hallway. "I've got two other executives and the head of tech in the room down the hall. I've told them as much as I can about it. We're excited about the software."

As we walked past their sales floor, I was immediately struck by how much it looked exactly like every movie I'd seen about Wall Street, minus the nervous breakdowns. Computers in rows, filled with what I assumed were traders talking at breakneck paces. Not a millisecond of time wasted.

"Thanks for the Imagine Dragons tickets, by the way. I have to take my son to the concert, " the guy said.

"Oh yeah? How old?"

"14, you know. Loves them. I'm a fan too, but this was a real treat. Seats were great too."

"That's what I'm here for, you know? Customer service."

The guy chuckled. "Yeah, you guys in Utah sure know how to do it right."

I scoffed. "Bet that's the first time we've heard that."

I was led to a standard-looking conference room with one of the fastest and spanning views of New York City I'd ever seen. Two other people were there. Both of them wore suits. I could tell which one was head of tech, though. The guy with the messy hair and glasses. Could have been a beer guy with the way he was built. The other guy had the brownest suit I'd ever seen in my life. Don't remember that much more about him.

I set up my laptop next to the projector they had in the center of the room. The three suits were whispering in the background. I paid them no mind. I pulled up the slideshow.

"Alright," the main suit said, "so what is cloud technology?"

I saw the head of tech roll his eyes for a millisecond. He acted like it was fine, but he was totally trying to hide his contempt. Honestly, the guy hadn't even let me speak yet.

"Um, well, yeah. Let's start with that if you're not familiar." I said, keeping my cool. "Cloud technology allows you the ability to transfer files to the 'cloud,' which is a server that multiple clients can access simultaneously. It consistently updates every time a client makes a change to the information and can be used in tandem with spreadsheets to generate data and charts without having to build them yourselves."

I clicked next on the slide. "What Mantiss does is specifically use this for professional data organization. Sales, marketing, sorting analytics, with real-time updating and collaboration to make sending files back and forth a relic."

The head of tech pushed up his glasses and wiped his face. "So, what we're really worried about, or should I say have questions about, is security. Especially if changes are reflected on every client's end."

"Security?"

The main executive picked up from there. "We're in the finance business. We're worried about interference from China, Russia… If our software has any flaws in it or your servers don't hold up for even two minutes, we could be losing tens, hundreds, billions of dollars. Having that happen system-wide could be a problem."

China? Russia? I mean, I had to take their word for it, but I found it hard to believe at the moment that China was going to raid an investment firm I hadn't even heard of.

"Well, I can tell you that Mantiss has the server and software to protect you and your business. We've got 50 companies in the same sector across the United States, all sizes that are happy customers."

"So, what kind of encryption do you use? And what other security measures do you have for firms like ours?"

Encryption? All they'd told me was how to sell and not worry about the tech. "I… couldn't tell you that off the top of my head."

"Well, we need to get information on that, and quickly. It sounds like it'll function. But it's a deal breaker. We're wasting our time if your encryption doesn't meet our standards."

I didn't know and I had to think fast and get somebody else involved. This was the one thing I hadn't been prepped for. I decided to go with honesty. With a kicker. "Um, listen. I can talk to one of my associates, his name is Yanni. He'll know more about the specifics if you need them and if you want, we can discuss it with you guys over drinks after you wrap up your day. On us. We've got some places."

The brown-coated exec and the head of tech raised their eyebrows.

"I mean, I'm not free tonight," said the main executive, "but if any of you are interested you can go and relay back to me."

The brown-coated exec looked pretty damn excited. "I'm always down for free drinks and a chat. 5:30, you both want to meet up for a happy hour?" He pointed at me and the tech guy.

"I mean… how about PDT? My associate really likes that place and told me all about it. Apparently, it's a pretty tight-knit place that only you locals know about."

The main exec spoke up. "I've been there. Great selection, let's head there after work."

"Sounds great! See you then!" I said, trying to hold back my concern. I'd saved the deal for now, but I needed to get a hold of Yanni."

CHAPTER 30

I picked up an Uber and called Yanni in the car. He answered immediately. "Hello?" He asked.

"Hey, man. You never told me these guys care about security. In fact, you told me they wouldn't care at all. They were asking me about encryption. I didn't have an answer yet, dude."

"Hey, hey. Give it a second. The first meeting's always tough, just what did you say?"

"I gave them a short pitch and told them I'd bring you to drinks so you could explain it."

"You told them you'd bring me?"

"The whole crew is in town right now, right? Do you think you could meet me at Please Don't Tell in about four hours? I know you don't have an event tonight. I'll pay for your drink since it's taking time off for you."

Silence over the phone.

"Okay, yeah, no problem. I don't have to meet a client tonight, fortunately. Let's do it."

"All right, cheers," I said, hanging up the phone and mentally fist-pumping. Christ, could I still turn this ship around?

PDT looked like a hole in the wall from the outside, but it was bigger than it looked. There was enough room at the bar to sit us and our clients. You had to walk through a restaurant to even get to the fucking place; that's how legit it was. It was a speakeasy – once you left after the restaurant's phone booth and through their secret door, it turned into a calm, cool cocktail bar. Plus, all the taxidermy animals on the walls and scattered on the bar floor reminded me of the Peruvian Bar. But with more pizazz. Nobody could tell that we were down there, much less who we were and how much money all of us were making.

Yanni had already bought the two cocktails for the duo and had regaled them with all the business stories he had about Mantiss, including a nod to who else but Cary. I sat and tried my hardest to relate – the tech guy's parents were originally from Ireland, so I popped a few friendly jokes at his expense. He shot back like a true sport.

Yanni laid his hand out on the bar table. "So, you guys go to the Adirondacks a lot?"

They both nodded their heads. The brown suit guy responded first. "I go every year with my wife and kids. Tradition, you know?"

"Yeah, I get that. I went once a long time ago, probably when I was… twenty. Did a bunch of skiing. Stayed in a lodge with my family. Beautiful area, right?"

"You're telling two locals."

"Hey, I gotta test you then, right? Have you been to Utah? You think the skiing compares?"

Yanni was fully in his element, ever the smooth talker as he attempted to keep them engaged.

"All right, here's the down-low on the encryption." He said, spreading his hands out on the table. "It's in-house and we've got an entire team dedicated to keeping it up-to-date. We're using AES and tailoring it to our systems."

The exec with us nodded. "AES is good."

The head of tech gave a nod as well. "Yeah, that's basically what we expected, but we just wanted to make sure."

Yanni smiled. "And listen," he said, "if you have any other questions about it, I can get you a direct line with our IT department as well as the teams maintaining our servers. They'll know a lot more about this than us. We're just getting everyone on the site."

The exec laughed. "Yeah, you know about all the Dodd-Frank laws and all that, right?"

Yanni waved off the problem with his hand. "Yeah, yeah, I know it's hard to get everyone. But it's just our job to try. I think we've been doing a pretty good job so far."

The techie raised a toast. "I'm sure once I have the talk with my boss, we'll be in touch pretty often. To a new partnership."

I raised my glass. "To all of us!" Everybody clinked their glasses and downed their drinks.

As the two went over to order some more cocktails from the bartender, Yanni pulled me aside. "Don't worry. You weren't even close to losing the deal, especially if the guy told you he liked the concert."

"I wasn't worried. I knew you could help. And that was all they needed? The fucking name?"

"So yeah, most of these guys' worries are about security, but they barely know anything about it; they let their tech guys handle it. There's nothing wrong with our systems. Or well, *that's* not what's wrong. All you need to do is explain that we focus on encryption and all that and we've got plenty of high-profile clients that trust us with their security."

"I did that."

"Some of the guys are sticklers! Never gonna be happy with anything but the best. I mean, you heard what I said.

You got this now. I don't need to baby you; you're perfectly capable of selling this software."

I took another drink and responded to Yanni. "Are you sure there's not anything else you're forgetting to tell me?"

"Dude, it's just because we don't get a new recruit to the Manhattan team very often! You're out in the Big Apple schmoozing with some of the richest people in finance because they think we're cool, alright? You proved your worth with the tickets and the presentation. We're supposed to be the breezy guys who know enough about a conversation topic to hook them in, and then we can send them to people who actually operate Mantiss. Forgive us for this one mistake, there'll be plenty of banks and firms for you to flex your knowledge on. We've trained you as much as we need to. We might be competing later on, but we're friends for now."

I just kind of gave Yanni a flat mouth and a head shake. I'd been on my toes, I'd done everything I needed to, and they were still putting me in the dark. And now he'd kind of made it sound like it was sabotage. I knew that I was already an outsider due to everyone at the company knowing I was partying in Manhattan, I didn't need the people with me being a hindrance.

At least PDT was nice. As the night went on, we drank a few more times with our business partners before they decided to step out for a second to get a quick smoke, leaving Yanni and me alone.

My phone buzzed in my pocket. It was Calvin asking how the meeting went. I quickly texted him back, telling him that everything was going well and that I'd brought Yanni in to help me close the deal. He answered with something to the effect of "Good to hear, glad those concert tickets paid off in your first sale." I closed my phone. Was it really all about the gifts we were giving out?

"Yanni?"

"Hm?"

"How many of these sorts of gift exchanges actually end in a sale?"

"I don't know. How long they take varies, but I'd say about ten, thirteen percent?"

"What? Seriously? That low?"

"Subscriptions and long-term clients out here are worth any of these concerts fifty thousand times over, dude. You're a whale hunter now, man. That's what everyone out here is doing. Just roll with it a little."

And then, in the middle of the conversation, he just stood up and continued talking. "Hey, I gotta go use the restroom; I'll be back in a few." That was all he said to me before bolting off to the men's room.

The finance guys walked back into PDT and sat next to me, but they very quickly noticed Yanni's absence. Their eyes darted across the room, looking for him.

"Where's Yanni?" the head of tech asked.

"Oh, he had to go take a leak, I think."

"Yeah, I wanted to follow up on the skiing stuff with him. After that, I'm probably off."

I looked down at my glass. The work I still needed to do flashed before my eyes. I wasn't going to close the sale, I'd already kind of messed that up, but I decided to pull out some tricks I learned at Samurai Brewing.

"So, you two got any plans with families this week?" Innocuous enough question. But if you remembered anything of what they said, these guys would fold over backward for you. Didn't need Imagine Dragons tickets with personal relationships, although the tickets didn't exactly hurt your chances.

The exec answered first. "Actually, my birthday's in a few weeks, I'm taking the family up to Vermont to visit my parents. Norwich."

Ah shit, fuck yes. I didn't even need to ask them anything about their birthdays. "Damn, what day? Congrats, by the way."

"Thanks, man. The fifth. Two weeks."

"Cheers to that. Hope you have fun up there. Honestly? I also have an idea for a present. Keep an eye out near your birthday."

"Awesome! I mean, I'm not gonna say no." He laughed.

Awesome. Nearly always worked on executives. They loved being the center of attention, and they loved when you followed up with them. I was going to, write a handwritten birthday card and buy him one of my new favorite books, "Leadership Strategy and Tactics" by Jocko Willink.

The plan was still simple, but everyone was surprised by salespeople who actually cared. Made them feel like you actually cared about the professional relationship, and set you apart from every other guy giving you concert tickets. I'd have to wait a second to send it, but if I sent it right around his birthday, I'd hook them for good.

Yanni threw the door open and seemed surprised by his own strength. He threw himself across the room and over to the seats where both me and the finance guys were sitting.

Yanni looked anxious. Coke anxious for sure. He didn't look at the guys, only at me, whispering in my ear so as not to let them hear. "Hey, are we getting out of here soon? I've got some places I want to hit before the hotel."

I rolled my eyes a bit. He was on drugs. Probably had just done them, and had probably done them before he got to PDT. Please Don't Tell seemed like a more apt name with every moment I spent with Yanni. He wasn't going to pick up on my minute expressions at this point, so I groaned loudly. "Places?"

"Yeah, yeah. You know, out on the town, some strip clubs, you know…"

I narrowed my eyes. He was going to be forward about this. I hadn't been to a strip club in probably seven years, for someone's bachelor party, and it couldn't have been in Utah. Were they… 'better' out here? For a guy like Yanni?

"Umm… did you want to go to a strip club?"

"Yeah, yeah! To celebrate, you know? It's a treat. We're going to Times Square to celebrate. You being out here and helping the team out."

"I mean, it's okay and all, I don't need that, but I'm down if you want to go."

"Alright, let's bounce."

And he bolted without even saying goodbye. The guy turned as he left, confused. The head of tech stopped us as I tried to catch up to Yanni. "Hey, hey, where are you going?" he said.

I responded. "Times Square, I guess."

"Ah, okay. Broadway, right?" he said, nudging me pretty fucking sarcastically.

Yanni butted in faster than I'd seen anybody ever pick up a conversation. "Yeah, yeah, we both know what's going on. You can't come."

The executive feigned surprise. "Aww, okay. Maybe next time you'll invite us."

Yanni and the head of tech thought that was gut-busting, for sure. "You already know more about us than you should. Get back to us once we have a deal." He winked.

CHAPTER 31

And then we were out on the street. We'd showed up by ourselves in an Uber from the hotel, so it was up to us to catch a train or a bus from SoHo to Times Square. I took Yanni by the arm and tried to lead him down the stairs to the nearest train station – 4th Street and Washington Square, but he was already pulling out his phone and calling an Uber.

"Come on, we don't need that."

"Hey, come on, it's gonna be less than thirty bucks."

"So is the train."

Yanni laughed. "I'm not gonna explain this to you again. We don't need to! You don't need to worry about that anymore, so stop it! I got this, I got this!"

A sleek black midsize rolled up right next to us about a minute later, and Yanni folded himself into the car. I followed. He was still sniffing non-stop and rubbing his nose. I sighed.

There's a chance that even if someone's aware of the glitz and façade of Times Square, they'll at least know its history as a sleazy part of town. Well, the minute Yanni stepped out of the car and outside of the square itself, we were flanked on all sides by gentlemen's clubs and smoke stops, just like the stories of old. Everything looked like it was built in the 70s and 80s, and only about three-eighths and only about three-eighths of the lights worked at any given time. However, as we passed these buildings, Yanni violently turned right into a nameless building with a bodyguard at the front. I passed the bodyguard – the guy didn't even look. Inside, I saw plush couches and a linoleum stage lit up so bright you couldn't even tell it was night. Tonight it was just me and Yanni, as nobody had agreed to come with us, nor did anyone know we were here. I guess that was good for Yanni. I didn't know how much anybody else knew about this.

But it seems like he was well-known around these parts. A man wearing a Tommy Bahamas button-down threw his hands up in the air the minute we entered the room. "Yanni!" he called, going up to pat him on the back. "How's it going with Mantiss?"

I was immediately a bit confused. Yanni wasn't Mormon, but he'd gone to BYU and had a wife. Going to a strip club every once in a while made sense, I wasn't new to it, but this guy two thousand miles away knew who Yanni was and what company he worked for. And he worked at a strip club. It was fairly obvious that this was more than the occasional "treat" he'd pitched the journey as.

Yanni pulled out a card. I hadn't seen him use it at any of the previous places we'd gone to, but I also hadn't seen him use really any credit card yet. I couldn't imagine that he didn't share a bank account with his wife so I was sure this was a company card. Or something along those lines.

I looked around some more. A few girls were on stage, pole dancing. They weren't topless yet. But with the amount of money being thrown it didn't look to stay that way for long.

As we walked up to one of the dancers, she stopped and looked at Yanni straight on with a smile on her face. Looked genuine enough, although I was in a strip club.

"Heyy Yanni…"

Oh my god. The way the lady sultrily said his name. Even over the noise of the strip club, I heard it loud and clear. I shook my head and stepped away from the dance floor. This was too fucking funny.

The dancer continued. "I see you brought a friend. From the company?"

Yanni grinned. "Yeah, he's new."

"So, your other friend's still 'doing gangbusters' or whatever you said?"

I bit the bullet. I had to know. "How do you know about Mantiss?"

Yanni slapped me on the back. Quite hardly, actually. "You don't like confiding in the secrecy of strangers?" He said with a smirk on his face.

The dancer stood up and looked down at us in her tall white heels. "Oh, Yanni's told me *all* about all the cool things he's done. Places he's been, money he's made, all thanks to that cloud stuff."

"I'm about to close a six million dollar deal over three years," Yanni bragged, "Should be going through in the next month or two. The commission fees they're gonna pay me for this are gonna solve everything."

The woman, still standing three feet above us, arched her eyebrows and kneeled down to talk to us. "Wow, sounds like you're pretty successful at that company these days."

I looked at him with a tentative smile. "Looks like you're pretty popular around this place. Or your wallet is, at least." I winked.

Yanni just chuckled and then put his hand behind my back. "So, this is one of my co-workers, Edward."

Holy shit, he was introducing me to a stripper he knew. What was I supposed to do? Shake her hand? Say "pleasure?"

Fortunately, she moved first. "Heya, Edward. Nice to meet you. I'm Janie."

"Yeah, nice to meet you too," I said, giving as little effort as possible. She didn't put her hand out, so I didn't offer mine. This was all a bit much for me.

"Yeah, we were just in the Financial District," Yanni bragged, "he's trying to follow up on his first leads, and I tagged along for drinks."

"You're really living the dream, aren't you? Working with high finance and all that…"

I scoffed at the absurdity of it all. This was just completely over my head.

Yanni coughed and sat down. "Alright, ready to enjoy the show, man?"

Fuck it, you know? When in Rome or Babylon, maybe. Sodom? Whatever. One of those. I took a seat on the couch and watched as Yanni leaned right up against the stage and stared at the dancers with another one of his classic sly smiles on his face. I'd watch from a distance. Yanni's being this into strip clubs was almost entertainment enough.

We paid for our own drinks. They had a bunch of specialty cocktails. We were in the center of New York, and although this place didn't look sophisticated from an outside perspective, it still knew how to have a party on the inside.

And so Yanni and I talked into the night as the women danced for us. Yanni didn't have cash, and so was using his credit card to tip the dancers – with a card I'd never even seen before.

And then I woke up. Like I'd been on anesthesia. Not a lick of what happened was still in my mind. At least I was in my hotel room. The alarm clock wasn't blaring or anything; it was actually quite peaceful. The room wasn't trashed; just some sheets were thrown on the floor. I assumed I'd gotten home through another overpriced Uber, but I didn't remember anything about what had happened last night.

"Do you remember anything about last night, Yanni?"

"Not after the strip club, no. I woke up with a text to Calvin, saying I was gonna go out and spend all my money on hookers?"

"What the fuck?"

"Don't worry, Calvin's used to this at this point."

Wait, what? Calvin was *what?* "I mean, did you do what you said you were going to?"

Yanni groaned. I could hear the grogginess in his voice and felt his hung-over struggle as he went silent, presumably to look around his room. "I mean, not that I'm aware of. I don't see any signs of sex or women in my room."

God, Yanni still didn't have a clue what to say and when to say it. Unless it was a business meeting, I guess. I grabbed my forehead and pulled my face.

"Well, it looks like it's fine over here. We didn't call anyone else? Or do anything?"

"No, no."

I scrolled through my phone, looking at my most recent messages. I hadn't texted anybody, but…

"Holy shit. I called the executive last night."

"What? No, no. Really?"

"No, no! It didn't connect! It didn't connect."

"What? Dude, just tell me that part first!" Yanni laughed, and I smiled after all this. I started laughing. I put my head against the wall of the hotel room and slammed my fist on it. The second fucking night, I was in Manhattan, and I'd already been to a strip club with a coworker that had offered me cocaine. On a night I barely remembered doing a business meeting that involved using Imagine Dragons tickets I'd given to the CEO. I'd sold beer before this. Jesus.

CHAPTER 32

"Dude, you didn't tell me that I was gonna get the most important territory in Mantiss!" "Hey, it wasn't my idea!"

"Yeah, yeah, not fully. It's not entirely your responsibility, I get it. Hide behind Calvin and Maurice, I gotcha." I winked. I was just having fun at Thomas' expense. Manhattan over the past few months had been as crazy as advertised, and more.

Thomas shook his head dryly. "It wasn't my idea, Ed. It's alright. You're handling it, from what I've heard, so it's all good."

I didn't have much time to talk to Thomas these days, much less about work, so this was a nice time to bring up his nearly unbelievable amount of confidence in me. We'd been able to hang out every other weekend or so when I wasn't with the Manhattan clique. When we did go out, it was usually just us and Ashley, who was still dating Thomas at the time.

Thomas was hanging out with Ashley these days a lot more than before I started working at Mantiss. I'd known Ashley for longer than Thomas had known her, but there really were no hard feelings between us. At this point, Ashley and I were completely platonic friends, having been separated irreparably by our work at the time. She'd been a real estate agent at the time I met her, and I was a beer salesman who traveled the country once a week. There just wasn't any time.

Either way, today Terrance and Maurice were with us, hanging out at the Park City Wine Festival during Oktoberfest. We were doing Savor the Summit out in the downtown area, meaning that the streets were lined with picnic tables where everyone sat in a long row that stretched down the mountain. We were headed to Snowbird later in the week, the big blowout event for the Manhattan crew. Today, we were sitting around, mid-day drinking and taking in the sunshine, just like all the other well-off people at the event.

Ashley put her arms up on the table. "Did you hear? Laurie's getting divorced." I stopped eating. "What? Laurie? Really?"

"Yeah, she doesn't want to be Mormon anymore. Her husband wasn't too happy about that, but she's committed to getting out. So they're separating."

Terrance leaned in. "I could see it, honestly. She never struck me as someone who loved that lifestyle anyway. Getting married that young… She's thirty now? She's outta there. Honestly, good on her, you know? To freedom!"

Thomas concurred. "Yeah, no kidding." He raised his glass.

Right after we all pushed our glasses together, Ashley started going off again. "Yeah, so Laurie is totally using a bunch of dating apps, right? She's matched up with a ton of people outside the company already. Once a week, twice a week, she's gone on a ton of dates, and I think I heard somewhere that she's matched with, like, ten guys already! God, wish I was her." She said, grabbing tightly onto Thomas' arm. Terrance rolled his eyes.

The group all laughed except for Maurice, who chuckled slightly. I'd almost forgotten. They were totally hooking up. How did he even feel about that?

Ashley leaned in towards me. "You know, I know a few people interested in widening their dating pools. I think I even heard some people around the office might be interested. Courtney, maybe. Planning around their newfound freedom if you're interested…"

It was my turn to roll my eyes. She was always doing stuff like this to me, trying to set me up. Just because I'd been single since we broke up, and she thought I'd be 'perfect' for one of her girlfriends, especially if they were just divorced. Honestly, I think she just liked playing matchmaker. "I think I'm good for now, Ashley. Mantiss isn't Samurai Brewing, but it isn't easy, either. I don't have the time." I said, sipping on some more Pinot Grigio. She shrugged. "Have it your way, you're missing out. They're interested in flings…" she said, raising her eyebrows a couple of times. But I just raised my hand. She'd tried to set me up with a few of her friends before, but the dates didn't really go anywhere.

CHAPTER 33

Over the next week before Oktoberfest, I spent every night connecting with someone from work over some extravagant Utah outings. Yanni and Terrance both invited me to Utah Jazz games with front-row tickets near center court – right up in the action. All around town, the Mantiss crew got me into the best restaurants and bars at peak hours. Brasseries, Sushi, and at least four steakhouses where we'd drop a bill of fifty per visit per person on food alone. These guys hung out and partied, not like they were on top of the world, but because they were on top of the world. They didn't have anything to worry about; like Yanni said, the software practically sold itself.

The day before Oktoberfest I pitched the idea of going to a Real Salt Lake game to Terrance, and he accepted. He'd just been able to score a suite to the game through a local business we'd sold to in entertainment or something. Seats in the boxes in the front row.

I took my seat in the leather chair and nudged Thomas. "Hey, football, right?" Terrance took a swig of beer like a champ. "Alright, fuck you, man!" I shot back jokingly.

The game started and Terrance started going into full 'local sports fan' mode, alcohol and everything. Underneath the screaming of the crowd, he was screaming orders. "COME ON, THAT GUY'S OPEN!" and "THAT WASN'T A FUCKING PENALTY!" as he threw things on the ground. I was shocked. A completely different guy showed up to the game than I'd seen working.

The ball hit the net, and the announcer screamed, "GOOOOOOAL!" and Terrance let out a guttural scream. I felt like I was in England for a split second as I saw him yell like a madman at football. Terrance was breathing heavily after expelling that much oxygen. He looked at me and laughed through tempered breaths. "WHOOOOO!" He yelled as the players returned to the center of the field.

Post-game Terrance and I stepped out of the arena, with Terrance basically sweating his entire face off. "Holy shit," he said, wiping his brow, "what a fucking game."

"What did I tell you? Football in Europe's always better. Now we just gotta see the Jazz, and who knows? In Manhattan, are we going to raid the Empire State Building? Parachute off the Statue of Liberty?" I said sarcastically.

"Dude, you're joking, but this is just the tip of the iceberg. Just wait until we get back to Manhattan."

"Oh yeah? Well, I don't think it's going to get fucking crazier than the night I had. Yanni and I went to a strip club!"

I howled but immediately noticed that Terrance didn't have a similar reaction, so I stopped myself. He kind of just scoffed and played it off.

"So wait, you all know what Yanni's doing?" I asked.

Terrance put his hands in his pockets and sighed. "Yeah, Yanni definitely does coke and tries to lay the charm on while he's out. And I mean, I can't stop him. Not my place, not my interest. Nobody can stop that guy. I'd do the same if I were him."

Yeah… that was a way to put it, I suppose. "And so you all know about what he's doing in Manhattan."

"Nah, all the executives know, man. They'd never tell you, though. He's basically like Mantiss royalty. That six-million-dollar deal, he's not joking about that. He's an asset. He's basically a lucky charm at this point."

They hadn't fucking told anyone yet? For how long had he been getting away with it? I looked at the moon and reflected. "I guess it's not hurting anyone but himself right now."

"Sure, and it's not like he's a jackass or anything. We'd probably give him a lot more shit if he wasn't meeting his quotas. But he is, so we don't. Them's the rules."

Terrance stumbled into his car. As he leaned with the window open, he gave me the peace sign and drove off.

CHAPTER 34

Oktoberfest was the next day, and the entire executive branch of the company showed up. Laurie was there, Yanni, Thomas, Terrance, and Maurice were there, and all their assistants had also showed up too. That meant Christa was there as well, as would Laurie and Courtney.

I hadn't seen Christa a ton around the office, but she'd done her best to wave towards me every time she saw me. I waved back when I noticed. Laurie had also been hard to catch, especially outside of business hours. I'd only met Courtney within the past week, with plenty of meet and greets from Ashley involved. She was Australian, and I had slightly ribbed her for being English myself. She was about as tall as I was, skinny, with long brown curls and brown eyes, and she was always smiling. Not that that set her apart from every other salesperson I worked with, but hers seemed slightly more genuine than most when she talked to me.

That October hadn't been cold, but we were still up in the mountains. Everybody had their sweaters on, moving together between the billowing white tents to keep warm. Thomas and Ashley were mostly schmoozing with some of their corporate friends that evening on the other side of the room. Laurie and the girls were sitting in a separate corner,

I assume to discuss the upcoming Mantiss girl's night in about a week's time. I tried to listen to their conversations and while I heard some names pop up – Maurice, Laurie, Christa, Shelley, mine, I didn't hear exactly what they were talking about. They were giggling, though. Having fun talking.

Maurice had pulled me aside and we were talking business. "So, we're about to try and strike a final deal with Tiffany and Co. It's on the last leg of the journey; just have to reel her in. Ten million over two years if it goes through."

"No shit, that's fucking massive! Who's on it?"

"Drew."

"Drew?" I looked over at Drew. He was a blonde guy with a bowl cut that had about five empty clear plastic cups near where he was sitting. I hadn't really talked to him too much despite him working in my territory. Yanni had told me once that he was alright but nursed the bottle a bit too much.

"Honestly, I hope the guy's ready for it. It's always the last few meetings that are the hardest. They love you, but the more they get to know us, the more we have to be on our game. You get that?"

I shrugged. "Sorta."

Maurice tagged himself out to go get some more sparkling water. I looked back over at the girls. They were staring at me. But the minute I looked over, they all turned away and giggled. As I sipped on some pumpkin beer, I saw a familiar face push through towards me. Christa. She was wearing a fairly formal dress and skirt for what amounted to a giant kegger for thirty-somethings.

"Hey, Edward!"

I finished the sip of my beer and set it down for a second. "Oh, hey. Christa, Thomas' assistant, right? I've seen you around."

"Well, no need for introductions, then I guess."

I laughed and she leaned up against the corner of the wall. "I guess I don't need to ask how you're fitting in with the Manhattan clique yet either then, right?"

"Oh, Christ. Yeah, they're a rowdy bunch."

"That's what I've been saying! That's why I elect to stay here in Utah, you know? Something about over there seems like it'll drive you crazy."

I wanted to tell her so badly about all the shit I'd seen Yanni do, but I couldn't just spill that out to his boss' assistant. I was so tired of keeping track of who was supposed to know what. On second thought, she also probably already knew, but whatever. "Well, you're not wrong," I said instead. "Those guys are rowdy when they're unsupervised."

Christa lightly laughed. "Life must be interesting for you over there."

"Oh, don't get it twisted, it's still work. I think that Mantiss might just be rowdy in general.

I mean, we're at a work party in Snowbird, for god's sake."

"Oktoberfest is fun, though! You're not Mormon either, right? This should be like, your haven!"

I scoffed. "Bold of you to assume I feel comfortable here. I don't think I've ever socialized with the upper class as much as I have this past month."

"I'm sure that you partied here when you worked at Samurai Brewing, you everyman you." She punched my arm.

"Hey! You could learn a thing or two from me," I fired back. "You don't even know what kind of world I've lived in."

"Yet." Christa smiled smugly.

"Is that a promise?" I asked.

Out of the corner of my eye, I saw Ashley take one look at us with her eyes lighting up, with the biggest smile I'd ever seen on her face. Bigger than when she was around

Thomas. Her excitement felt ravenous, even from the other side of the party. Oh my god. Was she pairing us?

Suddenly, Laurie appeared out of nowhere and pushed past Ashley from behind, carrying a cup of beer in her hand. "Hey, you two…" she started, "you guys enjoying the festival?"

"Um, yeah," I said. Christa just nodded. I gestured in Christa's direction. "Me and Christa… we were just talking about the beer here at Oktoberfest, you know?"

"Yeah! Yeah. It's good. It's good." Laurie said, swirling her own drink. "Listen, I wanted to ask you, Edward. After your guys' and our girl's trip, I was thinking about having a party. Across the sales teams only. Would you be interested in coming? Me, Courtney, and a bunch of other people from both Manhattan and the other regions are going to be there. Are you interested?"

"Um, sure. I guess. A bit of a way out, I feel, but sure."

"Great! I'll text you and get you the address and time!" Laurie said, pulling out her phone to do just that.

"Eh, well, I guess I'll see you around the office," Christa said, smiling faintly at me from behind where Laurie was standing. "I know you're busy traveling, but maybe we can get together near Salt Lake sometime."

Whatever Ashley and Laurie's plan was, I could tell that Christa was interested. Even when Laurie had seemingly sabotaged our conversation. Accidentally. She was cute, and I was willing to take a chance, even if Thomas – oh, wait, fuck. Thomas.

"Let's just take down each other's numbers right now and we can figure something out if I'm free," I said. I couldn't right now. Not with the commotion, and not with Thomas tentatively knowing.

"Alright!" She said, pulling her phone out of her skirt pocket. We quickly put down each other's numbers and Christa then ran off, saying "Talk to you at work!"

CHAPTER 35

The guys and I had to also plan our trip. Both the girls and the guys planned separate trips at Mantiss as celebrations. The girls were off to Beverly Hills to stay at the Beverly Hills Hotel, where they'd go get spas and manicures and massages. We had different plans. I think it was actually Maurice who had suggested we go to Key West and do deep sea fishing all day, buying an Airbnb to accommodate everyone. We joked that since the girls decided to go to Los Angeles, all the guys said, "Hell no!" and just went a small distance away toward the Keys.

Of course, we took a mid-day flight down to the Miami International Airport and spent the rest of the day driving through the fifteen or so bridges needed to get to the rented house. It accompanied all ten of us that went and was right next to Jimmy Buffet's recording studio. As we got further and further down the Keys, it felt less and less like we were in the United States and more like we were in the Caribbean. It felt like a resort across multiple islands – golf carts, mopeds, live music every night, and a bar on basically every landmass we visited.

Our backup was always San Diego but Maurice and Yanni had both heavily suggested going to Key West instead.

Apparently, they'd both been a few times and liked this area miles better. As I looked out the window, I could see why – it was a complete turnaround from Manhattan.

Even out here, Yanni and Terrance couldn't keep back from being wild, throwing themselves into pools and waves of alcohol, chatting up beachgoers, and talking about how successful they were on dry land hitting the beach immediately and then stopping at the Ernest Hemmingway House on the first day, as well as the Truman Little White House. We came back and crashed at our Airbnb.

Yanni had bought some canned cocktails in Miami to split between the ten of us, so the party didn't stop once we got home. The house had its own pool as well. We all crowded around the beach chairs and the barbecue cracking open more and more mojitos and rum punches as the sun set over the ocean.

Back inside, Yanni and Maurice were sitting on the couches in their bathing suits, still wet from the pool. They hadn't bothered to dry themselves off yet. "So, what's going on with Christa and you?" Yanni said nonchalantly. It immediately raised a few alarm bells, as I knew exactly what he was thinking.

"Nothing much, we're just talking. How do you know about it?"

"I mean, Ashley was all over it. She couldn't stop herself from telling me."

God damn it. Even when it didn't seem like she was directly involved in my love life, she found a way to push herself back in. "God, she doesn't know when to under-share, does she?" I relayed.

"Fuckin' A, man."

"I mean, Christa's nice. We didn't get a chance to talk too much up at Snowbird but I got the ball rolling."

"Well, that's nice. 'Getting the ball rolling.'"

"Hey, cut me some slack, okay? I want to. Fucking trust me. There are real issues. She's my friend's assistant! This is a business, I'm a salesman for it. That's what I'm here to do. I don't know if that's what I should be doing."

Yanni set his drink down on the round glass table in front of him and coughed.

"So, did she give off any signs or what?" "Signs?"

"Like, that she was interested."

"Well, she started talking to me about Oktoberfest and Manhattan, just made some light conversation, and then asked if I wanted to hang out around Salt Lake City. I mean, I might take her up on that."

Yanni slammed his hand on the desk. "Ed, she's totally into you! She wants you. Holy shit, that's golden."

I sighed. I already knew that. And I wanted to take her up on that. But Yanni was acting crazy. "The fuck do you care, man? It's none of your business."

"Dude, Ashley told me something; I don't know, I just thought I'd ask, but holy shit, man, you need to go after it."

"Listen, she's attractive. I like brunettes. Always have. Especially when she was at Oktoberfest, she looked like a northwestern belle, you know? A Utah nine, for sure."

Terrance rammed himself into the conversation. "Yeah, don't know where she got that body." He motioned short curves with his hands.

I shook my head and huffed out a laugh. "Yeah. Anyways, she's funny, she's causal, not wild like you fuckers…" The crew laughed. "She's got stuff to talk about, I like that, but I don't know if I can, plus there's—"

Yanni jumped on the couch and started bouncing up and down like a fucking teenager.

"Dude, you gotta take advantage of this, you gotta take advantage of this! You could date Thomas' assistant!"

"That's the thing, though! I know Thomas is gonna be a fuckin weirdo about me dating his assistant, and I'm not sure if I want to do that!"

"Nah, dude, just go for it! Don't worry about Thomas, he's gonna be protective of his assistant, but it's not like it's his daughter or anything."

"I mean, that's kind of strange, is it not?"

"Dude, this place is a fucking mess when it comes to hooking up. Everybody's repressed,

working at an upstart–"

"I don't think a six billion dollar valuation qualifies as an upstart–"

"Let me finish; they've got the cash to throw around and the confidence to pursue their co-workers; of course, it's gonna be a breeding ground, you know? I can probably name like, ten separate business consultants at this company that are hooking up with account executives. Maurice is hooking up with Shelley, the digital marketing manager!"

Maurice's whole demeanor turned sheepish at that. "Come on, guys. It's not that serious."

Yanni kept dogpiling on him, though, laughing drunkenly through the whole scenario. "Don't you have a wife and kids?"

"Dude, it's not like that! I'm just getting to know her, okay?"

"Nah, they're totally fucking. Don't let him lie to you."

Maurice scoffed, but I could see it in his face. No matter how much it hurt, Yanni, in his inebriated state, was right. I couldn't believe it; Maurice was taking pills and was a Mantiss guy now. But even through all of that, I didn't know the extent he was engrossed in the company culture.

Yanni continued his rant. "It's not Thomas' job to keep the workspace pure or whatever, and if it is, he's been doing a pretty fucking bad job of it. You know he hooked up with someone on the sales team, right?"

I gave him a confused look. "Umm, really? Like, recently?"

"Yeah, no, it was a while ago when Mantiss was first starting, but it happened, I swear."

Terrance walked in, apparently having heard everything, busted into the room, and said, "Yeah, you remember Pete, Yanni?"

"Holy shit, right, Pete!" And before I even got to ask Yanni who Pete was, I got a lecture. "Pete was at the Annual User Conference trying to hook up with a client and was getting wing-manned by another guy, and he got there with them, and he got found out!" Yanni was nearly on the verge of tears at this point.

"Well, what happened?"

Terrance picked up the story. "They got a wrist-slap from HR. I think one of the guys that.

works there actually hooked up with someone else." He said, snorting a bit.

"Anyways," Yanni continued, completely sidelining me, "all this is to say that Thomas shouldn't be a weirdo about it! You should just hang out with her. Christa's hot, too. Don't miss your chance. Listen, maybe that party in a few weeks is something you can talk her up at."

"Listen, I know she's attractive, but you think I should talk to her at Laurie's party?" "She's gonna be there. Don't know why she wouldn't."

"Be careful," Terrance butted in. "Laurie told – told Harrison –"(some guy that worked below us and had been 'hanging out' with Laurie) "that she wants to get with you too. And then he told me, I think."

"You're out of your mind."

"I swear! I swear on my life." Terrance said.

Holy shit, that was a lot to take in. I didn't know what to think of what Terrance had just said – I couldn't even separate reality from fiction anymore. There weren't any crazy orgies or anything happening anywhere else that I'd worked, so there was that first. It definitely seemed like one of those things I should have chalked up to the Mantiss lifestyle. Plus, all these words coming from Yanni didn't make me feel like going out with Christa was the right thing to do. I just tried to push back and get him to calm down, taking a second to walk outside. As the guys continued to dive into the pool and swim across, I took another sip of rum punch and looked out at the green-blue ocean. I sighed. I didn't know what I was supposed to do.

The next two days or so were the days that we spent deep sea fishing, looking for Mahi Mahi, Black Fin Tuna, and all sorts of snappers and lobsters. The third day we were there, a truck pulled in in the morning, packed with about seven to ten mopeds, one for each of us at the rental house. The truck backed in, beeping loudly, waking everyone in the house up. Yanni was the only one outside.

I walked out of the house, still rubbing my eyes, and saw Yanni grinning ear to ear. "Look at this! Are you fucking pumped for this?" He yelled over the truck engine.

"Holy shit, you rented all of these?"

"Yeah! You don't even know what it's like riding Key West on a moped, do you?"

I shook my head. "Can't say I know yet."

Yanni began unpacking the mopeds out of the truck and threw me and the rest of the team's helmets to boot. "So what are we doing, playing Fox and Hounds or something?" I asked.

Yanni laughed. "What, you mean grab pop guns on these things and try and shoot each other?"

Terrance responded. "Yeah, off the islands? Through the streets on the tip of Florida? That sounds fuckin' sick."

"I'll be real," Yanni said, turning to me. "That's a bitchin' idea, Ed. Let's do it."

I was kidding at least a little bit. It was a game I'd played in the woods of England with my friends as a child, but I didn't think they'd actually go for it. I thought maybe we'd go to a less inhabited part of the city, but I didn't think we'd be speeding in between traffic in downtown Key West. And yet, in a split second, the ten of us had split into two groups, and the Foxes were already speeding off.

Fox and Hounds was a game I expected some of the Mantiss people to know about, but I didn't expect there to be this much support. It was a hunting game, just about the Hounds team catching the Fox team within a specified time limit. I knew Utah was a big hunting state, or at least from what I could tell, but I didn't think everyone was just going to be into it.

"Let's tear up the Key West streets!" Terrance said, motioning for everyone on our team to load and start the chase. I clicked my helmet, took a breath, and got into position. I revved up the engine on my moped for about ten seconds, then jammed out of the rental house's driveway. We tailed the other team towards downtown, where about three of them took a left turn. I followed the group past a group of hotels and beaches on the ocean, trying to keep close to my targets. They looked back for a split second as I chased them down. While on my moped, I aimed my gun at the back of one of the salesmen from the Northwest market and took a shot. Direct hit on the back. The guy spun out and stopped while the other two continued down the road. I couldn't stop to enjoy the scenery or say hi – there was hunting to be done.

The game probably took an hour, but the Hounds eventually won – it was always easier once they'd been caught. Yanni was the first one to take off his helmet back at the rental. "Alright, round two?" He said.

"Sounds good to me!" Terrance answered. "Switch sides, let's go!" And this time we were off. The game lasted until sundown, at least. We probably played three or so rounds before we called it quits. Eventually, Yanni called the moped rental place, and we all packed the mopeds back into the truck. What a rush.

After spending the next few days exploring the reefs, visiting the Southern Point of the Continental US, and going out to the American Shoal Lighthouse for an afternoon, we all boarded back into our vans and headed off the island chain. As I scrolled through my messages and saw Christa's 'just checking to see if this is you' text she had sent me at Snowbird, the conversation with Yanni reappeared in my head. God, was everyone at this company exactly like him?

The day after we got back from Key West we were back to work. I still had leads I needed to work on and now that I was fully in the swing of things, I was calling executives back to back to get them signed up with Mantiss. Maurice had made it clear to me that we also had to plan for an event that Thomas and Cary were holding. It wasn't close, but it was up in Park City. It was during Sundance when he said that they were going to be holding a party for a bunch of Wall Street bankers, I and about five other representatives were tasked with calling every banker we knew to pitch them the trip. Cary and Thomas would handle it from there.

CHAPTER 36

Thomas and I decided to head out to a Jazz game he had tickets for that night. He'd gotten a corner lounge and was hanging out with a couple of other tech CEOs, but just as a get-together, not like a business meeting. Everyone was wearing Prada, Dior, Versace, and Gucci sweaters, and they were all bouncing between watching the game and watching it on our television.

As I scarfed down some chips, Thomas approached me with his hand grasping a club soda. "Hey, Ashley came into my office today and told me that Christa was interested in… dating you?"

"Oh, my god, Thomas. I'm sorry about all this. Honestly, it was my fault for even talking to her. We don't need to talk about work–"

"No! I mean, I told her that it was too close to home to work, trust me. This wasn't my first idea either."

"Okay, I guess I understand."

"She said Christa was a bit disappointed after she talked to her and that she felt like it was me holding you back. And I don't want to be a total stick in the mud, right? So here's what I'll do –" he said, "I'll give you three dates. To see if this is going anywhere. So don't fuck it up, alright?"

Um, "Cool." I said. "Uh, thanks. Yeah!"

"But listen…" he said, putting his arm on my shoulder. "Don't fuck the help!"

I felt a shock run over me. What the fuck had he just said to me? The help? As in, did he see his assistant as a maid or something? And he told me that? What the hell did he just say? Did I hear him right?

Thomas looked askew at me. "You got it?" "Yeah. Got it."

Thomas smiled and slapped my shoulder. "Good. Don't worry. I'm not gonna be spying on you or anything. Just want to make sure nothing bad happens or goes wrong, you know? Sorry if I freaked you out there."

"No worries, man. I guess. I'll try to take her out next week after I go to Manhattan again."

"Sounds like a plan, then! Excited for you two."

Holy shit. I needed to get some overpriced stadium beer at that point. I walked off, heading to use the bathroom, trying to make sure Thomas didn't see the absolute stupefaction that was on my face.

Life returned to normal, except for me having a hyper-awareness of all the hooking up that was happening across the company. I started to notice on our nights out that every night, all of my co-workers were heading home with someone new, driving home, doing god knows what, and then partying the next day like nothing had even happened. Marketing, sales, business consultants, and client success managers- it did not matter who it was; it was getting out of control. The day after Thomas gave me the "go ahead," I guess I'll call it, I saw Yanni take home one of Laurie's friends, and Terrance left early to go… somewhere. Yanni was fooling around with everyone he could, but he had eyes on Laurie and all of her friends. He'd talk to anybody, but he knew Laurie's group the best. He really didn't tell anybody he was going to leave; he just kind of left, usually followed out the door by another woman. He didn't tell us he was going home; that was all I remembered. I even saw Drew hooking up with someone in marketing.

One night, another woman, Shelley, a woman who worked with Laurie, came up and taunted me. She worked in Digital Marketing, and she was the manager, but it didn't seem like she wanted to talk about work. She just smiled with wily eyes and told me that she "heard Laurie and Courtney wanted to hook up." I'd just laughed. "Well, that's too bad if that's true. Kinda sucks. I've already got someone I'm interested in. Already had other propositions." That morsel of gossip got her off my back. Even the mystery of me getting asked out and going out with someone unnamed was enough to drive Laurie's group wild with speculation.

And I still had Laurie's party, which I had to attend. Holy shit. By the time all this had gone down, I was exhausted by all the auxiliary shit I had to deal with from Mantiss. It is not even work-related, but I could hold it together. I wanted to go and mingle.

The night of, I was sitting on my couch. Over the past week, I'd been trying to separate myself from Mantiss a little bit and take a break. I took a second to visit Dan and Hal at The Beer Crew earlier that day and was now past two beers and exhausted in my apartment. That's when Courtney texted me to make sure I was showing up at the hotel. I don't think Laurie had rented the room, I think it was Maurice's. Her message read; "Are you coming to the party tonight? Everyone's coming over. I think someone here is interested in you."

I paused. "Wait. Who would that be?" I sent it back.

"Only one way to find out!"

"I've gotten tired today, but I know you planned it. I've already been out every night this

week. I need a break."

"Alright, well, hope you make it."

And that's when a familiar number showed up on my phone and buzzed in my hand. It was Laurie. She'd texted me. "Hey, are you gonna make it to my party tonight?" "I told Courtney I'd consider it, but I also told her I'm tired. I could really use a chill night…"

"Come on, it'll be fun! Plus, I think someone's interested in you…"

I texted back. "LOL. Heard that before."

"LOL," she sent back. "So, does that mean you're coming?"

I thought about it. "Fine," I sent back. "I'll stop by for a bit, but I'm not making a promise."

"Alright, we'll be waiting for you here. Starts at 6. See you there!"

I rushed to my fridge and crushed an energy drink. I knew this would be a longer night, despite them making it seem like I had a choice to leave. They always had a way of cornering you to extract workplace gossip.

I showed up at 6:30 sharp. I knocked on the door and heard someone from inside say, "One second!" in a cheery voice. Fucking people.

Laurie opened the door topless. Oh my god. It was like I'd been struck down. She was still covered, sort of, in her underwear and pants, kind of, but something had been going on before I got here, and she wasn't being subtle about it. "Well, come on in!" She said, tilting her finger slightly towards her. "Time to celebrate."

My eyes darted to anywhere but Laurie, which was hard because she was standing right in front of the doorway. Behind her, I caught a glimpse of what was going on. I saw Yanni, Maurice, Drew, Courtney, everybody buck naked. Was that… I saw someone. Was that the soccer mom from Atlanta – Emily? What in Christ's name was happening in there?

Thomas' voice rang in my head. "Don't fuck the help!" It had sounded like crazy shit when he'd said it. It still did when I heard it again in my head. But I had no idea that his advice would ever mean anything. There'd been a real reason he said that. He'd known what was going on.

I didn't know what to do. 'Don't fuck the help.' Jesus. Don't fuck the help. Don't fuck the help.

CHAPTER 37

After all the craziness I endured, I finally got to see Christa. I didn't know what she would be like, away from work, and I was more than a bit concerned. We'd only talked in the context of Mantiss, and now that I had *more* context, I didn't know what she knew and what she was willing to talk about. Hopefully, she was more interested in me tonight than she was in talking about work. It hadn't even been that long since Laurie's celebration.

We'd decided on a Broadway show – something she suggested, but I had suggested the Book of Mormon. She'd agreed, which was already a hopeful sign that Mantiss hadn't fully gotten its grasp on her. We both thought it was a good way to break the ice and have something to talk about over dinner afterward. I picked her up at her apartment, and we drove downtown together.

It was already darker when I pulled into the parking lot. I locked my car and walked Christa across the street. She'd dressed a bit warmer and more formally for the occasion, as had I, but her face read more like she was looking for something casual and fun. I was down for that, especially to start. "Hey," I said, "so, you ready to see Mormonism laid bare?"

Christa laughed. "Never been more ready in my life, Edward. Let's do it."

The show was a riot, as to be expected, and it seemed like Christa was enjoying herself as well. She laughed and rocked back in her seat, almost like she knew people who acted exactly like it. It was a classic joke in Utah at the time that the Book of Mormon was nearly a documentary about people everyone knew. Christa and I knew all these characters too well, and so did everyone else from the looks of it.

As the lights went up in the theater and people filed out, Christa sat with a pensive face for a second. I couldn't tell what was on her mind. After noticing my eyes on her, she giggled and then got up. "That was fun, right?"

Afterwards, we had dinner at Masuri. The food was stellar as always, and we were content sitting at the sushi bar finishing up our sake and water. We'd mostly just gone over the show while eating, with her confirming that she'd seen her close friends in the characters on stage.

Christa swirled her glass and took a drink of water out of the straw. "Hey, sorry about Thomas again."

"What are you apologizing for? It's not your fault he's a stick in the mud about this. If anything —"I stopped myself. Whoops. There were a thousand reasons not to go into what

Thomas had told me. "Well, whatever. Listen. Let's stop talking about Thomas. I want to know what you've been up to."

"Well, I've been eyeing a couple of concerts that I'm going to go to with some friends outside of work; Ed Sheeran's going to be in town sometime in the next few months; I might go see Harry Styles with some of my family in Colorado… you know. I like going to those sorts of events."

"Harry Styles, eh? So you're into Englishmen, huh."

Christa nearly spit bubbles into her water. She smiled. "I guess I am. All types, as well, I guess." She thought for a second before continuing. "Crazy that you got here, you know."

"Yeah, I guess. I didn't even really know Utah was a place when I was growing up. My parents had talked about it once or twice before my mother and I came down here. I grew up Mormon, for god's sake, but I couldn't imagine what it looked like or what actually went on inside, you know what I mean?"

"Yeah, I mean, my family's from Colorado, so same here, except I visited a couple of times. Went to the University of Utah, you know? That's why I'm here. Not as interesting of a story as yours, but it's not surprising."

"Well, whatever brought us here, I'm glad that I got to meet you."

Christa grabbed her sake glass and fake-clinked it up against the air. "Yes to that." She then tilted her head back a bit and downed what was left of the sake.

We walked down the street to the valet parking in silence, just looking up at the night, taking in the atmosphere of downtown, and then that's when our eyes met. I took Christa up and kissed her. She made a surprised sound as I did, but soon reciprocated, putting her arm around me and keeping her mouth pressed on mine. We recoiled, with both of us breathing heavily.

I grabbed her again and went in for a make-out. Christa accepted. We probably stood in the cold for ten minutes, holding onto each other and keeping each other warm.

And then I was off to Manhattan again for the third time. It was time to reel some of these accounts that I'd established relationships with and start closing some of them. Or at least set them up to be closed.

CHAPTER 38

By this point, I was fully engrossed in the Manhattan crew culture. I had hopped on a flight with Yanni this time, and we were going to meet Calvin for some drinks. Over the next few days, we had plans to meet with every single representative we knew, including Laurie, Terrance, Drew, and a few other friends of Yanni's, whom I was excited to meet. This week was the week of the big Yankees versus Red Sox game, so Thomas would also be flying in. I still hadn't gotten back to Yanni for helping me keep that deal alive, so his drinks were on me this week. I was a little scared of that, but he'd helped me. I had to pay him back.

Calvin met us at the airport, and we piled into his car once again. As I packed my bags into the back, I took a second to address him and give him a handshake. "Hey, Calvin! Surprised you were able to get off early to spend the weekend with us."

He just shook his head. "I got a seven-figure deal on the line this weekend, so my Jewish Princess gave me a pass. We've come to an agreement this weekend that I need to decompress."

Yanni yelled through the window on the other side of the car – "Well, I'm rolling now, and I've got a whale on the line, and mine could be HUGE. Bigger than yours, even."

Calvin was quick to recover. "You're only rolling right now because you dropped your pants on the last day of the quarter and didn't finish the deal. You're making up for lost time, buddy. IT, Finance, and Procurement are all gonna beat you up."

"Yeah," I said, "Isn't the last day of the quarter when you're supposed to make the *most* money?"

Yanni took it on the chest. "A deal's a deal, no matter when it happens."

Calvin just looked back at him and scoffed. "I guess you don't need time management skills when you're Yanni." Yanni winked back at him.

We'd picked up Emily and headed to PDT once again with our party of four. I'd messaged Terrance, but he was still on his way. We decided pretty early on not to split up if at all possible. Yanni knew the head bartender by this point so he was able to get us reservations. So we crowded around a booth and started ordering mixed drinks like we didn't have to go to work tomorrow.

We got to know Emily better as the night went on. She'd had kids and used to be a stay-at-home mom, but neither in attractiveness nor energy level could you tell. She'd joined Mantiss, climbed up the ladder quickly, and was now one of the best Enterprise Account Executives. She was killing it.

"Alright," Yanni said, "what do you want to buy with the money?"

Calvin leaned on the table. "The money, huh?"

"Yeah, I mean, Mantiss's raking in the dough right now, and we're feeding off of its success... It's time to start dreaming big. I will make fifty million when we go public, not to mention all the commission I'm making in the meantime. You know, the whaling scene out here. You absolutely will too, Calvin."

Calvin just sipped more alcohol. "Wish *my* college friends gave me fifty million in stock."

"So what's your dream purchase?"

Calvin took a sip and contemplated the question.

"Well, I mean, I have a family to take care of–"

Yanni jumped in. "Aw, come on, that's no fun!"

Calvin slammed his hand on the table and laughed. "*As I was saying,* I'd use my money to buy an Aston Martin DBX. You know. An SUV for the wife and kids."

Yanni raised his eyebrows and mulled it over respectfully. "Okay, okay. More admirable. And what about you, Edward?"

"Oh, me?" I said cheerfully on my first drink of the night. Yanni'd actually outpaced me, and I wasn't about to drop several hundred dollars on drinks. "Yeah, I don't know, probably some old liqueurs, bourbons, scotches, and wines and my own place. Get out of that apartment downtown, you know? Probably also buy a car, though, if I'm being honest. Land Rover? Defender 110?"

"Shit, an off-roader?" Yanni replied.

"Yeah, I'm an adventurer."

"Admirable, admirable. Don't know what the fuck is with you all and your British cars. Italian's the way to go. I'm going for a Lamborghini."

We all burst into laughter. One of Yanni's friends nodded along. "Yeah, okay, Yanni."

"I'm serious!" He said, wiping his area clear of drinks, "A Huracan. Powerful, looks badass, exactly the right type of car for me. I like my cars fast and my women faster, motherfuckers."

That statement sent the whole table into more fits of laughter. We couldn't control ourselves. I shot back and jabbed Yanni a few times. "It certainly fits your personality. The only thing faster than your cars and your women is how fast your credit card's going to get swiped."

Yanni once again laughed it off. "Hey, what can I say? How is that a bad thing?"

Terrance then busted through the front door, looking like a storm had hit him. He was bundled up like he was in a storm as well.

"Alright, guys!" Terrance said, slapping his hands together. "I know we're all out casually right now, it's the weekend, and even though you guys are doing well, I need you all to kick it into overdrive and step it up!"

Every single one of us looked at Terrance like he'd just passed out on stage. Yanni gave him a confused look. "Alright. Nobody gives a fuck right now, man!" he said, starting to laugh as he said it.

Terrance laughed to try and lampshade his embarrassment, but you could see his flushed cheeks from a mile away. "Okay, okay. But we do need more multi-year deals, and we need to improve our client retention rate so that our profits become more–"

Yanni waved his hand. "Predictable, yeah, yeah. I'm working on it, I'm working on it. I told you about the whale I'm reeling in right about now, right? We can talk about it for a second, but I need another drink, that cool?"

Terrance shook his head and then shrugged, seemingly accepting that his rallying cry to do more work had gone over pretty fucking poorly. He sure was a businessman and a manager at heart.

Emily took another swig. She laughed. "You know, speaking of making hard cash, I've been making some progress on sales too. My commissions are probably going to pay for a new Rolls-Royce by the end of the year?"

I looked in her direction. "Oh really?"

"Yeah, If I'm going to play Soccer Mom, I should at least be doing it in style. I'll finally be able to stick it to all those other designer parents. You know, those *Big Little Lies* sorta people."

I didn't know what the hell that was, but I guess I could compare them to the people I was around currently. Most of my co-workers back home were already rich, married, and had kids.

Yanni took the stand and faced Emily directly. "Hey, I don't know if the self-proclaimed 'soccer mom' is going to smoke us this year, but you know what? I'm always up for a little bit of a challenge. Wanna bet on it?"

Emily looked smug as all hell. "Loser has to buy a Rolex?"

"Sounds good to me."

I mouthed '*a rolex?*' to Terrance, but he didn't seem too torn up about it. It seemed like he was just used to the Yanniendorsed Mantiss's lifestyle at this point. What the fuck ever, I guessed. It *was* a wild bet, and I was all for it.

Emily pounded on the table with her hands. "Oh, it's *on,* motherfucker! Thanks in advance for the free watch."

The whole table burst into laughter and cheers again after that one. Yanni yelled "NO CHEATING!" over the noise and then doubled over in laughter.

Calvin looked at Yanni like he'd just said the stupidest thing he'd ever heard in his life. "You two play *CLEAN?* That's fucking hilarious!"

And the jokes just kept on coming. Calvin was still smiling, but his face and body were sagging. He was exhausted, probably because all we'd been talking about since we got here was work. "Round's on me!" he decided, "but then I'm done, all right? Let's make Mantiss rich but that's enough about business for now. I think we've exhausted that."

CHAPTER 39

The morning after that conversation, I woke up with a slight headache. I climbed into the taxi for my first meeting of the day, which was still a little bit hazy. It was fine. I could still pick up a quick coffee at Starbucks or ask for one at the company I was visiting. As we drove down Park Avenue, I felt a light buzzing in my pocket, but I didn't think anything of it at first. Then I heard it again. I didn't even check the caller ID; I just hit accept and put my phone in the ear.

"Have you seen Drew?"

It was Calvin's voice. What was he – Drew? Oh, fuck, right. The Tiffany and Co. guy. I barely knew him, and I'd been hanging out with Yanni, Terrance, and Calvin all night. I didn't even know he was in town. "Uh, no. Is everything alright?"

"No," Calvin said and then hung up. He was fucking *miffed.* I could tell. At least he wasn't miffed with me, but I was worried. Great thing to carry with me for the rest of the day.

I was meeting with another investment firm that day, one I had already convinced to go to the Yankees game. Mantiss used this opportunity to prospect people and companies and introduce Thomas and Cary to the executives.

We'd already discussed the details and where we were going tonight. Mantiss pulled out all the stops to fill the suite, and they weren't about to let how much the suite costs get in the way of their sales plan. We were going to use this to our advantage. Hell of an advantage to have.

I walked into the elevator of the skyscraper with a tablet and a briefcase. I took a deep breath, mentally preparing myself to work off my tiredness. As the doors were closing, I heard the trampling of feet. BANG. A hand gripped the side of the elevators, and the doors stopped. A sweaty man stepped through the crawlspace and into the elevator. He wiped the sweat off his brow and looked at me. Suddenly, he did a double take.

"HEY, man! How's it going? So, how's the game going to be tonight?"

Oh my god. That fucking guy. Over the past week or so, he'd been trying to gain the company's favor. This guy kept getting in the way. I knew he wanted tickets first. A lot of these guys with no say in the company tried to weasel their way into Mantiss's events. I guess I couldn't blame them, I mean, we were getting suites at Yankees games, but these guys were always blood-boilingly annoying. Lower-level executives want to live a high life. They were already self-interested go-getters, so putting a live sports opportunity on the line made them go absolutely ravenous. And the companies were one hundred percent willing to send them our way – if they could get a free gift and not have even to consider our software that was a win-win for them.

This guy was no different from the rest of them. The last time I'd been here, he'd basically pretended to be a high-level executive, pushing himself into conversations, asking basic questions about the company like, "What do you do?" and "What department will you be working in?" None of these questions were unique, and I caught on quickly that he wanted our goodie bags. Fortunately, I'd scouted out who already mattered on our software back in Salt Lake. He wouldn't brown-nose us. We always aimed straight for the top.

I leaned back against the wall of the elevator. The guy looked eager for a response. "Oh, um, good." I was not going to be there to have a conversation with him today. I still had Drew on my mind. I was still trying to clear my head.

"Yeah, yeah. Must be crazy. Hey, if you've got an extra seat…"

I scoffed politely. "Yeah, no. Got a lot of other attendees at the game tonight."

The guy shook his head. "Exciting that you get to go then, lucky you."

I sighed. I guess. Life still wasn't perfect. "Yeah, yeah. I got stuff I have to do."

"Work hard, play hard, right? That's how I live too. What you gotta do to make it out here in Manhattan. Nothing like out there in Salt Lake City, right? That's where you're headquartered?"

This guy didn't know anything about Salt Lake. "Yeah, sure. Maybe it's not like the Big Apple right now, but it's fucking getting that cutthroat."

The guy rolled his eyes. I could tell he wasn't happy. But whatever, he probably was just pissed about not getting tickets. I wasn't going to fucking rest on my laurels at the game. I still hadn't closed the deal. I needed not to lose sight of that.

I was tasked with bringing my client to the game, but we were going out on the town beforehand, along with Yanni and Terrance. They'd be bringing prospects as well, and we'd all be in a box at the game. We'd all be going to the Yankees game together for a thirty-minute ride in a limousine. We hit up a bar first. Usually, we'd go someplace upscale and good for gatherings in the financial district, like Underdog, The Dead Rabbit, or Lounge on Pearl. We'd usually rotate which one we went to, just so we could keep it interesting for ourselves. Each one had its own distinct vibe, with Lounge on Pearl being the most extravagant. I usually went for Underdog myself when talking to clients on one or two, which fit my style a bit better.

Either way, tonight we were taking them to Death and Co. before heading to the stadium. Death and Co. was one of the originals, classy old-school interior and, ramshackle exterior. We were just there for the drinks as they had some of the best mixologists in the country.

The prospects had already met each other – assumedly through business. Drinks were on us tonight and none of us were driving, so we each ordered two strong cocktails and downed them quickly.

Next was business. I had to hear Yanni, once again, tell the story about why Cary was so great. After having heard it so many times, it was really starting to grate on the ear. Especially because Yanni really didn't focus on switching the story at all. Plus, they all asked again about how good our security was. Every single one of them had the same question, "What kind of encryption do you use," god, it felt like the whole experience was on a loop.

Eventually, we packed into our limousine for the night and took our seats at Yankee Stadium. We took the elevator up to the boxes and suites and found ours – The inside was packed with every kind of media, retail, and finance executive you could find. Pretty much all SVPs and Managing Directors dressed like they owned the entire league, plus the occasional C-suite executive. The fridge, stacked high with Cutwater Vodka Mules and the like, was right next to an overhang looking at the game. It's like the Jazz game but fifty times as expensive and about five times as nice.

I saw Thomas chatting up some management types and executives. He was still fairly business casual, in a button-down. He was completely calm and collected, even though he'd flown in this morning. It almost felt like a power move. "I'm headed up to the Hamptons tomorrow," I heard him say. "Business trip with the crew, you know?" They all laughed.

I took some biscuits from the catering table and stood beside the glass. The game hadn't quite started yet. Staring down from the suite, I felt like I was looking over the edge of the world. This was as close as I was going to get to the big time. I didn't even know what my father or anyone from England would have thought about where I was standing right at that moment. It was nearly too much to take in. None of the people in this box had celebrity, save *maybe* Thomas and a few CEOs. They didn't need it. All they had was enough money to buy a suite and enough power to write it off as a small business expense.

Yanni rushed over to me about two minutes later. "Hey, Ed. You all good?"

"Yeah," I responded. "Just starin'."

"Did you hear?"

"What?"

"Drew missed his appointment today."

"Wait, are you serious? That's why Calvin called me today?"

"Yeah! Calvin called me too. He told me they had to put together an entire plan for a video call. They were dodging calls probably fifteen minutes after the call was supposed to start."

"So wait, was he drunk? Why did he miss it? It's fucking Tiffany and Co.!"

"Well, Calvin's the one in New York, so they sent him over and got security to let him in – he walks in and he finds lines of blow on the dresser, and they can't find him – but get this, they find him half-wedged between the wall and the bed, naked from the waist down, half empty gallon of spirits."

The story brought me right back to reality. No more introspective shit, just… what the fuck had Yanni just said? I barely felt like I understood him. "Holy fucking shit, man!" I told him.

"Yeah, serious shit. Calvin called me this afternoon, and it really shook him; I mean… I could hear his soul escape as he talked, man. God, I'm glad Drew's door was locked. Security was there to call the paramedics. Calvin didn't enter first. Can you imagine busting down the door when you're fifty, seeing that on the floor by yourself? Jesus, fuck."

I looked out at the party of businessmen all shuffling around on the floor. "What do you think will happen to him?"

"Dunno," Yanni said solemnly, downing another sip. "HR'll get involved. He'll either be fired or go to rehab, I think. Only two real options."

"Fuck, dude."

"Yeah, just wanted to let you know. I know it's heavy, but yeah." Yanni paused. Then he snapped, making a single finger gun, and then slipped back into the crowd of high-rolling executives. He didn't really regain his smile until he was fully engrossed in the sales culture again. I was left alone again to look out over the baseball field.

A voice in the back of my head just started talking – *what were we doing here?* It said. I was on one drink from earlier and two biscuits. I felt sick to my stomach a little bit. I hadn't known Drew that well, but looking back on the party from last night, were we that much different? Even if we were, were we on the brink of acting like that?

I excused myself quickly and rushed to the bathroom. I took the stall and just sat down, rubbing my head multiple times. Good god. The speed of it all – I could handle it, but Drew had just crashed out. Christ.

My stop wasn't long. It couldn't have been. Over the next four hours, we needed to convince every single one of these guys that Mantiss was worth using. There were probably ten or so companies represented here, we were looking to close deals with all of them. There is no time for grief, pity, or anything else. Barely even time for the game.

I walked over to Thomas. My job was to get my prospects some face time with the co-CEO of my company. Thomas was his own best hype-man, able to take any conversation and make it a positive time. Honestly, a godsend for a time like this.

"Hey, man! How's sales going?" he said.

"Ah, great, you know? Got a ton done this week. Close on a few that I want you to meet, yeah?"

"Yeah, sounds good, sounds good! We'll catch up this weekend. Where are they?"

I pointed over near the televisions, and Thomas rushed over to talk to them. Quick, efficient, but I was left alone again.

I made my way back to the catering table. The hunger was getting to me. I mostly stayed back, watching the game on television and interacting with prospects when they had questions. I mostly got to eat sandwiches, though. After about twenty minutes, I noticed Thomas was done talking to my prospects. Thomas made a victory motion with his hand.

"I got them to close!"

"YES!" I said. I threw out my fist, and we bumped ours together. "That's what we're talking about."

"Three down, seven to go."

And then he was off again. I felt a little better knowing I still had him around, and however wild things were going to get, Thomas wouldn't let Mantiss get out of control.

The night was a success. Six out of ten of the prospects had agreed to a deal – a great success for us. The Yankees hadn't done poorly either. Yanni and Terrance had successfully pushed through extra sales as well, getting more teams to sign up for Mantiss than we could have ever hoped for. We were ready to fucking celebrate.

CHAPTER 40

It was true; Thomas, me, and the gang were all headed to the Hamptons. Just for two days, but that was what constituted a vacation up here in New York. Thomas had actually just flown Ashley in that day, and Terrance and Yanni were able to bring their wives on short notice as well. I was chilling by myself, but it was going to be chill hanging out with my co-workers. There was no talk about work other than the successes we'd had.

Thomas got us all two blacked-out Executive G-Wagons all the way from Manhattan to Southampton – yeah, it was as expensive as it sounded – and we both stared out the window as the New York Bay passed us by. The GPS took us downtown and past a bunch of buildings that looked like they were stuck in the Civil War. We took a few stops to pick up beer, wine, liquor, and groceries while we were in town. After that, we stopped by Rowdy Hall, a classic pub in the area with a ton of fresh seafood. Terrance's wife was really excited to get the oysters.

We passed estates so large that we weren't able to actually see the houses behind them. And finally, we entered a private property on the beachfront, looking out over the ocean. Thomas had rented a fucking mansion. Great Gatsby would have been jealous. We drove in on gravel past endless trimmed hedges, passing a garden that had to have been its own acre-wide.

We all stepped out of the car. I was in fucking awe. Thomas was the first one in, as he had the key, with Yanni and Terrance right behind. The outside was stone and glass. The minute I stepped inside into the foyer I was bombarded with luxuries – stained glass ceilings and marble floors.

Yanni jabbed me with his shoulder. "Italian marble. Direct."

He wasn't fucking around. I looked down at the ground and started at my reflection. This was beyond anything I'd ever seen in my life or even read about. This was the fucking high life.

After setting the beer, wine, and liquor on the kitchen table we all made a beeline for the back where the swimming pool was. Terrance yelled, "It's cocktail time, motherfuckers! This is gonna be a great spot for the weekend, Thomas."

Thomas smiled and rolled his eyes. "Alright, Terrance. Glad I got your approval, you schmuck."

We all laughed. I pulled out some cocktails, and since I was the one with bartending experience, I started cranking out Vesper Martinis, Mojitos, and Mai Tais like the old times.

Thomas raised his glass first. "Sold three and a half million of product this week!"

Terrance let out a guttural yell. "YyyyyyyYEEEEESSSS!"

"To one hell of a week!"

We all cheered and then jumped in the pool.

After we all dried off, we decided to explore the compound. We walked around the backyard gardens and the guest houses, looking down at the secret entrances and finding the private beach.

I stood looking out at the ocean. I turned to Thomas. "You really outdid yourself on this one."

Thomas just laughed again. "You know, I try. Besides, we've got our significant others this weekend, what did you expect."

"Nothing but the best, I guess!" I joked.

"Hey," he said, "If it goes well, maybe you can bring Christa up here next time. Just remember what I said."

Oh, right. God, "Don't fuck the help." How could that not stick with me? Jesus.

The rest of the weekend was a breeze. We all needed the moment after the Yankees game. Someone would volunteer to cook each night, family style. Terrance cooked one night and Yanni cooked one night. I bartended instead, as I was never the best cook and I was the only one trained to make mixed drinks. We drank by the poolside and on the beach, and Thomas got a few board games out of his bedroom for us to try.

We ate late that night, mostly the barbecue Yanni'd made plus some snacks we'd gotten from town. I hadn't talked to Ashley a ton over the past two days, but she was obviously chomping at the bit to know how things were going with Christa.

"So, how did the date go?" Ashley asked.

Thomas' eyes looked up from his food. "Date?"

"Oh, yeah! The date. Went really well. We went to see the Book of Mormon and get sushi after; it was nice."

Thomas arched an eyebrow. "You didn't tell me you were going on a date."

I shook my head. "I guess I forgot. I'm sorry. You're learning about it now."

"No, what the fuck!" His face went red. "Seriously, you take my executive assistant out, and you don't even tell me you're doing it? I thought I told you to tell me!"

Ashley clapped once. "Nah, good going, Ed. Sly dog." Thomas gave Ashley a side-eye.

"I just don't tell you everything, trust me," I said. "Mum's the word."

Thomas resumed eating. "Fine, fine," he said, "As long as you remember what I told you."

Holy shit, I didn't know this was such a big deal to Thomas. I rolled my eyes. I knew what he was fucking on about, but I didn't need to hear it again. Yanni butted in from across the table. "Oh, did he give you that lecture?"

Ashley eyed Thomas. "*That* lecture?"

"No, no," he said. "It must be something else."

"He told you not to fuck the help, didn't he?" Ashley asked me.

I scoffed. Ashley gave Thomas a good slug on the shoulder. "OW!" He jumped back in pain. The rest of us laughed.

CHAPTER 41

The next day was our last day. I started the day with my phone already ringing. It was the first company I'd gone to – the one that I'd gotten Yanni to help out with. They'd bought the software already, so it was strange to be receiving a call from them. "Hey," the CEO said. "You're our account executive, and I know you're in town right now… could you come down today? We've got something we want to discuss."

"Uh… yeah. Does twelve sounds, okay? I get out of my other meeting at eleven thirty."

Yanni and I started the night at a Knicks game, front row, with a client from a pharmaceutical manufacturer. We'd gotten the Head of Marketing to come with, and he'd be the one making the order. Apparently, they were heading towards a product launch within the next year and they were desperately looking for anything that would help them with that.

The Knicks were struggling in the game we watched and while being front row was fun and all, it certainly wasn't helping business when New York was behind. Having listened to everyone talk, I kind of wished we'd been trying to sell during the 1992 season.

The company was overseas, can't remember which one he was from exactly, but this guy was definitely an American, yelling at the ref and nearly jumping out of his chair. Right in the front fucking row, too.

The game was loud. There were thousands of fans in the stadium that night, all roaring lowly looking for the Knicks to win. I still had to sell. "All right!" I yelled. "So not only is this going to help your team's productivity, it is also going to give you access to a bunch of data visualization for points you didn't have before.

"Dude, the rate's fair, everything's good and ready."

Yanni's voice came from the other chair. "Then why don't you do it?"

"Well, what's the catch?"

Yanni laughed. "You think there's a catch? We're taking you to a Knicks game and you think there's a fucking catch?"

I wasn't about to tell the guy that our systems seemed to be struggling, but it was on my mind. I continued anyway. "Listen, man. The software is priced competitively. We're pretty much first to market on the data visualization and cloud integration stuff, so the setup isn't even going to cost you that much time in the long run.

Yanni pushed farther. "That tech conglomerate I told you about? The one that Cary left? Doesn't even have a platform yet that's like this. We don't even really need you to do any setup other than downloading the software. If that doesn't sell you, I don't know, man. This is a good deal."

"You guys will help with onboarding?"

"Fucking… absolutely." Said Yanni.

"Alright. So I'll just talk with you guys tomorrow, and I'll get the ball rolling on it. Deal?" And he held out his hand to me.

"Deal." I shook on it. Holy shit.

The Hawks scored another basket. The guy immediately threw his head back and grabbed his hair. "Awwh, my GOD!"

Eventually, the Knicks lost, and the whole stadium emptied out into the streets and subways. I picked up the car this time. Yanni and I waited on the side of the street for our ride, thousands of cars passing by and people running into the streets after them. Yanni then doubled over and screamed, "YES!"

I felt the excitement as well. I screamed too. "FUCK YES!"

"ONE MILLION, MAN!"

"WE'RE FUCKING DOING IT, DUDE!"

With all the breath left in his system, Yanni yelled into the street. "We're fucking drinking tonight! And you're done paying for my drinks this trip – this one's on me, man!"

We met up with everyone who was in the territory for the week late that night. Calvin, Laurie, Yanni, Me, one of Laurie's friends, and a few of the Northeast account executives decided to go to one more bar I hadn't gone to yet – East Market, another classic Calvin had previously recommended.

The crew was rowdy. My week had been filled already, and from the sounds of it, everybody else's had been too. I got told story after story about how people were tagging along with prospects to concerts, dinners, and parties. Calvin was allowed to visit us tonight even though the weekend was over. We probably wouldn't be returning for another three weeks or so.

There were a variety of beers and cocktails swirling around the table that night. Mojitos, rum drinks, and some Manhattans on the rocks were passed around, all on the company tab. A lot of people I only knew in passing were there, so I got to meet and catch up with a lot of reps and tell them about the deals I had just landed as well.

"Well, this has been a wacky fucking roller-coaster of a trip, hasn't it!" Calvin stated.

"Yeah, ups and fucking downs is right, man," Yanni said. He looked at Laurie. "Did you hear what happened?"

"Oh. Drew?" she responded.

"Yeah, Drew."

"Aw," Laurie's friend said, "Yeah. I just heard about it today. What happened? So sad."

While all the other tables stayed rowdy, ours immediately fell silent. This was the first time all of us were sitting at a table, trying to talk about what had happened the night before. Looked like everyone had been shocked.

Calvin noticed everyone's trepidation first. "Listen," he said. "I know we're all thinking about what happened this week. We all knew Drew in some way or another, and we all knew this was coming. We just didn't know when. And god, of course, it happened on the worst possible fucking day of our work lives. But all we need to do is slow down a little bit on everything out here that's not work."

Laurie responded. "Yeah, that's a good idea. Is everyone okay with slowing down on that?"

The rest of the table nodded. Calvin took another glass into his hand and raised it slightly. "Alright, everyone. To Drew."

We all clinked, with half of our table clinking water together.

It was then that I noticed it'd been about two hours since we'd gotten there, and Terrance was missing in action. I checked my phone and messages to make sure that I told him we were meeting up, but he hadn't responded to me since this afternoon. I looked at Yanni, who was tapping away at his phone as well. "Where's Terrance?"

Yanni's eyes perked up. "You remember that girl I was talking to about the bet the other day? Emily?"

"What, did something happen between you and her?"

"Nah, nah. Terrance, man. Terrance hooked up with her this time!"

I shook my head and staggered back. This time, huh? "Terrance hooked up with her? Just so I'm getting that right."

"Yeah. That's why he's MIA tonight. Hanging out with her again."

"Sheesh, really?" I laughed and set down my empty drink. "His wife was here *yesterday!*"

Yanni shrugged.

"I didn't know he had it in him." I said, "Well, congrats to him, I guess. I *guess.*"

"You'd be surprised. You'd be surprised." He winked and slid me another drink, presumably on him. He was trying to be sneaky, but it was an open secret at this point. The women who were invited to these parties were the best salespeople in the company, no doubt the country, but the guys loved their experience. A lot. Maybe more than they should.

Laurie raised a glass. "To the last day of New York!" We all clinked our glasses together. "Get your fun in, *responsibly*, while you still can." I gave a half-smile to that sentiment as well.

CHAPTER 42

And then the rush was over. I flew out of JFK with Terrance the next morning, not saying a word to him out of respect for his sleep schedule and mine. I touched down in Salt Lake City, and about two hours after I landed, I got a text from Laurie. *Are you still going to Shelley's Dinner Party?*

Shelley's dinner party, right? The festivities never ended. Shelley was Laurie's other friend I knew – Digital marketing manager for the company. She was shorter than most of us, about 5 foot 5 inches, with longer brown hair and a smaller figure. Columbian, ended up in Utah due to her parents. Laurie, Christa, and her were all hosting her birthday this week and I'd nearly forgotten.

I responded with a single *"Yep!"*

Laurie got back to me immediately. "See you there! I'm gonna get a suite for everyone for the night, just so we don't have to commute all the way from the valley. What are you getting her, Ed?"

"Oh, I'm not sure exactly, she's got everything. Maybe a bottle of Dom and some high-end chocolates. Safe, but it works for sure!"

"Wow, okay, planner over here!" She texted back, adding a smiley emoji. "You got anything I could give her?"

"IDK, another bottle of Champagne. Can't go wrong with that."

A laughing emoji was sent my way. *"You're right!* Laurie said. *"It'll be fun to see everyone.*

Yeah! Laurie responded, especially *after the last party.* And she ended it with a winky face.

I drove to River, an upscale restaurant downtown. Shelley was already there, her fiancée by her side. Laurie, Christa, Yanni, and Thomas were already there. I hadn't learned Shelley's fiancee's name, but he looked like every other lower-level executive I'd met. It didn't matter what industry; plain guys who wore business casual would always exist. Some just made more money than others.

It was all a bit strange, knowing that Shelley was getting with Maurice.

Shelley seemed like she was talking to the others about her vacation plans this summer. Her fiancée wasn't necessarily uninterested as much as he just looked bored like he'd already heard these plans before and wasn't concerned with rehashing them.

The table was set for twenty people, but sitting by myself it looked like an empty throne room. Shelley had already gotten table assignments. Fuck. There were already appetizers laid out – mussels, pork belly, and beef tartare – but nobody was here yet to offset how still everything looked. I placed my single box of chocolates, my champagne, and the card I'd gotten on the tablecloth. Laurie and Christa followed suit.

As everybody from Mantiss filed in, the center of the table filled up with drinks of all sorts – mostly wine and champagne. Yanni eventually showed up with three bottles in his hands and between his arms. It was going to be a rager by the end of the evening. The whole place was going to be underwater after we were through with this.

Shelley welcomed everyone and showed us all to our assigned seats. "Glad you all could make it. I know Terrance is going to be late."

Laurie interrupted with what everyone else was thinking. "What else is new?"

The table chuckled. And then the champagne was opened. And passed around like soda. And then Terrance showed up with two more bottles in his hands. The whole table gave him his shit for being late, he slammed the champagne on the table as an apology, and two more full bottles got added to the alcohol pool for the night.

Christa and Shelley were sitting next to me with Laurie directly across from us. The server approached Shelley first. "Welcome to River, everyone!" he said, staying formal. "Everyone enjoying their appetizers?"

We all nodded. "Good," he said. Looking at Shelley, he leaned in. "Just wanted to grab you for a quick second. So you said you wanted this to be on one check or –"

"Separate." It was Shelley's fiancée who'd answered the question. I'd heard him answer. Yanni and Terrance looked like they'd heard as well. That was… strange.

"No, no! Just checking. We're all good. Just wanted to confirm." And the server pulled out his notepad. "Alright, what does everybody want to eat today?"

I was just left scratching my head. Were they not on the same tab? Why did they want to stay separate? It stayed with me as I watched Shelley order. I didn't have much time to process it, as once the server left the table everybody started talking up a storm. It's not like we had our own room or anything so a bunch of people started giving us glares from across the restaurant. We attracted attention, but you could tell that they were intrigued.

Christa leaned in towards me and talked under her breath. "So, where do you want to go for our second date?"

"Oh, me? Um… yeah. A concert sounds nice. If you know one around."

Christa smiled. "Sounds like a great time. If you know any, you know."

I felt someone's eyes on me. Laurie's. God. I knew I had to come up with an excuse to leave early. Keep them on their toes.

I'd gotten a Porterhouse, and I'd gotten about three-quarters of the way through it. Same with my glass of wine. I stood up, walked over to Shelley's fiancée, and threw 200 dollars down on the table. "That should be more than enough for my share."

The guy just smiled an 'alright then' smile. I mean, I was in the same boat at that point. With Laurie's eyes on me, I felt out of fucking place. Shelley's fiancée didn't know me at all, neither did I, but they had invited me to dinner. I was appreciative, but I wanted to relax, and I couldn't. "Thanks, man!" He said. "We really appreciate you coming out and for the gift, too."

"Yeah, anytime! Thanks for the invite."

I walked up to Shelley. It was her birthday after all. "Hey," I said. "Hope the rest goes well."

Shelley looked a little mad at that one. "Where do you think you're going? We're just getting started!"

"Emergency. Sorry."

"What kind of emergency? Is it one that you can put off dealing with so you can celebrate my birthday with me?"

"A friend had something really important come up. Can't talk about it." I don't know what I was supposed to say to her. "Sorry, but I wish I could stay."

That's when Shelley grabbed me by the arm. She turned away from her fiancée and leaned in. "I hear you've been quite the Casanova lately."

I scoffed. Shelley looked back at me pleadingly. I looked at her fiancée. He was lost talking to some of Shelley's co-workers. He might have seen it, but he had no idea what was going on.

"Al—alright," I said. I pulled my arm a bit back towards my body. "Happy birthday, Shelley. Maybe we can go on a double date with Christa sometime soon. I do have to go."

Christa perked up. She looked at me with a confused face. I shrugged.

Shelley pouted. It felt like everybody in the room had some sort of awareness of the fact that I was dipping early. It didn't matter. I strolled out of the restaurant.

The next morning I awoke to both Shelley and Laurie texting me – not in the group text but separately. "So, where did you run off to last night? What's her name? I still can't believe you left…" Laurie texted me.

They had no idea that I'd run off to the Beer Crew to talk with Dan and Hal and hang out in their mancave drinking bourbon. Dan and Hal had been receptive, although there was also no way I was talking about what was happening at work with them. I needed to decompress.

Shelley texted me again. "I can't believe you didn't even present your birthday gift. You left before everyone else did." She sent along with a smile.

I didn't know what that meant. I mean, I had an idea but I didn't want to jump to conclusions. It felt like we were talking around each other. Jesus. This was a struggle to deal with. Christa hadn't texted me since the day before. God, what was going on at Mantiss?

CHAPTER 43

Back to Salt Lake. It was almost like being back to reality, almost. My old boss Hal and I were meeting up in Vail, Colorado for the weekend to catch up. I hadn't seen Hal in a while. He was older, but he was really trying to stay in shape these days was all I knew. Bald, California-raised, looked absolutely the businessman type. A bunch of collared button-downs in his wardrobe. A bit old-school compared to the Mantiss world.

We'd picked the weekend of the Strong Beers, Belgian, and Barley Wine Festival to hang out. When I was working for them, it was hands down the premier beer festival in the country and my personal favorite. Founders and Master Brewers from the best craft breweries in America came to showcase their brews. Every single hot-shot beer distributor in the nation would bring their executive team to get face time with the brewery staff, and it felt like a gathering of the best scientists and creatives in the country brewing the highest caliber alcohol in the world.

I wasn't showing up as a salesman this year, which means a load was off my back. Hal was mostly there to meet with distributors and show off this year's line of Barrel-Aged Stouts and Sours. They were currently high off being the number one beer brand in Colorado. When we weren't at events, we jammed the main bar at the hotel. The place was also filled with industry veterans, no surprise. They'd all donated their rarest and most obscure beer to the bar for the hotel to put on tap. Everyone had an absolute blast catching up, having fun, and even doing business at distributor meetings and whatnot.

I also took the opportunity to catch up with Hal. Samurai Brewing had been running steady for quite a while now.

"Ah yeah, Mantiss. Silicon Valley guys, right? Yeah, yeah. Utah loves stealing other people's ideas." He chuckled loudly. "Even California's wacky-ass business strategies."

I laughed, but I had to ask. "What do you mean specifically?"

"Well, you tell me. How much are they spending on customer acquisition?"

"You don't want to know."

"It's a fucking boatload, right?"

"Yeah, they swear they're going to make money in the long run. I don't know if I believe them. But it worked the first time."

"Fuckin reckless. That's what it is. How are they going to turn a profit? In any other market, they'd be dead in the water."

"Well, they're in the hottest market in town right now, right?"

"Yeah, I guess if I had seventy different angel investors looking at the brewery I'd take the money." He laughed. "Even then, you know?"

I doubled over. "I don't fuckin' know man, it's their money, you know? May as well ride the wave."

"It's a fuckin wipeout waiting to happen, it is what it is, Ed. Be careful out there."

"Thomas' assistant, huh?"

I'd told Hal already. We still kept in touch and he was always interested in what was going on behind the veil at Mantiss. "Wow," he said. "So you're life's better now too." He swirled his beer and then eyed me again, smiling – "You've drunk the Mo' cool aid."

Holy shit. Right for me. Mo meant Mormon. Hal had always been blunt – he wouldn't have tried to start a brewery in Utah otherwise. He was always fighting the system. At every point, the government had tried to push back against his business, and he'd won through perseverance. Still, it'd hardened his personality a bit. I knew he didn't mean it at this point. But it was direct of him. He was joking, and I knew he was, we shit-talked the Mormons all the time when I worked for him, but that was a fucking step out of line.

"Alright," I said, trying to push back toward the topic at hand. "That's not what this is. You couldn't get me to switch back to Mormonism. Not for any amount of money. It's not some cult initiation, I actually wouldn't mind less of that."

"I know," he said, "just pulling your leg. Thomas' got everything under control. Except for finances, I'm sure. I mean, he spirited you away from Samurai Brewing, so he's got one good instinct."

Thomas had been ruthless after the New Year's Eve party, like Mantiss's life, hinged on having the best salespeople in the country to the detriment of everything else. I was still working for Samurai Brewing at the time, so we didn't have too many opportunities to hang out, but I heard from him at least three times every week saying something along the lines of "So, when are you going to start?" or "We've got everything lined up, just have to do the interviews."

"Hal," I said, "you remember back right before I left when I went to Harry O's then, right? That's what sealed the deal for me."

"Aw, yeah, barely, but I remember you talking about it."

About two weeks before my first shadow and interview, I'd gotten a text message. Innocuous enough, I got tons of them. But this was from Thomas. *Hope you're in town next weekend... it's the opening weekend of Sundance. I just booked St. Regis and got VIP. Eminem (probably) at Harry O's.*

The fuck? Harry O's? He'd gotten in? I texted him back. *I'm in town, count me in if you're serious.*

Another buzz. *Fuck yeah!*

I responded. Cool! Looking forward to it. Let me know what I'm gonna owe you.

Thomas got back to me within seconds. This one is on me, I just take care of meals and bar tabs, but Harry O's Concert is my treat.

I sent Cheers man, out with Samurai Brewing right now, but I'm back tomorrow night. See ya next weekend.

Thomas just responded with a thumbs-up. I closed my cell phone. Holy shit —that weekend, when Park City got the most action, Harry O's was nearly impossible to get into. Park City was rich, but anybody who went to Harry O's during Sundance was richer. I didn't know what the Mantiss lifestyle was like yet, but I already knew Thomas was obsessed with the high life. Might as well take advantage of it.

Friday afternoon. Thomas' condo downtown was our designated meeting spot. Terrance and Yanni were already there loading their bags in the back of Thomas' Tesla. I didn't know them too well yet, so I just shook their hands and introduced myself. Thomas had asked us all to carpool with him. Showing off his Tesla again.

We went through the light snow-up Parley's Canyon. There was just enough of a sprinkle left to admire on the mountaintops.

As we pulled up to the St. Regis, Thomas immediately pointed off East of where we were, where a bunch of ten-million-dollar houses sat on the mountainside. "You see those houses over there? Cary's second house is just past that."

"Shit, man," I said. "Out here flaunting it, I see."

The bellman rolled a dolly up to us and shook Thomas' hand. "Good to see you again, Thomas, how's life?" The bellman at the St. Regis knew Thomas by name. That was huge. The hotel already looked like a country club on steroids. Notoriety didn't get passed around here for free.

The bellman took all of our bags while Thomas checked us all in. As we reached the elevator, he handed all three of us the keys to the rooms. "Alright, let's settle and meet at the bar in two hours. You guys need to get a Bloody Mary here."

"It's 3 o'clock," I said.

"No, no! You have to try it. Trust me. Even if it's late."

Upstairs, Terrance and I are sharing a room together. I open the door and it's the most extravagant two-bed suite I'd stayed in. Roomier than anything I was getting working for Samurai Brewing. I threw my luggage on the bed and then threw myself onto it as well. Plush, soft enough to sink right through. Holy shit, I was going to get the best sleep of my life in this room.

After settling in, I headed to the bar. Thomas was already sitting down with four Bloody Marys on the table already. Jesus, he was really into these things. I took a seat and Thomas immediately started talking about the drinks. "These things are as old as the bar, man. Every St. Regis has a different version of these, and the Deer Valley one is absolutely money. Oat distilled, completely local, a classic. Tastes good all day. This one's on me, but I can't be held responsible for the rest!" He said, laughing.

Thomas raised his glass and clinked it with ours. "Good to be back. Thanks for coming this weekend."

"No yeah," said Terrance, "thank you, Thomas. None of us would be here without you. Like, literally. At this hotel."

We all took a chuckle at that joke. This is what happened when you were friends with the co-CEO. I pulled out my phone. I thought I might finally treat everyone to a night out. I texted one of my Samurai Brewing clients yesterday. I kinda knew whatever I picked had to impress Thomas, so I decided to go all out and ask for a favor. I looked at my phone – my contact had gotten me in. "So, I made reservations for the ten of us tonight at RiverHorse on Main for dinner– and it's on me," I said.

Yanni looked awestruck. "Shit man, really?"

Thomas looked at me with concern. "You got those last week?"

"Nah, yesterday."

"The fuck? That place is impossible to get into."

"Samurai Brewing connections, you know. You're bragging about how you get to live the high life? Well, I do that by knowing everyone in town."

Thomas pounded the table with his fist. "That's what I'm fucking talking about, man!"

"Dinner's on me," I said, "as long as Terrance doesn't buy several thousand dollars' worth of wine. I'm not on the hook for that."

Terrance just laughed. "Yeah, right! Fucking whatever, Limey…"

Right as we were talking, the bar manager came up to us.

"Edward, right?"

"Yeah!"

"HA! It's been a second man!" He threw his hand back and we basically high-fived. "You want a Samurai Brewing to wash down that Bloody Mary?"

"Uh, yeah! Give me the Pilsner, man."

Thomas raised an eyebrow but seemed almost proud of me. I still had a bit of charisma left. I think he knew what I brought to Mantiss right there. Coolness and street cred.

"Good to see you still carrying Samurai Brewing! Glad we've got some pull around here."

The manager smiled and gave me a salute. "You're running with Thomas these days?"

"Yeah, you know—" I stopped myself. Of course, he knew Thomas. He was essentially a celebrity up here. I changed my demeanor. "I've known him for a while now. Friends for a long time."

The bar manager basically whispered to me. "Pretty good friends to have."

"Hey!" I said, "These guys are no slouches."

Yanni clicked his tongue twice. Terrance gave me the thumbs up without looking away.

"Alright, I have to go," The bar manager said. He turned to address Thomas dead-on. "Keep bringing us your clients, alright?"

Thomas grinned. "I'll try."

That night we went out to the restaurant. Riverhorse on Main was a four-star Forbes Restaurant in the middle of Main Street – one of the most celebrated restaurants in Park City.

They were, as advertised, crowded as shit. There were also no available spots when we walked in, save for the reserved table I'd gotten for the whole group. The night was rowdy, but it didn't compare in the slightest to the chaos I'd seen in other states. I think that Utah itself suppressed the volume of the conversations. We were still ordering alcohol and tapas like Pierogies, Oysters, and Buffalo Tartare, all on me that night.

The next night we decided to head to Stein Eriksen Lodge for apres, skiing, and cocktail hour. The place was massive, a rustic resort built like an 80's ski resort, European Chalet style, with million-dollar views and the atmosphere to match. The only problem is that it was also going to be a crowded fuckfest. When we got there, it absolutely was.

"Fuck! It's a two-hour wait for the ten of us." Yanni said, looking genuinely pissed.

"Don't worry! Don't worry, I got this." I said. "I've got it handled. You think you guys are the only company that deals with millionaires?"

Yanni rolled his eyes a little. "Alright, of course, you do."

These guys loved Samurai Brewing, as we stood out as the most "real" beer in Utah. I'd been able to hook them up with all sorts of products, and they rewarded us handsomely. I'd texted one of the execs beforehand and set up a table for the Mantiss crew. Thomas was about to see that I could swim with the big fish as well.

After a quick conversation, I ran back to the group. "We're in." As I looked at their faces, I decided to rub it in a little bit. "No need to thank me."

Thomas looked with confidence at Terrance and Yanni. "Told you, he knows everyone in this goddamn state."

"That's a fuckin' understatement," Yanni said.

After drinks, we headed back to The St. Regis to freshen up and head back out on the town to go to Harry O's. We arrive and there's already a line a mile long down the street. Thomas waved his hand at us, just walked up to the front of the line, talked to security, and then walked back to us. "We're all good to go." He said nonchalantly.

"And *I* know everybody, huh?"

Thomas rolled his eyes. "It's the money, alright? It's the money! I know why I can get in, let's not discuss it further."

I still couldn't believe I was even here. That's when Thomas gave me a strong pat, enough to startle me. "Okay, Ed," he said, "we've got about two dozen more people from Mantiss showing up tonight. Sales, Marketing, and Executive Assistants tonight."

"Cool! So obviously everyone coming up tonight is cool?"

"Oh, yeah." Thomas nodded with his mouth pursed. "They wouldn't be invited if they weren't."

I walked in and the place was packed. People wall to wall, drinks clutched tightly in hand, it looked like a bunch of sardines. "Holy shit, is it always like this?" I asked Thomas.

"Yeah, yeah. But you see that roped-off area right there?" Thomas pointed all the way to the dance floor on the other side of the club. "That's for us."

Holy shit, he wasn't kidding about being a VIP. Right as rain, there was a quarter of the dance floor roped off with white leather couches. The rest of the club was packed, but there was an empty space specifically sectioned off for Thomas. During the biggest, most expensive event in Park City. Harry O's usually wasn't the most prestigious club but during Sundance, it was packed with wealthy locals, New

Yorkers, Californians, and the occasional in-the-know celebrity. I couldn't believe it.

While it was just ten of us there with everyone en route from the valley, I finally felt like a true tech nerd. But that didn't stop Thomas from partying. This felt like the future – and mine, in more ways than one.

Everyone on the dance floor was staring directly at us, wondering who the fuck we were. It was almost uncomfortable how many eyes we got on us during the party. It didn't matter. We were knocking back drinks left and right and when Eminem finally came on we went wild, shouting, cheering, and dancing.

Before the night wore down completely, Thomas slapped me once again. "Hey Edward, I've got connections too. Guess where we're going next?"

"I couldn't."

"Club Tao! Open to 4:30 AM. Put your big boy pants on, man! We're just getting started."

"Game on, man! Game on!" And we left to hang out at a separate club before heading home.

I woke up late, around 10:50, and Yanni wasn't even up yet. I clutched my head. How long had we been partying last night? I groggily walked over to the bathroom and took a quick shower to try and wake myself up.

Yanni rolled off the bed onto the ground, pretty much following the same routine as I did. Upon texting Thomas it sounded like his experience wasn't too much better. We still needed to get brunch downstairs though.

Straight from the St. Regis, we hit the Deer Valley slopes, and we got about two hours of skiing before we all decided to go to Montage. It was a giant resort in the mountains that was accessible by the slopes. One of the nicest resorts I'd been to in my life. It was the last day I had available. Sunday afternoon. On the slopes, Yanni and I were shredding down black diamonds basically all day while the rest of the crew chilled on blues. "Hey, can we go back to St. Regis and hit the party tent?" I asked.

Yanni breathed heavily in his skis. I could tell he was tired from the night before. I didn't know what he'd done. "I'm dragging ass, man. If I lose you, how do I get there?"

"Um, the most direct route should be Ontario to Homeward Bound... take Homestake up, and then Little Stick to Deer Hollow. That'll get you to the party tent."

"Alright," Yanni said through another heavy breath. "See you there."

We rolled up to The Party Tent with some of the group still struggling. The tent, however, was fucking packed. There was a DJ cranking tunes, people spraying bottles of

Moet all over each other and generally making a mess. Thomas just looked at all this and smiled. "This'll do nicely."

Terrance responded next. "This'll get us going again! Look at all these snow bunnies… Jesus!"

I laughed with Terrance.

I went over and grabbed a drink from the bar while the rest of the group scattered across the tent. As I walked past, with my vodka mix in hand, I saw Thomas chatting up some people who I could only assume were venture capitalists. Or maybe just interested parties. Whatever was going on, Thomas was keeping their attention. "Not only is our technology world-class," he said, "our latest round of funding values us at five billion." I heard the silent gasps from his captive audience. I was fucking blown away as well by that statement. *Five billion?*

"Everyone who's invested so far is world-class. Real superstars of the industry. Can't disclose them, you know, but we've got a real good board and I think we're going to succeed a ten-billion-dollar valuation."

It'd been about thirty minutes since we'd got there and Yanni finally showed up at the tent. I looked over and went up to greet him.

"Now this is what I'm talking about!" He said through stifled breath, "Look at all these snow bunnies. Holy shit, time to relax, right?"

I didn't know him like I did now. I didn't know that this was probably the tamest thing I'd hear him say for the next four or five years. I didn't even know I'd be hanging out with him. To me, he just seemed like another guy like Terrance. "You know, Terrance said the exact same thing."

He blew a raspberry. "Would have never fucking guessed."

Thomas waved us over and then motioned to another sectioned-off area. Couches, finally. Bottles were ordered but the seating was the real draw. I raised my glass. "Cheers," I said, "to a hell of a weekend, Thomas!"

"Yeah man, when are you going to help us make those killer connections you were talking up?"

Everyone laughed. Terrance followed Thomas up. "Sounds like you're coming to work at Mantiss, even if Thomas has to tie you up and steal you."

Yanni rebutted. "Hey, man. We're all making our millions over here near Mantiss. If you want to join us, the door's always open. Especially if you've got Thomas on your side."

Yeah. Thomas had been my gateway. At that moment, I had to consider it. This world already seemed better. And as we all clinked glasses in my memory, I snapped back to reality. Hal was just swirling some beer on the table, looking at his phone. In the past year, so much has changed. I wasn't making as much as Hal but he respected how much I was making, even if he didn't agree with who I was working with.

I guess Hal knew a little bit. That these guys *could* try and bite me in the ass. At that point, it didn't seem like anything was going wrong. But he was wary of Mantiss just due to their ties with Utah culture. Something he'd been ultimately dealing with since he started his brewery. We both had no idea how far it would go. It felt like I was still on the rise. We'd sold so many products. With time, I'd feel like an integral part of their team. I already sort of did.

CHAPTER 44

I really wanted to revisit London. Every time I had been in Manhattan a pang hit me right before I went to sleep – New York was the closest I'd get to England in terms of where my work would take me. Honestly, that was what I wanted to do with the money I'd saved from Mantiss first. I was on my way to moving out of my apartment in the city, but I wanted to do something for myself. Plus, I had time over the holidays to myself.

The first place I decided to travel to was the Middle East. Petra, Tel Aviv, Jerusalem, Istanbul, and Athens, I got a good rest every night and went out to visit every attraction I could in the morning. Everything I could think of -- Petra, the Western Wall, the Tower of David, Old City, Dome of Rock into the West Bank to see Bethlehem, Hagia Sophia, and The Parthenon. The break I got to take was exquisite. It felt like I'd hit the payload and could sit back and relax. It felt like total freedom.

I boarded an airplane to head to London afterward. It'd been a while since I'd been. Over the holiday, I'd made plans to meet with two of my old friends from back in primary school and see what they were up to. We decided to meet up at Mr. Fogg's Tavern in the city, meaning they had to book it for a couple of hours to get into the city proper.

Mr. Fogg's was about as homely as these bars got. Right inside Covent Garden decorated floor to ceiling with British paraphernalia with a bunch of knick-knacks, it truly felt like home rather than some upscale tourist trap or rowdy nightclub.

Pete and Connor had both been my friends back in the day, but I'd moved to Salt Lake with my mother when I was a teenager. It was honestly striking how much they'd grown up. Pete was super skinny, and Connor had put on a few pounds. Both of them looked like they were down for a drink, though.

The minute we all got our beers, I jumped into my tales of success at Mantiss. They both just continued to lean back in their chairs and shake their heads, laughing like they didn't believe me. And who would? Even for people who didn't live in the countryside, could anyone from Britain believe that I'd gone to America and was selling cloud analytics to executives from Manhattan? In Utah? It was unlikely.

When they gave me a moment to relieve ourselves, I decided to scroll through my phone. I'd set up a date with someone over Instagram, Charlotte. Everything I was experiencing at this point was so casual that I thought I'd be fine finding someone in London to hang out with. I'd gotten a few messages, but one had caught my eye, and I was meeting her tonight. Pete and Connor returned right as I chose a conversation to start.

"Can't believe you get to live the high life, mate," Pete said. "We're all bloody married with kids, and you're still single. The freedom you have, man. Can't imagine."

"It's not all fun and games. And the stuff that is fun and games, well…nah. It's still pretty good." I said, smiling, ribbing Pete a little.

"Eh, well," Connor said, "We're all looking for freedom out here, man. A lot of people from our old school are getting divorced and moved to London. You remember Charlotte?"

"Oh… yeah!" Huh. The person I was planning to meet tonight. And I knew she looked familiar.

"Well, she's one of 'em. She was a smoke show back then, and she still is now. I'd get that if I could."

"We all would!" Pete said.

I looked back at my phone. No shit. Yeah. I smiled and laughed.

I totally had a date with Charlotte.

The date was scheduled at Sexy Fish in Mayfair, London. I showed up early, having changed from my clothes into a suit, a Giorgio I'd rented, at my hotel before going out again. While I waited for a table, Charlotte showed up in a long, stunning black dress with her brown hair pulled back behind her ears. "Hey Edward, nice to see you again." She said.

"You too, you too. I heard from Pete and Connor that you lived in London. You know, after we chatted."

Charlotte smirked. "Those two are jokers. I miss them. If you see them again, tell them I said hi, will you?"

"Yeah, yeah. I will." I said.

We took a seat at the cocktail bar while we waited to be seated. As we did, Charlotte looked me up and down. She was eyeing my suit. "Can't believe you can afford that these days."

I shot right back at her. "Same to you."

"No, but you left England! That's incredible. Made your money, right? And in tech, too."

I knew I worked in sales, but it didn't matter. I knew what I was talking about pretty much to a tee at this point when it came to cloud computing. Charlotte continued. "After everything you did at school, I would have for sure thought you would turn into a Hooligan or something."

I could only laugh. "I mean, you're out in the big city right now, you know? Congrats on that."

"Yeah," she said. "Thanks. I live in Notting Hill now. Divorced. Still have joint custody of the kids. You know how it is, rich family, and my ex was wealthy as well."

Sexy Fish was great. I learned that Charlotte had a housekeeper who was taking care of the children and that she was completely financially stable, even with four children. I told her all the stories I could about the tech world, still trying to hold back the craziest parts, but even without all the partying, glitz, and glamor, she still seemed smitten with my success.

We then headed to Mr. Foggs' Residence. Charlotte had apparently called ahead and managed to get us in. We chatted and drank cocktails until midnight, playfully flirting the entire way. As we left Mr. Foggs, Charlotte put her hand on mine, got close to me, and walked her fingers up my chest. "You know, now that I'm divorced, I can live out a fantasy of mine."

I arched an eyebrow and smiled. "Oh?"

"I'm thinking Notting Hill. You know, the movie. With a twist. You sound so bloody American right now."

"Have I really lost all of the accents?" I teased.

"Oh, no! No. Not completely, at least." She laughed. "But I know if we did something right now, it'd drive my ex crazy. I think that'd be fun. And I do really like you. You should come back. Live in the best city in the world. London. And you can visit me anytime." She winked.

I laughed and pulled her even closer, our faces nearly touching. I spoke into her ear. Whispered. "I'll think about it," I said and then kissed her on the lips.

CHAPTER 45

In the morning, I needed to travel directly from London to Manhattan. With my first-class flight and boarding information, I was able to jam past security and get into the Delta Sky Club Lounge. The one at Heathrow was spectacular. Terminal-side views, a full-service bar, and plenty of nice leather seats and nice carpets. I'd been to mansions by this point, and I'd talked with the financial elites in New York. Didn't matter. This lounge outdid every lounge I'd been to in the United States.

I got to have a drink before boarding my plane, taking this last moment of respite before engaging with the sales world again back home. I thought about Charlotte. She hadn't said a bad word about her ex the entire time we'd been on the date. But she had told me that she was interested in one-upping him. She was competitive, but so was I. As I stared out the curved windows onto the tarsal, I took a sip of the IPA I'd been drinking. Could I really live in England again? After all these years? Had she been serious? I didn't know. What would my life even be like?

My phone buzzed, and I fished it out of my pocket. My flight was nearly here, straight to Manhattan. Every other New York rep had been in Manhattan for a few days. I wasn't behind, but I needed to keep up with them. My life was in America now. It was time to get back to it.

No time to experience jet lag. I'd slept on the plane, but the moment I touched down in Manhattan, it was back to reality. And then my phone must've buzzed seven times with text messages from Calvin and Terrance. "Call me back when you get the chance!" and "Hope your itinerary's good and planned!" and "You have to hear what Yanni's done!" Oh shit. What was that last one? Calvin and Terrance put up with a lot of what Yanni was doing. What was so crazy that they had to contact *me* about him?

I picked up my phone and dialed Calvin immediately. "Hello?" he responded.

"Hey, just checking up; what's going on with Yanni?"

"Alright, the story's long; you got the time?"

"I'm heading towards the rideshare area right now; I have time."

"Okay, here we fucking go." And then he laid out one of the most reckless things I'd heard in a long while.

Apparently, two nights ago, Thomas and Cary had invited a bunch of Mantiss's biggest and most lucrative clients up to a party at the Mandarin Hotel. They'd booked the penthouse – a crazy expensive suite that looked over Central Park and the New York City skyline. They'd gotten the event catered with champagne, wine, cocktails, food, everything. Thomas and Cary were looking to impress that night. Yanni and Terrance also planned to attend, with the goal of strengthening relationships with our top customers. Yanni, for whatever reason, had shown up with three to four beers already in his system. Calvin said that Cary had pulled Yanni aside to ask him if he felt drunk, but Yanni didn't even recognize that anything was different.

As Calvin explained the whole situation, I heard Yanni's voice in my mind at that party. "No, no! I'm fine! I'm fine. I go through drinks like this all the time," talking to clients as though they're his frat buddies from college, thinking that he's generally well-composed while near-staggering through the party.

"I heard that he actually tried to tell some of the clients about his 'escapades,' you know what I mean?" Calvin told me.

"No shit, man. No way! I've never seen him do anything like that at work before."

"Yeah, well, it's the first time in a while he's done something like this. Terrance told me that Yanni grabbed a whole bottle of red from the table – must've been a cabernet or something. It couldn't have been cheap; it was in one of the most expensive penthouses in the state. He just starts slugging it."

"Off the bottle?"

"Right out of the bottle! I swear, that's what he told me."

Apparently, a bit of the wine was rolling down his chin for the entire party to see. Cary and Thomas immediately clocked that some of their clients were giving him side eyes and troubled looks. Terrance could see Cary's face contorting into anger. He was the first to storm over, with Thomas soon behind.

Terrance couldn't see everything, but he did hear Thomas and Cary absolutely dressing down Yanni and trying to shepherd him out of the penthouse. They were livid. Cary was the strictest, telling Yanni that he 'needed to go back to the hotel before he lost his job.' Yanni wasn't having any of it. He wasn't going to hang his head, especially with liquid courage in his bloodstream. He fought back. He stood toe to toe with Cary and told him that "he wasn't going to take shit from them." He still had wine on his collar. Thomas told him, "You're not going anywhere, and you're not going to make a fool of yourself."

And that's when Yanni made a break for it. Past Thomas and Cary, with everyone watching, he rushed to the elevator and started mashing the button. Thomas used his weight to throw himself on Yanni. He frantically fished around for Yanni's wallet and grabbed it. Yanni wrestled his way out from under him, and he slipped into the elevator by himself. Cary was there a second too late, and he banged his fist twice on the elevator door as it went down.

They had no idea where the hell Yanni was headed, but they did know that he wasn't able to spend any money with his wallet in his hand. They tried to salvage the party and get their sales back on track, but the damage had already sort of been done. It's not like they didn't make more sales, but everyone was on edge.

Then Terrance got a call. It was from one of the managers at a bar nearby that he didn't disclose the name of to Calvin. It had been about an hour since Yanni's outburst. The manager called Terrence to tell him that Yanni'd shown up at their bar without his shirt on. And apparently, he'd run up some charges.

The minute Terrance informed Thomas, Thomas felt up his pockets and pulled out Yanni's wallet. He riffled through all the cards, and surprisingly every card they knew about was accounted for, which meant that Yanni had been hiding something from them. They didn't know what. Either that, or he was just racking up unpaid tabs.

Thomas, Cary, and Terrance left the party furious. They split up and had to start asking bartenders and people on the street if they'd seen Yanni without his shirt on. Cary was noticeably uncomfortable and anxious that he was even out at this time of night. They entered bars and apparently closed out a total of six separate bar tabs that Yanni had opened. He hadn't been paying. On the way out from every bar, he kept talking about "needing to wake up early tomorrow morning" and how he 'couldn't believe he was on the streets at this hour.'

Eventually, right as they're about to head back to the hotel and hope everything blows over, they see Yanni brightly lit under a streetlight, stumbling towards a street corner. Terrance ran over and grabbed Yanni. He was beaten to shit, but he was pissed as well.

Cary runs over and immediately tries to call a Taxi. Yanni was speaking with slurred words, saying, "No… No!" And as Cary continued the call, Yanni yelled "NO!" and yanked himself out of Terrance's grasp. Thomas once again took the lead and tackled Yanni onto the pavement, causing him to scream out in a fit of pain. Cary then dogpiled on and pinned him to the ground.

"They eventually got back, but not without Yanni throwing a tantrum the whole way."

"What… the fuck is going to happen to him?"

"I don't know. I really don't know. It's a conundrum they're all in for sure."

"So wait, he's not booted?"

"He's still the best we've got. I don't know if he's replaceable, especially with how much experience he has."

"Jesus, what a shit show."

"You're telling me. He's still recovering from the other night."

It wasn't like I hadn't experienced events like this before; I'd worked in the craft beer industry, for god's sake. When I was working for the brewery, I met all sorts of people who all had different tolerances for alcohol. We'd had plenty of meetings with people who held their alcohol, though, and everyone always tried to stay professional, even at events outside of work. If someone in the beer industry did something like this, they would be fired. I'd seen it happen firsthand at least three times – never at Samurai Brewing specifically, but I'd seen people get in fights and then get dragged out of bars by their managers. It was fucking crazy the fortitude the tech industry had – much less Cary for tolerating his college friend.

Calvin's voice got peppier immediately after. I could tell he was kind of done relaying drama. "Anyways, how are you doing? How was your Middle East adventure?"

"Oh, it was awesome, man. Real vacation. Have you been to Israel yet? For your birthright trip, right?"

"Nah, nah. Haven't gone yet."

"Well, you should go. It's amazing. Can't believe you didn't take that opportunity."

"Yeah, I know, I know. I was a bit busy. I was on the grind, you know? Had to get a rock for my Jewish princess."

"Sure, sure. Well, when you get the chance, you gotta make sure your kids end up there."

"Yeah, on your recommendation."

I laughed. "Alright," I said. "Well, is the pipeline still looking good? What's on the verge of closing?"

"Ah, man. It's looking good, but once I take down the deals already in the pipeline, we're gonna have to ramp it back up again."

"Welp," I said, walking out of the airport, "once I'm back in Utah, we can hit the ground running again."

This Manhattan trip was short – pretty much a stop to catch up with one or two clients before heading back to Utah.

CHAPTER 46

I'd planned to meet up with Thomas and Ashley when I was back, so we decided to meet up at Masuri and talk about my vacation.

I showed up a bit early, which meant that as I sat down, I saw Thomas stroll in, looking as casual as ever. He looked the same as when I'd left. He didn't seem like he was stressed about Yanni or anything.

"Hey, Edward! Good to see you got home safely." He held out his hand, and I brought him in for a bro-hug.

"Thanks, man! Good to see both of you. You kept up with my vacation?"

Ashley chimed in. "I mean, I saw all your pictures on Instagram, so I know that it was a great time, at least. Looked amazing. Where did you go again? Just want to make sure I didn't miss anything."

"Ah, London, Petra, Jordan… Tel Aviv, Jerusalem. Stopped by Bethlehem… Then I went to Jericho in Israel…"

Thomas interrupted me. "Whoa, all that in two weeks?"

"I'm not finished yet!" I laughed. "I went to Istanbul, Athens, then returned to London, then got on a plane to head to Manhattan. Now I'm back in Utah."

"Jesus, and you weren't scared over there?" He asked. "I can't believe you went by yourself without any security."

"Ah, I was fine. Fun, even. Especially when I was whizzing in and out of the West Bank. That's a trip, man. It almost feels like you're in a Jason Bourne movie."

"No, no, I agree! It's just crazy that you got back in one piece, you know?"

I shook my head. "Yeah, yeah."

Ashley raised her glass and took a sip, looking me dead in the eyes. "So, how was your date in London?"

"Oh yeah! Nah, it was great! Got some good food in Mayfair at a high-end Sushi Restaurant…"

"Wow, sounds incredible. Do you think there's something there between you?"

"Well, sure. We both had chemistry, but there was this small problem, you know? It's called the Atlantic Ocean; you may have heard of it."

Thomas and Ashley both laughed. "So it didn't bother you that she has four children already?" Ashley continued.

"Hey now, *no*. It didn't. But don't get ahead of yourself now."

"All right man, don't fuck the help, and I can see what I can do to get you transferred to London."

I rolled my eyes, and Ashley rolled hers. Honestly, I hadn't seen him say it in front of anyone else yet; he'd just made references to it. I knew what it meant by this point; I had no fucking clue why he kept harping on and on about that shit. "I mean, I'd love to go…" I told him, "But not like this, man. I'm good here. For now. But I'm still listening."

"Anyways, we do have something to tell you," Ashley said. It was clear that she was trying to get away from the topic and focus on something else. But she did seem excited. She set her hand on the table, gesturing her eyebrows for me to look. Holy shit – she had a huge gold ring on her finger with a singular diamond. "Oh my god! Is it finalized?"

"Yep! We got the rings etched too. We were in Florence, Italy, a few weeks ago, and Thomas got down on one knee in a vineyard in Tuscany."

"Wow, congratulations! You romantic, Thomas!"

Thomas laughed and said, "Yeah, we've already booked everything. Dates, hotels, venues for the wedding and honeymoon. Ashley bought her wedding dress while we were there.

"Yeah, I'd expect you two to be on top of things, although it took you forever to get here. I thought it was never going to happen, honestly."

"Well, we're here, you know? We're here. All of us, honestly. We wanted to tell you in person because you've always been for us. You know. Through thick and thin. We appreciate you."

"Thanks, man. Much appreciated. Same to you, honestly."

"Alright, but now that you know, I'm immediately going to text everybody else in the group." And he did. He pulled out his phone, and Ashley and I laughed.

I got a quick look at what Thomas was sending to the chat. Every Mantiss Elite was there. He quickly snapped a picture of the ring and sent a picture off to the group. Thomas furiously typed in the chat. "Save the date, the second week of April. Florence, Italy. We got engaged, and everyone in this thread is INVITED! Our venue's in Tuscany. More details to follow."

As we continued to eat and drink, Thomas' phone probably buzzed at least thirty times. I took a second to parse what just happened.

"Second week of April..." I mulled. "Isn't that less than a month and a half away?"

Thomas smirked. "That's how we roll, man. All in, baby."

And we finished our dinners, Thomas' phone bussing at least ten more times.

CHAPTER 47

I drove home and looked out the window at the foothills of Salt Lake City. As I pulled up to my modest apartment – or at least modest compared to where I'd recently been, I looked back at the downtown lights and thought about how small Utah felt when you looked around at the rest of the world.

I walked over to the fridge and took out a beer. I sat on my couch and lit a cigar I had sitting above my fireplace. The trip, Manhattan, and the people I'd been with were all too much to handle. The world was so big now. How did I get here? How did I end up in the Mecca of Mormonism while at the same time witnessing all the lavish indulgence that Mantiss had to offer? Witnessing everyone doing drugs, having sex, and drinking booze had done things to my perception of reality. I'd never imagined when I was a teenager in England that I'd end up here.

We'd grown up working class, in the countryside, with my father being a cab driver in London. He worked far away from us and mostly provided for us while staying unseen, only coming back to visit our family every once in a while. I had a few siblings, and my mother looked out for us.

We'd also grown up Mormon. I guess that meant that moving to Utah wasn't out of the question. I'd fallen off of the religion pretty early in life. I was already rebellious by the age of eleven and I already wanted to leave the church, mostly to play football on Sunday rather than get lectured for three hours. However, my mother really didn't give us a choice. I was there until I was 18. I chose to leave. I'd always been a rule breaker.

I didn't live in a horrible situation; our father was able to meet our essential needs. However, it wasn't a fancy life – far from it, but I found ways to make fun. Football, cricket, fox, and hounds, cycling around the countryside, going village to village, heading to town on a bus to shop for sports gear, CDs, and Percy Pigs. It was those moments where I felt like England had most of its charm, in the simple acts of enjoying life. When we weren't in the house we were in the park playing around, and we'd often bump noses with some of the Pakistani immigrant children that lived across the block. We were the only British white boys around, so we'd often have our disagreements that would turn into fights. Both of our parents had to try and break it up. I often got a scolding.

My mother was swamped coordinating my family, so probably once a month, we'd all get dropped off at my

Grannie's for the weekend. God, that was bad. It was my mom's mother, and she was the most Mormon person in England. She lived on a council estate and also lived in a rough part of town, and always told us that if we didn't pray and read the Bible, we'd go to hell for sure. Every day, probably about five times a day, she talked about the next life and lectured me about how I, *me specifically,* was going to hell for misbehaving and all that. It sucked.

As the years went on, I could tell my mother was getting tired of England. She wasn't happy and always envisioned a better life for us. Our father was too busy to take care of our family, and she wanted something more, I could always see it in her eyes. Eventually, my mother got a divorce, and when I was fifteen, she and I took off across the ocean to live in America.

I hadn't had a conversation with her since I started at Mantiss – she was busy with work, and so was I. I wondered what she would think about all the things that were going on and how different my life turned out. She always supported me when I was working at Samurai Brewing, even from afar. If I were back in England, I'd probably have been living similarly to how I did when I was bartending in Utah. Going down to the pub on Friday nights, then back again on Saturday for Premier League Football. Meeting up with my old mates Pete and Connor had told me as such. It was simpler, but in some ways, I wondered if I could go back. The high-speed world of sales at Samurai Brewing and Mantiss was just a completely different lifestyle. I'm not sure I could live that life again.

Then again, I'd never been one to tap out early. This whole world, with Thomas, Cary, Terrance, Calvin, Laurie, Yanni, and everyone else in the Mantiss Crew – it was a challenge. And I was going to try to see how far I could take this. See how much I could sell, how much I could make, what kind of network I could build. I thought about my childhood friends that I hadn't been able to reconnect with – a lot of them just didn't pick up – and I wondered what they were up to. But these different paths, I could appreciate them and forge my own. At the time, Mantiss had seemed like the perfect place to trailblaze. Man, they were crazy, though. If I couldn't wrangle them in, maybe I could find a way to tame the bull.

CHAPTER 48

Despite being at the forefront of cloud technology, Mantiss did have *one* other competitor. Dream Team, a company headquartered in Boston, was doing a very similar thing to what we were doing. They were offering cloud services for marketing and sales purposes, the same as us. Same price, essentially. Ours was maybe a little bit lower. But they were visual, and we were data-driven.

We didn't do any direct slander, but we definitely fired our shots when we were in the office. They'd thrown shots at us and gotten on our nerves over the years. Everyone from outside the company was used to treating us like we were just rich kids, and while everyone at Mantiss knew there was truth in that statement, it didn't mean we were happy about that simplification. Terms like "fuckwads" and more childish, sane names like "nightmares" were thrown around when discussing them.

We were rarely asked about Dream Team when selling, we tried to be in their offices giving gifts before companies even knew we had competition, but when they did ask, we were asked to convince them that our support, systems, and security were better overall. And I mean, I had no reason to believe that it wasn't true, and they didn't either. It was a mutually beneficial ignorance.

Anyway, this all was to say that it started to become more and more of a problem as time went on. I'd go on a trip to New York, and I'd get more questions like "How is your product different from Dream Team's?" and "What can you offer us that's better than what Dream Team is providing?" I'd often have to point to the gifts we were giving them as "part of the relationship." Our presents were still working their magic. But Dream Team was still on everyone's mind.

And then, one Friday night, I was about to fall asleep when I got a text from Yanni. *Hey, can you give me a ride to the airport tomorrow?*

God, it was late, and he was asking for a ride at 11 at night. I still couldn't say no. I was free that morning, and I wasn't super opposed; I was just tired and wondering why he was texting me so late. *Sure*, I wrote, *what time?*

Noon.

Okay, at least that was reasonable. *See you then.* I sent and then rolled over and passed out.

I woke up at 9 and grabbed a coffee before heading out to pick up Yanni. As I pulled up to his house in the valley, I saw him hug his wife and kiss her goodbye before running over to me. It dawned on me as I waited in the car that I had no idea where he was headed.

Yanni opened the door and jammed his seat belt on. "Thanks a bunch, man." He said.

"Yeah, no problem. Short notice, but I'm here." I said back. "Are you going back to Manhattan?"

"Nope, nah. Can't tell you where I'm headed."

I gave him a sly look and pulled away from his house. "Sounds like 8 balls and hookers might be involved, then."

Not skipping a beat, Yanni responded. "Nah, I fucking wish. I could use some time off right now. Maybe spend some time with Christa? She'd do nicely." He said, elbowing me in the arm as I tried to make a left turn.

I rolled my eyes but took his words. "Fucking Yanni, never at a loss for words. Whatever. Can you tell me *now* where you're going?"

"East Coast is all I can tell you. There's a bunch of us going."

"Wait, so this is for Mantiss?"

"Yep."

"Then why are you being all weird about it? What are you guys doing?"

"I had to sign an NDA for this one. Everyone else had to too, but I promise I'll tell you as soon as I get back. Or when I can."

I mean, most things Yanni said to me were suspicious, but this seemed doubly so. "Sounds like Mantiss is going all cultish all of a sudden."

Yanni laughed it off like he always did. "It's good! It's a good thing. We're going to make a splash."

I shook my head and laughed with him. "Just update me on what's happening."

I pulled up to the Salt Lake Airport drop-off next to the Delta curb and saw about a dozen other employees. A few who I recognized, like Maurice, and a few I'd just seen around the office. Cary and Thomas weren't there.

Yanni rolled down the window as I pulled up and yelled at the top of his lungs, "DRINKING HOUR MOTHERFUCKERS! THE LAST ONE TO THE LOUNGE BUYS DRINKS!" Everyone laughed back.

Yanni practically tumbled out of the car. He grabbed his suitcase and started running towards the terminal like he didn't need to go to TSA pre-check like the rest of them. I pulled away from the curb. I needed to drive back to my apartment and it was mid-day. I had things I needed to do.

Not twenty minutes later, I got a call from Maurice. There was a cacophony of background noise behind him. "Everyone's going crazy in the Delta Lounge, Ed!"

"Where are you going!" I said, trying to cut through the noise.

"Can't tell you, man! Nice try!" I shook my head even though nobody could see me as I was driving back downtown.

"Is that Edward?" I could hear faintly. "Let me on! Let me on." It sounded like there was pushing going on. Suddenly, I was put on speakerphone. The commotion in the Delta Lounge overwhelmed the speakers in my car. "Hey Ed, how's it going!" Yanni's voice said, ringing through loud and clear. It sounded like he'd had a drink or two.

"Good! Good. Just driving home, you know?" I said.

"Yeah, yeah. Can't believe we're about to do this?"

"Still don't know what it is…"

Maurice interrupted. "I mean, I'm game to take you guys across the country, but what Thomas and Cary are doing isn't actually all that professional."

"Like you're professional, too, man," Yanni said. "I know it's an act. Seriously. This is about winning and getting deals. And I'm going big next week.

In the background, I could hear a bunch of commotion. I couldn't hear what they were talking about, though. So this was about sales, but nobody at that airport could tell me what was actually going on.

About three days passed, and I'd nearly forgotten that Yanni and Maurice were somewhere in Massachusetts. I was doing some work at the office, catching up on some prospects I was researching from home base, when I got an e-mail. It was an article – the headline read something like "Mantiss Crashes Dream Team Expo." Yanni'd signed the e-mail. *"Check this shit out motherfucker! Game on."* Holy shit.

My phone buzzed nearly instantaneously. Yanni again. He was trying to FaceTime me. "Did you get my message?" He said, his face framed poorly and the picture shaking as he walked.

"Yeah, yeah. I did. So you're poaching over there? That's what you're doing."

"Poaching with *style,* Ed. Poaching with style. We're just playing the game. Watch this." Yanni tilted the camera to show off the building. It was huge and had a wildly showy banner with Mantiss's name on it. Yanni then tilted his phone across the street to the Dream Team expo across the street. A bunch of Mantiss employees were soliciting outside and trying to get people across the street with signs and t-shirts. The strategy was working, too. People were walking away from the Dream Team conference and towards the Mantiss conference. "We got this last week, we've been setting it up, and we've hired a team to furnish this entire building." Yanni explained, "It's a pop-up user conference! All the fucking bells too. Catered and everything!"

I laughed and leaned on my laptop. Those guys. "Cary and Thomas set this up? They're there?"

"Yeah. They even got some more music acts to show up in Boston. Future and Post Malone!"

"Post *Malone?* Of course. Of course, they'd show up to that kind of event. What else would they have done?"

"I wish you could see how the Dream Team people are reacting."

"Brilliant. Brilliant! Are you kidding me? I would've shown up if I'd been invited. What does the CEO look like right now?"

"We're not going into that building, or the CEO'd have a conniption, so I gotta canvas out here. But you wanted an update, so here's an update."

"Hell of a fucking update. Shit, Cary and Thomas'll do anything to win."

"Damn straight. You think we don't do this kind of shit?"

Yanni was right; they were playing the game. These sorts of tactics were part of their plan. Force their way in. Made all the sense in the world but I didn't think they'd be so quick about it.

"Alright, I gotta go. Whale hunting never stops, right?" Yanni said, and he stopped the video call.

Damn right, I guess. Whale hunting never stopped. The tech industry was full of tactics like this, but not on this scale, and they didn't get Post Malone. I was sort of relieved I wasn't in Boston doing this kind of work, especially given the corporate sabotage that was going on. Cary and Thomas played dirty. They just had the money to play dirtier than everyone else.

CHAPTER 49

The wedding was a week and a half away. There were a few things that needed to be wrapped up beforehand, and I'd heard that Cary was planning some sort of surprise, but it still hit me hard that this was happening. I'd be jetting out to Florence, Italy for my boss' fairytale wedding. It'd been tough keeping up with the Joneses, and while I wasn't low on funds due to my work at Mantiss, I was blowing through a sizable chunk of change. I was, again, going to Florence, Italy. Shit wasn't exactly cheap.

I needed cash. I cared about Samurai Brewing, but my life was so much bigger than it was before. In the beginning, in order to get me invested in their growth, Samurai Brewing had given me shares as part of my contract. Divesting the shares would close up my relationship with Samurai Brewing, but maybe that chapter of my life was over. Maybe it was time to sell and reap my profits.

I dialed up Hal and he immediately answered. "Hey Ed, what's going on?"

I was blunt. "Hey, Hal. I know you're probably busy, but I'd like to divest my shares. Do you want to buy my shares out?"

Hal seemed surprised but also seemed on top of it. "Oh. Um, yeah, man! I get it, no problem. Cashing out, right?"

"Yeah, you understand. How quickly can we do that?"

"Uhh, I'll get my accountant on that right away. You know what we have to do, procedure and all that. Call you back in, like, two hours, maybe three, with a quote?"

I went to lunch in the meantime, picking up some bar food and a stout. Hal rang me.

"Alright, we ran the numbers, and you're set, honestly. How about 250 K for your shares?"

250, huh? Sounded good to me. It wasn't chump change, not by a long shot. "Done. When can we sign the contracts and the payments?"

"Next week? That work?"

"If it's like Monday or Tuesday, that works for me."

"Alright, talk to you then."

And with that, it was pretty much done. I went down to Samurai Brewing's office on Monday morning and signed the contracts. Hal looked at me and laughed. "Man, it's been good having you on the team. Best wishes. Keep in touch."

"Happy to have been a part of this." We exchanged a firm and hearty handshake. It was done. I had breathing room. I was back in business.

CHAPTER 50

When I got home that afternoon, I'd received another text. Always something going on. No, this time, I'd gotten a direct message from Cary. It was a group chat, but it was still from Cary himself. *"Bachelor party. Tonight. 6 PM. My house is in Deer Valley. Be there."*

I'd talked to Thomas once about this. I thought he didn't want one. I remember what he'd said pretty clearly, something like, "Nah, man. Been there done that. I gotta focus to make sure that I'm not fucking this up again. I don't need another weekend in Vegas with all of you."

I mean, he was probably right. Didn't want a Hangover situation with Maurice or Thomas stuck on the fucking roof. These guys weren't the best influence. I just quickly texted Cary back. *"Are you sure?"*

"Sure as all heck, man. If you're not there, I'm calling my assistant and canceling your flights. LOL." Strange that he was talking in such a casual manner. I couldn't tell if he was kidding, honestly. I hadn't even heard a lick from him since, what, the flag football game? But whatever. You couldn't stop Cary from doing what he wanted, even if his co-CEO, for more than six years, had told him otherwise.

Cary decreed it, and so it was. I scrambled to get myself together. All the guys I worked with showed up around 6. Nobody knew what to expect, especially because Thomas (and Yanni, for what it's worth) hadn't shown up yet. I pulled up at the ten-million-dollar home around the same time Terrance showed up and buzzed the doorbell. The door opened automatically and we stepped inside. After stepping past the foyer, we were greeted with high society shit we'd never seen before.

Somehow, Cary had been able to secure a Utah celebrity chef that I'd seen on TV and at food and beer events around town. He'd set out an entire catering table with, like, market fresh sushi (probably flown in, somehow), Japanese A5 Wagyu, Australian Lobster Tail, Stone Crab, and the list just kept on going.

Cary had bottles set out of Prosecco and Reds even though I knew he didn't drink that much. Behind the food table, there was a makeshift bar outside next to the swimming pool. I recognized the mixologist he'd hired from my days at Samurai Brewing. Honestly, I think I'd seen him around the Beer Crew a couple of times.

Thomas arrived late with a hand plastered to his face in embarrassment. He just shook his head and said "God damn it, Cary." Under his breath. Yanni was the keystone to the party and showed up about twenty minutes late. After crossing the foyer, he brought attention to himself immediately. "Holy shit, is this a BYU party? Fucking feels like it."

Cary eyed Yanni and walked over to him, chuckling. "Be careful. Don't party like you're back at BYU."

Yanni scoffed. "Yeah, if you're talking about how lame it was. Bunch of uptight missionaries. But hey, a hell of a fucking spread, Cary. You fly out today to get this Lobster Tail?"

Cary laughed. "Yeah, no. But everything here's pretty much the freshest stuff you're going to find in the state."

"Well, what other kinds of tail you got here? Where's the strippers, Cary?"

Everyone joined in on the laughter. Some of the employees raised their glasses to that.

"There aren't any strippers tonight, Yanni," Cary said. "We're flying out to Italy in the morning, so nobody's going to fuck off things for anyone."

"And thanks for that," Thomas said, clasping his hands together.

"Well, whatever for you two, what about us? You didn't bring strippers? To a Bachelor Party? Are you serious?"

Yanni yelled. Cary nodded. "We're staying clean tonight." He said.

Yanni burst out. "Ahh, fuck that, lame! You got all this sushi; you could at least have gotten us Nyotaimori Sushi. Just eye candy or something, man. Anything!" He said, bursting out into laughter. Nyotaimori. Of course, Yanni could just pull out that name out of a hat. And everyone laughed along with him.

Sure enough, there weren't any strippers. Not one. It was just boy's night, bacchanalia everywhere and laughter echoing through Cary's high-ceiling hallways. Everyone who wasn't still a 'good Mormon boy' had already had about three to four mixed drinks, just like in Manhattan. It was still a bit off-putting, as it was the only bachelor party I'd ever been to without strippers. Just a bunch of guys hanging out in Speedos and masks running around the hallways playing fucking *tag*, jumping in the pool, just basic shit, nothing crazy.

Finally, we all ended up in Cary's steam room, where the hot tub and pool were. Cary turned the heat up, and the place became near a sauna. By the time we got out of there, everyone was exhausted. All of us who had drunk that night were stumbling around and finding our way out of the sweltering room. One last time for the night, I wanted to sit in the hot tub. After getting cooked in the steam room, so I moseyed on over and nearly jumped in.

I woke up to two guys yanking my arms and legs out of the water. Thomas was the first one to run over after they fished me out. He took me by the shoulders and hoisted me to a sitting position. "Jesus Christ, dude! What the fuck, thank god you're alive!" He said.

"Huh?" I said, still recovering from exhaustion.

"We came back into the sauna, and you were face down in the hot tub, man! Hey!" he motioned with his hands to Maurice. "Stay with him for thirty minutes. We need to make sure he's okay."

"Water. Water!"

"Oh shit, yeah! Absolutely, man!" And Thomas ran to fetch me a jug of water. I must've drank a gallon just to make sure I stayed awake and alive. After the near-death experience, everyone was more than ready to leave. Thomas helped me up off the ground where I'd been sitting and looked at me solemnly. I could see the disappointment in my eyes. "Here. We'll get Cary to drive your car home, and he can ride with me back. It's gonna be okay. Fuck, man."

CHAPTER 51

I woke up hungover. No surprise, but I felt like shit. My phone was ringing loudly, and it felt like it was stuck on my eardrums. I slapped my phone on my nightstand with my hand and answered the call. "Hello?"

It was Thomas. "Wake up call, man! Flight's in two hours; are you on your way?"

"Fuck!" I said, now jumping out of bed, "Yeah, I gotta get moving. Thanks, man. I would have totally missed my flight."

"And when you get here, we need to chat."

"Yeah! Yeah. Gotcha." I knew what it was about. No way around it.

As I threw on some comfortable flight clothes, I checked my messages as a force of habit. One was from Cary – a picture of me and four other guys carrying me to bed with the caption, *"That was some party you guys threw! Thanks for coming!"* and it ended with a winky face. I knew he meant well, but almost dying wasn't exactly my idea of fun. It took me about a millisecond to realize that that wasn't the reason he'd sent me the message. He had some leverage on me now. Honestly, though, it didn't matter. I didn't give a fuck; I wasn't some Tech or Wall Street CEO.

I shot down I-80 towards downtown, with my only saving grace being that, in my then-sober moments, I had packed the night before. I rallied to the long-term parking and ran toward airport security one more time. Fortunately, I'd set up a Delta One ticket with Sky Miles from when I was still working for Samurai Brewing. The whole trip to the airport had taken an hour.

I beelined for the Delta Lounge. Everyone was there, and I recognized everyone who had shown up to the bachelor party the night before because they were all battling hangovers as well. All their wives and partners were there, trying to find out what we'd done the night before.

"So…" Terrance's wife said. "What did you guys do to my husband? I've never seen you all this way."

Another wife interjected. "I've never seen them act this way! My husband didn't come home last night. Are you sure everything's okay?"

Yanni came over to me and patted me on the shoulder, immediately filling me in. "I think a few of them didn't make it home last night. Slept it off in their cars on the way down."

I just nodded as everyone laughed it off. Everyone knew the bachelor party was good fun, for the most part.

And upon thinking that, Thomas approached me. "Yanni," he said, "can you give us a moment?"

God, here it comes. Yanni just raised his hands and backed away. Thomas pulled me aside to a separate table.

"Ed." Thomas wasn't messing around. "I know it was a bachelor party, but you had us all scared as shit. You doing okay?"

"Yeah, man. I really appreciate you all looking out for me."

"Dude. You almost fucking drowned. I've never seen you like that; you were face down in the hot tub like a fucking frog in a cauldron, man!"

"Yeah, I know. I'm just glad it wasn't game over for me. Thank you. I really mean it."

"We need an everyman, a tank during business hours and at bachelor parties, but in Italy, I need a groomsman. Edward the gentleman, Edward, the one who understands everything I've been through. I've seen it before, it's why I asked you to be my groomsman. We've been through hell together. I get you more than anyone else here. I believe in you; I just want you to be safe."

"I'm not planning on dying before the wedding, Thomas. I can do that."

"I know, I know. Let's just… when we get back, let's chat. If you need outpatient treatment, or AA, or something, let me know. Even with your salary, I want to do everything I can."

I scoffed. "I'm not an alcoholic, Thomas, I'm English. Alcoholics go to meetings. I don't."

Thomas chuckled. "English, huh? Always deflecting." He sat in silence, and so did I. I knew that my drinking had turned for the worse since I worked at Samurai Brewing. At least over there, it was beer. Now that I was living the high life at Mantiss, it was all wine, champagne, and cocktails, stuff that you could down like candy. And everybody else did, so I went along. But I knew Thomas was trying to keep everyone in check at the time. And it was hard to control these high-rolling salespeople. "Well, I'm here," Thomas said, pushing himself off the table. "I just want the best for you. You helped me when I needed it, I'll do the same."

I looked over at Yanni and the crew, with Yanni already pregaming the flight. He'd bought rounds for everyone, six champagne bottles. "Game on! To Thomas and Ashley, cheers!" he said, and everyone raised their glass. I looked back down at the table. We were all already drinking. The group then started shuffling towards the gate, so I finally mustered strength as well and headed out with them.

CHAPTER 52

We landed in Florence at about five in the afternoon and headed straight to Saint Regis to throw our stuff in our rooms before heading to Thomas and Ashley's reception. Everyone who wasn't tired from the flight crowded into the absolutely decked-out lounge, where there were already about three dozen bottles of wine and champagne from all sorts of family, friends, and business associates. We all cheered loudly and often, with everyone getting a chance to pat Thomas on the back and say congratulations. Ashley yelled over the crowd, "Dig in! There's no way we're going to get through all these bottles before we leave. We've got, like, twenty bottles in our room as well." Everyone laughed. I took it as an opportunity and drank with my co-workers until midnight. We got rowdy, but Thomas had gotten private access to the room, so nobody was pissed.

The next day, those of us who, like the day before, didn't have hangovers met for breakfast and then attempted to tour the city by foot. The first place we visited was the Cathedral of Santa Maria Del Fiore. As we all walked through the stone floor, I heard our footsteps echoing through the hall. This place was centuries older than the United States. The whole place had been what, built over the course of one hundred years? Passed over ten different architects or something? I'd read their names, Di Cambio, Giotto, Pisano, Ghiberti. And yet here we were, new money, pushing our way into wealth over the course of seven years. I looked at the ornate mural above my head. There was no way, Thomas, or even Mantiss would have this much of an impact on the world.

The second stop was Cantina De' Pucci, where we all searched for the miniature wine window. Terrance's wife was the first one to find it, and we all took a look inside. It was distinct, something that would have only existed in the old world, a port through which to *just* hand people wine. Classic upscale Italian food as well, old and rustic on the inside with beautiful views. Thomas had gotten reservations early, about two weeks ago for everyone at Mantiss. Thomas recommended the Cured Ham, but we shared some Lonzino, Cured Ham, Porchetta, Capocollo, and Tuscan Salami as well. I finished off with a spaghetti carbonara.

The last place we stopped by was the Rasputin Cocktail Bar, a small and hard-to-find upscale lounge. Brick above the bar so it looks like you're really experiencing the underground old side of Italy, even though they'd adapted to the times with their cocktail list. The others ordered Cezannes, Thaulows, Henris, and Vesper Martinis, but I took a Redivivus, something I knew I wouldn't get often. A smoky scotch cocktail with Naked Grouse, Laphroaig Ten Years, orange curacao, pineapple, and coriander syrup. Served with a crémant and egg white. The classiest drinks you could find in Italy. We all cheered again but savored our drinks this time as we all planned the Wine Tour for tomorrow under the influence of the most delicious beverages any of us had downed.

CHAPTER 53

The wine tour Thomas and Ashley had planned was to Barone Risacoli, a wild castle out in the countryside with forests behind it and acres of vineyards surrounding it. We'd gotten a private tour, so we were able to wander the halls of the castle and tour the towers and outer walls.

The rest of the crew walked ahead of me when we got to the courtyard but I wanted to take a second. Truly let the atmosphere sink in completely. Courtney looked back and didn't turn around but started walking slowly enough for me to catch up to her. "Impossible, isn't it? Or at least to a Utahn."

"Yeah. Only Thomas and Ashley would find a wine castle out in the middle of nowhere."

Courtney laughed at my comment. "I guess I just didn't know what to expect. Such a fairytale, you know? The modern world isn't like this at all. I wonder what kind of

I nodded. Courtney smiled. "So, groomsman, right?" She puffed out an exhausted sigh.

"Yeah, yeah. I'm not really nervous, though. I'm just excited for them to finally tie the knot after all this time. And you're a bridesmaid, right? How's that working out?"

"Well, okay, I guess. I'm excited, too; I just don't have your resolve, honestly. I'm a little bit worried. Not too much. I'm just jealous of Ashley, you know?"

I looked out over the vineyard. "Well, at least we're going to be in Tuscany with them, you know? After all this craziness, it'll finally be a day to relax, honestly. This can't be more stressful than work, right?"

Courtney laughed. "Cheers to that – oh, my god!" She pointed ahead and noted that the group was turning a corner. "Maybe not! We gotta run!" And we sprinted through the courtyard, trying not to lose the group, laughing the whole time.

We all spent the reception at the Grand Hotel Baglioni, drinking wines on the rooftop patio and looking out at the entire city of Florence. New-world partying in one of the most beautiful and old-world countries I'd ever been in. It beat New York by a mile. By midnight nobody was done partying, so we all decided to hit up an Irish Pub and drank until three in the morning. As our crew stumbled back, Yanni put his shoulder on mine drunkenly. "Dude, DUDE! They have a McDonalds here! I'm so fucking hungry. We have to go."

I grabbed my face and laughed loudly. "That's gotta be a crime. A thousand miles and tens of thousands of dollars to go to an Italian McDonalds?"

"I don't fucking care. I'm going in. I just drank… five glasses of beer now? I need this." And Yanni was off to wander the streets of Italy in search of a burger. What a guy. Oldest world, and he wanted to indulge in the world's shittiest comfort food. I guess I understood now why everyone was numb to his antics, he was just like this all the time.

CHAPTER 54

The day of the wedding. I woke up at ten with a major headache, but I was able to pull myself together in an hour. The lobby below was jovial, with everyone at Mantiss dressed more to the nines than I'd ever seen them. Yanni was wearing a *suit*. It was like the party had been going on since yesterday; everyone was drinking negronis and Italian Wine. Thomas had arranged a limo for the groomsman and Ashley had her own for the bridesmaid. Me and Courtney boarded our cars and everyone headed to the wedding early to take pictures.

As we arrived, everyone just stared in awe. On the drive up to the Chateau, I noticed the beautiful cobblestone road we rode up and the lush green countryside that surrounded it. We got out and as everyone took their pictures, Courtney and I walked into the vineyards to chat. "So," Courtney said, "Impressed? Nervous yet?"

"Nope! Not one bit, honestly. I expected to have some jitters, honestly. None at all."

"Alright, mister." She said, slugging my arm and then grabbing my hand. Wait, what? It took me by surprise for sure, but Courtney seemed taken aback as well by her sudden bout of confidence. We both stood up against each other for a solid fifteen seconds, both of us nearly paralyzed. She looked up at me, moving her eyes away, but she touched my chest. "I know it's just romantic here, it's Italy." She said, speaking slowly, turning her eyes upwards. "But Thomas and Ashley can't be the only ones having fun tonight, right?"

I huffed out a quick laugh. "I like your style, but let's not mess up each other's outfits. We're front and center; we have to look our best for them."

Courtney pulled me closer and pecked me on the cheek. She took a heavy breath. "It's not up to them what we look like. I want to have fun." And then she pressed her lips against mine. I was happy to reconcile. We took each other and made out for a while, trying to get the romance out of our systems before the wedding. And then we pulled ourselves away, still with a little romance left over. But it was time to go. I wiped her lipstick off of my mouth, and we both laughed.

The wedding was the most traditional wedding I'd ever seen in my life. Picturesque, right up overlooking another vineyard, exactly like every movie ever filmed, right down to the words, but I know that Thomas meant it. He, more than anyone here, was devoted to this. "For richer, for poorer," where everyone tried not to laugh – how was Thomas going to blow all of his money? "In sickness and in health, to love and to cherish…" all of that. And he was stern and strong the whole time. Everyone else I saw at the wedding was messing around with each other back home. But I'd never seen Thomas do that. I couldn't imagine it. What was he hiding? Was he hiding anything? It didn't seem like he could, not right now.

We left the vineyard and walked back towards our cars. The reception was the night before; they were just tying the knot. "Hey!" Thomas' voice appeared behind me. He looked miffed. "Why the fuck have I been telling you all this if you aren't going to listen?"

"What?"

"Ashley told me about Courtney."

"Oh, about *Courtney?* She knew that soon? You're giving me your little spiel about the help, right?" Thomas loosened his look but was still staring daggers at me. I tried not to roll my eyes. "She doesn't even work at Mantiss anymore, remember? She's just Ashley's friend, I think she's still in tech, but it's none of your business."

He had to think about it for a second. "Oh, fuck. Right. Okay. Fine. Sorry, it's hard to keep track of all this."

I sighed. "It's your wedding, man. I get it. Focus on that." I gave him finger guns, and after a second of contemplation, he shot finger guns right back at me. "Okay. Have a good time."

On the last day, almost everyone left, but Thomas, Ashley, Courtney, and a few others stayed behind for a few extra hours. We picked up dinner at Buca Lapi, another classic Italian architectural underground-looking building, before our flight the next morning. Ashley was giving me looks the whole time that I didn't necessarily appreciate, but Courtney took my hand the whole time, and I felt better. Thomas had his mouth pushed to the side the entire meal.

Courtney and I took a walk away afterward and ended up at the Arts Inn, a cocktail bar. We just sat mostly in silence, taking in the calming atmosphere after a whirlwind of a wedding.

As we walked out, Courtney turned back towards me. "Well, this is it, then, right? A near-fling in Italy. Just like every trip to Europe, huh?"

"It doesn't have to end."

Courtney laughed. "I guess you're right. Utah isn't the same, but… this was fun. I'd love to hang out with you again sometime."

"I'd love to do it again too. A gentleman's promise?" I said, holding out my hand.

Courtney rolled her eyes and grinned. "Ah, go to hell. Just be yourself when you get home. It'll be enough for me."

I just looked at her for a minute. In the darkness of the Italian sky, it all seemed too good to be true. I took her and kissed her one last time. "See you in Utah," I said.

"Yeah, see you too," Courtney responded, right before walking away.

CHAPTER 55

Ever since the Annual User's Conference, I hadn't stopped mulling over how calm and collected Thomas and Cary had been while still knowing their plan was showing cracks. So it was even more surprising when their star child, the one with the third most shares in the company, shared a cryptic message on Facebook saying that he was "worried his house was going to burn down." Picture and everything. Yanni never posted anything negative on his feed, so this was a warning shot. To who? Maybe the rest of the company, perhaps every other tech company in the valley, maybe just me and him, but I knew something bigger was happening when I saw that post. I needed to talk to him.

We arranged to meet closer to his place, at MEND, as I had with Terrance previously. I told him to book us a seat somewhere quieter, in a place where nobody could hear us. As I walked in, the lights were dimmed like any other upscale bar in town, and Yanni was in the corner with a glass of Moscow Mule sitting right next to him. Nothing festive, just plain and simple. His head was in his hand, and his eyes were glued to the table. He was tapping his fingers anxiously on the wood. Something was immensely wrong.

As I approached the table, Yanni's eyes turned to me and he jumped up, but I'd already seen him downtrodden. His whole happy demeanor, his man-hug, his charm, it was all off base. "What's up, Ed? Haven't seen you in a while!"

"Ah, nothing, man. Just evading the cops, you know?"

Yanni scoffed. "Hey, it's no rose garden over here, either, let me tell you." He obviously didn't know what I'd been through. Maybe Thomas and Cary would know, but I don't think even the Mantiss gossipers knew what the 'detectives' had set up for me.

I looked at the menu for a mixed drink to down myself. Yanni didn't say anything else. He just shifted his eyes from left to right. Fuck. I had to set the menu down. "So." I started.

"Yeah, so, huh." He responded.

"Everything alright over at Mantiss?"

"Pffft… you know?" Yanni waved his hand. "Everyone knows what's happening. We're tightrope walking over the Grand Canyon over here. Running, basically. You think if the New York crew knows what's going on with Laurie that everyone else in the company doesn't fucking know? Our IPO is supposed to go through in a few *months,* and this all drops. We all have shares in the company. It affects everyone in the god-damn business!"

"You're just spilling all the beans, just like that."

"You already fucking know, man. I have multiple horses in this race. We all do. It's a shit show, I'm not going to lie. Your investigation and Laurie and her crew's whole… hunt… It's a problem, man. The whole industry is on thin ice right now. I'm not going to pretend like I'm not on the edge of my fucking seat every day, Ed!"

"Well, you sounded like it was just my problem at the Annual User's Conference."

"I don't know, man, I don't know." He said, sighing heavily. "The whole case, it's got the entire company piss scared. Thomas and Cary are trying to hold up until we get out of the woods next month, but, like, they can't let investors know about this."

I squinted. "Is that, like, illegal?"

"I'm not sure! I know what I know. That's all we can do, right? But I don't think I've ever seen Thomas this angry. He doesn't talk to anyone these days and his face is like, permanently red, dude."

"Maybe it should be their problem," I said straight-faced. Yanni just gave me a solemn stare back. I did come here to figure out what all the panic was about, but after hearing Yanni talk, it seemed like he was more interested in the money. Not that I didn't expect it, but I expected him to be *somewhat* interested in my investigation. Or have questions or something. I chalked it up to the pressure of the sale, but I was disappointed. If Mantiss was going to throw me under the bus, then I sure as hell wasn't going to thank them for it.

Yanni just continued his spiel. "Whatever. Mantiss is supposed to be the big one, the one that proves that Utah can actually support big players in the tech market."

"So when you said the house was on fire…"

"Yeah, I meant it for Mantiss, and I meant it for every other tech company and conglomerate in the valley."

"Well, they can't be different from Mantiss, right? None of these places were run like a tight ship, right?"

"No, no way. A lot of them are worse than us."

"Then they'll all just try to sweep their incompetence under the rug and sell out before they're found out, right?"

"A lot of them already have, Ed. You know Couraa? They actually beat us to market. 6-billion-dollar valuation. Transit? 3.5. Same deal, they're public now. They're all rushing and now we're the ones that are behind. And then *this?* Are you serious?"

"So, Thomas and Cary can just sell, right? So, they're probably fine."

"Nah, they're worried too. Of course, they're not gonna show it, man! But we're trying to save face. We're also trying to get a six-billion-dollar valuation; a case like this could, like, halve that. Quarter that, even?"

"Huh." I mused. This whole situation was interesting. I thought to myself that I might be in a better position than I previously assumed.

"If this had come to light before, maybe we could have solved it before going public. After that, we would have already been able to sell our shares. Laurie knew what she was doing. Either way, it's getting hairy out there. You better be careful out."

I swirled my drink. "One has to be. But I also didn't realize I held so many chips."

Yanni squinted right back at me. "What is that supposed to mean?"

"Well, if this eventually goes to court, then maybe I could just let everyone know how fucked Mantiss is, you know? I know you all have some trade secrets."

Yanni sighed. "Listen, I do feel bad for you. You don't deserve this, and I know you didn't do anything to Laurie. I worked with both you and her. I *know*. I have the utmost faith and confidence that you're going to win. I believe in you."

I did know what he stood to gain from this court case. And even if I hadn't seen him go that far myself, I knew there were plenty of women at Mantiss who could've taken him down for harassment.

"For whatever it's worth," he said, "I hope it doesn't come to that. We're all pulling for you."

"Save Laurie."

"Well, yeah. She's saying things about like, you being a stepping stone to Mantiss. She and her husband have been telling most of their friends about it."

That's when it all hit me like a truck. Mantiss wanted me to go down so that every other point of misconduct, everything I'd seen, everything they were doing in Manhattan, Utah, everywhere, would be cleaned. They would look like they'd squashed the problem, cut it off at the source.

Mantiss had celebrities going to all of their conferences and some of the largest private investors in the world. That's how they made their money, keeping their underbelly under wraps from their funders. And they were about to blame me for basically everything they'd done to fix that. If this whole case broke during their IPO, it'd be over for them.

Yanni finally set down his drink. "Well, I mean, I can't stop thinking about it, but maybe we could stop talking about that tonight. I need some time. I'm gonna go piss, I'll be back." He stood up quickly and left me at the table with my thoughts.

So. Billions of dollars, to everyone at Mantiss, that was what was at stake, huh? Laurie had definitely planned everything perfectly. I knew that she was aiming for bigger fish, that she'd pinned it on me first to have leverage against the executives with the money to defend themselves.

If I went down, then I'd fucking let loose. I already knew about their fucking skeletons. And they couldn't just get rid of me now, not with the case about to go public. It was time to face Mantiss head-on, and I knew that they were scared. Maybe not of me just yet, but they would be. They wanted to cash out. We'd see how that went. If they were under pressure, maybe I could squeeze them for everything they were worth.

CHAPTER 56

"All the world's a stage, and all the men and women merely players."

– William Shakespeare

Grant ran his hands through his hair and leaned away from his computer. "Oh, god." He bemoaned.

"What? Is something wrong?" I said, sitting across from his desk. Grant looked more pissed than in despair, so I guess that was something.

"There's nothing wrong, just fucking annoying. I think you're going to get charged soon, and that means we really need to start hitting the gas. And hitting the gas means talking with Mantiss."

"I think they – Laurie and her husband, I mean, might have made a complaint to Mantiss."

"If Laurie and her husband threatened to make a complaint, then that means that Mantiss will probably also want to know what's going on."

"They already know what's going on."

"Well, yeah, but they want it on the books. I just want to know if they made an actual complaint or not. Same reason. If we know, we can plan our next move accordingly. But these corporate fuckers are douchebags. I'm used to dealing with all sorts of defense attorneys and lawyers and all that, but these guys are pushy and egotistical, and they'll bite your ear off if you don't tell them what they want to hear. But," and he gave an exasperated sigh, "I need information too, so I guess I'm reaching out to them."

"Shit. So what's like, the timeline on this? Do you think you can even figure out if they made a complaint?"

"We'll talk in a few days. I just finished up my other cases and cleared my schedule for this, so I'll be available."

Grant was obviously in a hurry, but I knew that he was going to do right by me. "Thanks," I said, "Let's beat these fuckers at their own game." I got up out of my chair. Grant saluted me as he typed furiously on his computer.

About two days passed, with me simply lounging and hiding in my apartment. I felt isolated, but I was feeling confident. I had Grant on the professional side of things figuring everything out and getting ahead. I'd texted him the day before, but he hadn't responded.

Grant was actually the first one to call me. I answered and started the conversation. "Hey, Grant, how's your investigation going?"

Grant was not excited over the phone, but he sounded "No fucking response, essentially. They ignored me and asked me if I could 'pretty please' send them your account of the situation like they don't fucking know we're trying to protect ourselves. Like I hadn't even asked them the god-damn question."

"Christ. I guess I should have expected this."

"This is the dance you have to dance but I hate tangoing with these guys," Grant said, exasperated. "They pretend I'm a dumbass, I flame them, and then the actual conversation can start. They're a bunch of rich spoiled fucks for keeping me going through this loop."

"Do you think they'll give you the information?"

"We'll see, I guess. We'll see."

I went back to sitting in my apartment impatiently, waiting for more news. Grant called me again.

"Hey, I figured it out," Grant said in an exasperated voice. "I went through all this shit, took me like, a week, and got our answer, but god damn if they don't fucking blow bullshit out of their asses."

"So, you got the info, how did that happen?"

"I basically hooked them by just fooling them into thinking that I was going to give them information about you. Made it seem like I might be willing to cooperate. Plus, I only needed to know one fucking thing. And no, they hadn't made a formal complaint to Mantiss."

"Great, we've got the upper hand then, right? That's awesome!"

"Just remember not to tell them anything, all right? If they pester you *at all*, call me. Because I told them the fuck off."

"You did *what?*"

He just turned his screen and pushed his chair away to look out his office window. I squinted at the text on the screen. *"To whom it may concern at HR,"* it began, *"My client is under no pressure to give you any information regarding the investigation. We are both aware of the criminal investigation, but Mantiss is not entitled to my client's account until a case is established. Further requests to contact Edward will be ignored. Thank you for your time and consideration. Kindest regards, Grant Harland. P.S. Man becomes great exactly in the degree to which he works for his fellow men. – Gandhi"*

"Wow. Kindest regards, huh?"

"Yeah, they gave me what I wanted." He snickered. "They give me the fucking run around; I'll want them to hate me as much as I hate them. I think it worked."

I woke up the next day to the sound of my phone ringing. As my eyes flickered open, I took a look at the caller. Unknown number. Great. I shut my phone off.

Immediately I got another call. Two, I could call it a coincidence, but it wasn't the same number calling me. I silenced my phone again – only to have another person calling me. Something was happening. I picked up the call.

"Hi, this is Rason Law calling because we noticed that you might be in need of representation for an upcoming –"

I hung up. Oh, fuck. Another call. I picked it up. "Hi, this is Brown and Trent Associates, and we're calling on behalf of–"

This was sooner than I expected. Shit. I hung up and dialed Grant immediately, still getting rung up like the paparazzi was after me. Grant picked up quickly.

"Grant? Hey, Grant! I guess I've finally been charged!"

Grant laughed a little. "It's public now. It's about to be a shit storm, man. Stay in the eye of the storm, alright? At the center but completely clean. Mantiss is about to have some trouble."

It felt kind of exhilarating, not to mention relieving that I was finally charged. No more dodging police, no more of these silly correspondence games. I just needed to get to court, and Mantiss couldn't take me down any other way.

"There's a bunch of two-bit lawyers calling me right now," I said. "I want to keep you, but I know that it's going to be tough."

"Listen, you've got a day or two to scrounge up fifty thousand dollars. I know you don't have a ton right now, but that's enough to retain. We can get started as soon as you get the money."

I pinched the bridge of my nose. After all I did for Mantiss I only had 35k left in my bank account. I'd been trying to find work, but I'd also been trying to lay low. Plus, only half my salary was really starting to hurt me financially. I needed to win the fight, and I knew that Grant was the guy that was going to do that for me. I needed help.

"Okay, I'll do what I can," I said and hung up. I immediately got another fucking call. I turned off my phone for a second. No doubt my mailbox would also be absolutely fucked as well, and if they knew where I lived, no doubt the police, warrant in hand, would be arresting me as well at this address. I'd have to call someone quickly to get money. I didn't want to call my mother. But maybe…

"Edward?"

I sat on my couch, my father's voice on the other side of the line. I didn't know what to say. It'd been so long.

"What's going on, Edward? How's everything going in Utah? It's good to hear from you."

"Yeah, yeah. I know it's been a second."

"No, I know you've been busy with that business you're working for over there. Got your father's work ethic, you know that?"

I felt a pit grow in my stomach even though I hadn't seen him in over five years. He hadn't had time for us, but that didn't mean that he didn't want to see us or talk to us. And now I had to tell him about this.

"Yeah! Yeah." I said. "Listen, I have something crazy to tell you, and you have to hear me out. I'm so sorry to call you.

I spent the next hour and a half explaining everything, from the job to the investigation to Elliot to Grant. There was nearly no response over the phone the entire time I explained it, save for the occasional stressed sigh. I reluctantly asked him. "I know it's a lot to ask, but I need twenty thousand dollars. Do you have that sort of money right now? I know this case… is a lot.

"Well, it's a fair amount of money. And I trust you. I know if you did it, you'd man up, and take responsibility. Maybe even find a plea deal. If you're going to really fight this and if you say you're innocent, I trust you. But… it's still a lot of money, Ed."

"I did not do it. The company is fucking me over. I just don't have the money to protect myself, and I promise I can pay you back."

"I'm sorry we had to talk like this rather than under some better circumstances."

"Yeah, me too, Dad."

"Maybe after this, you can come back to England for a bit. We can grab something." My dad said. I think he was trying to end the conversation on a high note considering the circumstances. But the irony of him asking me to come back to England after all this shit had happened wasn't lost on me.

"You know, Dad," I said, "every day that goes by, I start thinking it's a better and better idea." He laughed. I laughed as well.

CHAPTER 57

The money was coming in late. Surprising, as I knew it was pretty close to the dead of night, but I couldn't do anything about it.

This wasn't good. I was on a deadline to retain Grant, and I knew it was strict – it was now or never. The attorney calls hadn't stopped yet. Everybody was watching me like vultures ready to strike. The warrant was out for my arrest. But I knew that there was only one person that could even come close to handling a case like this.

I phoned Grant again. "Hey, Grant. I've got the money; I just need to wait for it to hit my account. I've got the check."

"End of the day's coming up soon." He said.

"I know, I know. I had to get the money wired to me, I know. I'm really close; just give me every second you possibly can. I've got the money."

"If it's a check, I have to cash it in today. Make sure it doesn't bounce."

"Copy." I hung up.

About an hour passed. I was getting nervous. Two more hours and Grant's office would be closed. Another hour passed, and I was officially beginning to worry. I got a ping on my phone, and the minute I did, I rushed around my apartment looking for my checkbook. I set it on the counter next to my keys and scribbled out a barely legible check for 50k, ripping it and taking my keys with me.

I barreled down side streets, trying to make it to Grant's on time. Five minutes to go before Grant was out of the office. I nearly tore my car door off, trying to get across the parking lot. I threw the doors open and made the split-second decision to take the stairs up the flights to Grant's office. Three minutes. I jammed the next door open and ran down the hallway, almost tripping over the carpet. I finally got to his office and threw the door open, where I saw Grant and his assistant preparing to leave for the day. The assistant looked shocked, but Grant just had a cheeky smirk on his face. "How kind of you to show up!" He said, laughing.

I slammed the check down on the reception desk. "It won't bounce."

"Great," Grant said. He threw his hand out, and I accepted his handshake firmly. "Let's kick their asses." He said with a smile.

I walked out the door. As it closed, Grant yelled back to me. "You got bail?"

"How much?"

"50K Cash! It was 500K, but I negotiated it way down for you."

Oh, Christ. "I'll get it to you!"

"Find a way to keep yourself out of trouble!"

That was right. I needed a place to hide. I texted Hal, and I texted Dan. I received a text back shortly after but from neither Hal nor Dan. It was from Terrance. I looked at it for a second and called him directly. This was too important to cover in writing.

"So, the word is out, huh?" Terrance said immediately.

"Yeah, I guess it is."

"I can only offer my support in words right now. I wish I could stop the cops from grabbing you, but I can't help in that case."

"It's all right. I'll figure something out, I'm sure. Even if I go to prison, it's not the end of the world. Although, it's totally avoidable if I'm smart about it."

"Well, yeah, watch out for Mantiss."

"Yeah, Yanni basically told me as much."

"No, yeah. I'm sure everyone wants to know about Grant's adventures fighting the company. It's the most pressing thing on our dockets right now. You've got a warrant out, and Mantiss is going to be looking for you. Press you for information, you know. The whole thing."

"Jesus. And what happens if they do find me?"

"Deny. I know you didn't do it, but don't say a word to these guys. Deny everything, don't say anything. I'm sure your lawyer's already gone through a lot of stuff with you like that, but that's what we'd do at Mantiss if something was wrong."

"Something *is* wrong."

"Well, you know what I mean. Listen, I gotta go. I'll call you back later."

I clicked my phone off and reflected on the call. Mantiss was after me. I knew it, but Terrance had confirmed it. Hal was the next to answer. "Hey, congrats on keeping Grant around." He said. He was trying to sound joyful around me, just like everyone else. They were all pretending that I wasn't

"Yeah, yeah. He's the best."

"I mean, he's basically a Utah legend at this point. It's really good news if you retained him."

"Yeah, but I got a warrant in my name."

"Yeah… that would be the next thing. Listen. I had a friend go through a criminal investigation and a charge, and I don't want you to end up in jail for long. You need to get out of your apartment and stay the night somewhere. You probably can't even park close to where you're going to stay."

"Fuck… I guess that's true. Fuck! I don't know how long they're going to try to lock me up for this!"

"Maybe Dan would let you stay at the Beer Crew for a few nights, but after that, I think it's couch surfing if you know anyone. Stay as small as possible. Leave your car somewhere and try not to be seen. Once you post bail, it might be better, but you need to make sure you can find the money first. I think… I think that's your best bet."

"Well, it sounds like I better hit up Dan, then."

"Yeah, I'm sure he would be willing to hear you out?"

Dan told me that The Beer Crew wasn't at all busy that night, so I drove my car over to give him the rundown as well. He hadn't heard about my charges, but they were public information now, anyway. Dan listened to my quick summary while nodding his head slowly. He looked concerned. "Is this really what you've been up to these past few months?"

"I just need you to hold me up for one night. I know it's a fucking mess."

"I mean, after meeting all those guys, I believe you. All those"

"I still need to post bail, too. Fuck. Right."

"Listen, as long as it's not a lot, I can help you post bail. Don't worry about it."

"It's a fair amount, man. But if you can help, maybe I can get some more of my friends and family…"

"No, no. For a long-time friend, I can post that kind of money. The full amount."

In all the anxiety, I'd almost forgotten that Dan had started this business with his family's money. This was pennies to him. And I almost couldn't say no.

"Thanks, man," I said, a bit humbled by Dan's generosity.

"At the end of all this, I just hope that Mantiss eats dirt. Those fuckers coming in like they own the state and then doing all this to everyone they know, that's fucked up."

"I can't imagine my life is the same after this, especially after fighting these guys. The whole Utah tech industry is going to fall down, pretty much no matter what. I'm just not going down with it."

Dan chucked. "You're never going down without a fight."

"Yeah, I guess that I was destined to ruffle some feathers with someone. It just happened to be with one of the richest companies in Utah. I gotta cover my tracks for now."

"Well, I wish you well. Tell me when you need bail. I need to figure out how to

As Dan locked up for the night, I laid down on the couch, looking at all the old bourbon and cigars in the cases on the wall. My car was across the street. Tomorrow, another life started. Different from anything I'd lived in the past. Bartending was so far behind me. Sales were behind me at this point. I needed to post bail. I needed to defend myself. I needed to play the court's games, and I needed to prove that Thomas and Cary were backstabbers who played everyone in Utah like a fiddle.

CHAPTER 58

I woke up disoriented – I wasn't used to Dan's mancave as a hideout. I had tossed and turned because the couch hadn't been a wonderful place to sleep. I woke up groggy. However, it was an early morning. I exited out the back of the building, and I was able to execute my plan without a hitch – I parked my car far away from where I was staying and hit up multiple acquaintances I worked with at Samurai Brewing.

Three days passed. The police hadn't found me yet. None of the situations I was in were comfortable. I was getting rides from friends, traveling around Salt Lake City, and trying to lay low. I was sleeping on floors and carrying only a fresh set of clothes in a suitcase I had. Soon enough, it was Friday the 13th. Dan called me quickly and gave me an update. "Listen, I'm having trouble getting the money moved over and I know you need it in cash. I can get it to you by maybe 11:30 or 12 at the latest."

"Shit. I need it today, man! This is the last day I have to post bail."

"I know! I know; I just had a holdup because of the cash thing. We're good, I swear."

"I'm sorry. I'm just stressed; I'm sure you can understand."

"No, I get it. Come down to the Beer Crew, and I'll pour you one on the house as well."

"Okay, cheers." I hung up.

Grant called next. Just a neverending sea of calls. I picked up. Grant was quick to speak first. "Mantiss might call you soon, Edward. They emailed me a document with a 100-point questionnaire on the back of it. It's about the allegations and whether or not the state intends to bring charges. Fuck these guys. Fuck 'em hard. Remember what we talked about."

"Right, don't tell anyone anything."

"You got it. Bail's today. Get the money to the courthouse before mid-day today, okay?"

"I still have to wait on a friend to get me a lot of it –"

Grant groaned. "Listen, Edward, I got you a huge reduction on your bail. I spent hours trying to get them to agree with it. The deadline is today! If you can't post it, it's going to be horrible for us."

"Grant, I got it, I got it! My friend just has to get the cash, and he told me he's getting it by twelve!"

"Twelve? Edward, you have to get it to the court in cash, by one!"

I knew he was pissed because he was in a stressful situation too, but I was the one who had to pony up the money. "I know! Don't worry. I know it's a tight squeeze, but I'm on my way to pick up the money. It's not easy retaining you *and* paying my bail in the same week." I said.

"Right, okay. Don't throw it all away now, Ed." He sounded disappointed but also stern. Grant hung up. All for the better, I supposed. I needed to get a move on. I hitched a quick ride to the lot where I had parked my car and sped off toward the Beer Crew.

There was nobody at the Beer Crew when I walked it. Immediately upon seeing me, Dan threw the money in a wad onto the table next to a beer he'd poured. I scooped it up in my hands, grabbed the beer, downed it quickly, and ran out. "After!" I yelled.

"Yeah, I'll talk to you then!" Dan said, waving sharply back at me. I barely got a wave back as I threw my weight against the front door, running out the door and into my car. I threw the car into reverse and then slammed on the gas pedal. The courthouse was only across downtown, but I had less than an hour. I spun into the parking lot and rolled out of my car.

Bursting down the courthouse doors and going up to the counter, I set the money down. The clerk looked at me funny.

I must've been breathing heavily from the running. "All there?"

"Yeah, uh –"Oh, shit. I hadn't even counted the cash. I thumbed through it quickly. Twenty, thirty, forty, okay. Christ. "Yeah, it's all there."

The clerk tapped away at his computer. "Alright, well, you have to stay here while we get it processed, but you're fortunately on time."

"Thank god." I shoved the money into the slot in the window, gave the guy at the counter a salute, walked over to a plastic and metal waiting room chair, and crashed down onto it with a sigh of relief.

Another fucking call. But when I fished my phone out of my pocket, I was surprised to find that it was Courtney. I hadn't heard from her since before this whole shit show started. I mean, her call had to be about the case, but still. I picked up.

"Hey, Edward?" Courtney sounded concerned.

"Courtney? What's up?"

"Hey…" She said, pausing afterward to think of what to say. "Just calling to see how it's all going. You know, with the case and all that. Now that it's public."

"I mean, about as well as it can be right now. Not perfect. I wish they weren't kicking dirt in my face right now, you know?"

Courtney chuckled. "Yeah, I guess that would be better. I'm glad you still have a sense of humor about it. This whole thing's got everyone in a fuss. Another company just sold for ten billion. Luck 13 AI, remember?"

"Yeah, vaguely. Chatbots and whatnot? Can't believe they got an offer before Mantiss."

I heard a hesitation on the other end of the line. "Listen… I called you for something about the case. Laurie tried to get me involved. I don't want any part of this, but I would have felt bad if you hadn't seen this. I'm going to send you a text log."

"Oh – okay." My phone buzzed, and I received a video feed with a text conversation between Laurie, Courtney, and a few other women on Courtney's iPad. It started with Christa, of all people, even though it did look like it was from the middle of a conversation. *"Count me in!"* It read. *"I'm always down for some corporate espionage. We can totally get Cary and Mantiss from here. I can keep you two posted."*

Laurie had responded. *"Hell, yes! All are coming together."* There was a smiley afterward. It was very casual of her to

"Well, I'm glad I got out," Courtney replied. "Can we get back to planning the girl's night?"

"Yeah! We're still planning it." Laurie texted back.

"It's still crazy what you're doing… you know you're fucking with a pom, right?"

"Pom?" Christa'd written. I guess they weren't up on their slang.

"Aussie thing." Courtney wrote. "Knowing Edward, I don't know if you know what you're getting into… those Redcoats aren't pushovers…" She'd signed off with a slanted mouth emoji.

"This didn't come from me, okay?" She asked me.

I scoffed. "Jesus, I knew Christa was leaking info for Laurie. Damn it. She was the perfect mole. Always at the top. They want to get back at Thomas and Cary without them knowing."

"Yeah, it's a pretty good plan. I still want nothing to do with this whole scenario."

"Well, it's a shit show on all fronts, so that was probably a good idea. You know, actually–" I laughed, "I showed up at the Annual User's Conference. Christa was there at the after-party."

"What? No way! You went?"

"Yeah, unannounced and everything. Crashed their party. You should have seen the look on Christa's face. She looked like she'd seen the Grim Reaper."

"Well, I'm glad I stayed out when I had the chance. I'll let you know about anything else that happens."

"Thanks, Courtney. It's about to be a blood bath. If all those tech companies sold, there's plenty more that still need to sell, and there's a lot of money at stake."

"I'm aware, I'm aware. Stay safe, alright?"

"I've done plenty of that this week already."

"Alright." She said, laughing again. "Well, continue to do so. I think you can get the people responsible for all this if you want to."

"I want to," I said, laughing in the courtroom chair I was sitting in. "Trust me, that's all I want."

CHAPTER 59

I sat in the pretty much empty courtroom next to Grant. Two or three people were sitting on the bench, maybe there for their loved ones. There was silence otherwise. The judge took a second to find his papers. "Don't worry, this is going to be very short," Grant said. The judge looked lazily at his papers and began reading the charges out loud, laundry-list style. Whatever. Everybody who walked in here already made up their minds. "How do you plead?"

"Not guilty," I said. I looked back at Grant. He nodded.

"Okay then, a pre-trial will be scheduled and your first hearing will be held…" the judge started. I sat back down. The judge read off the dates. I looked at the plaintiff's security on the side of the judge's bench. They were dressed in the plainest uniform possible and both of them had beer bellies hanging over their belts, yet I knew they thought they were the shit. Laurie and Mantiss were dirty but in the most corporately sanitized way possible. This was the land of money, corruption, and strict guidelines. Even with all the evidence I'd gathered second-hand, I wasn't sure I was going to be able to play the court's game. And if I didn't, I'd be the first under the bus at the hands of guys like these.

Grant pushed open the door to the hallway, seeming casual from the speed at which he was walking. "Those fucks at Mantiss are really trying to put the screws on me, man. Fuckin' snakes," he said.

I laughed, trying to match his pace. "You'd never let them, right?"

"They're trying to force me to 'cooperate' with them, sending me threats like they'll sue and all that shit. You know, classic Mantiss stuff. Making themselves look like idiots."

"Well, let's let them."

"They have weight, though. They've got money. Any information we give to Mantiss makes it look like they're not involved and that if we're cooperating, it must be our problem. Honestly, serving them a subpoena might be worth it at this point."

"What do you mean?" I'd heard the term before, but I'd never been in a court case like this.

"Ask them to appear, get them to show us their evidence, and get their business records. It'd get them off our back for a second and it would drag them directly into the limelight. It's usually not worth it, but if they're going to treat us like this, it might be worth the trouble. They won't badger us for information anymore, at the very least."

"Well, if it puts them in the hurt locker, it might be worth it, right? They're now last to the party on going public and if the whole world knows they're involved, they'll be fucked. Not to mention we could maybe turn the tides back on them."

Grant just kept his eyes forward, still walking and talking with a purpose. "Once we subpoena them, they're going to be fucked regardless. If they have to go to court, they won't be able to do jack shit, let alone go public."

"They're totally trying to go public before all this goes down."

"We can beat them to the punch. I'll start working on it. The sooner, the better."

"Fucking badass, Grant."

I saw a woman at the end of the hallway where the elevators were, seemingly waiting for someone to show up. She looked like she was also in a hurry. Lawyer types. Grant spotted her and immediately changed his course to meet her. She looked back and greeted him with a handshake.

"This is Yolanda," Grant explained. "We're going to be working as a team."

Yolanda was really short, definitely a full foot below me. Black hair down to her waist and she had it pulled back into a ponytail. She was dressed to the nines, long plaid checkered skirt and a red top to match. She had a professional smile on – one not too wide, just enough to make you trust her without being fake.

She greeted me with a handshake as well. "Pleased to meet you. Hell of a case, huh?"

I scoffed. "You're telling me. It's been one hell of a week evading my warrant."

I'd clocked Yolanda's accent as Columbian, and she did look the part. "You're Columbian?" I asked.

"Oh, yeah, yeah. You've been?"

"Yeah, once. I also have another co-worker from there."

"Great, yeah! My parents moved when I was in high school. You wouldn't know the area or anything." Yolanda said. "Anyways… I've heard everything, but we don't know what they're going to say or how they're going to play this case. I think I can help, though. I'm sure Grant's already told you all the basics. But I can dig more into Mantiss when Grant's busy, and I can also look into getting anything I can out of Laurie, her husband, and her employer."

Grant turned to me. "You're going to have to hire her too, just so you know. But it's gonna be a two-person job to defend against everything."

I sighed. "More money down the drain. Those fuckers are bleeding me! Can I compensate you if I win?"

Yolanda laughed. "It'll be fine. I can hold off for a second. We can talk again soon. Remember – no days unalert."

"Robert Greene quote?" I asked.

"Yeah. Stay out of prison." She answered.

Grant laughed. "I'm pretty sure Robert Greene never said that, though."

Yolanda walked away, leaving Grant and I by ourselves. I pointed at the elevator door, and Grant nodded. We headed over. "So, the subpoena," I said, trying to get back on track.

"It's not like it's entirely a rose garden once we file this. We get the upper hand and cause a shitshow, but it's still going to take time for us to get anything out of it. And in the meantime, it's going to officially burn the bridge between you and the CEOs you know over at Mantiss."

"Fuck 'em. This is what Thomas and Cary deserve. Everyone else is just peanuts at this point."

"You say that, but you're also saying a ton of money is on the line, right? There's a lot of people in that company. Stay alert, stay silent, stay under the radar."

Right. I didn't think that Yanni or Terrance would do anything, and yet I knew they were on the chopping block next. I gave Grant a nod.

"And I know it's going to be tempting to want to go get more information, but that gets a lot rougher now that we're having a hearing and a pre-trial date, all right? Remember. This is our advantage. We can't turn the tables on them if they turn the tables on us."

"Okay. I think we should do it."

Grant smiled. "They are going to fucking panic."

I laughed. "Make them run around like chickens with their heads cut off."

As Grant and I got in the elevator, he got serious once again. "I'll fucking hand-deliver this nightmare straight to their door tomorrow. The pact's been fucking sealed. One last time to back out."

I shook my head. Grant then gave me a salute. "Let's do this."

CHAPTER 60

It was too exciting to wait. I paced around my apartment. Grant said he was going to serve the subpoena to Mantiss mid-day, and it was only ten o'clock. I'd woken up the earliest I had in months. This whole case had been a stressor, but finally being able to stick it back to Mantiss was worth being up at the break of day. I poured myself a cup of tea and grabbed a bagel from my fridge. It felt good not to have to stay outside my own apartment for the time being.

I had to tell someone. And I knew just who to call. I pulled my phone out and punched in the numbers as fast as I could. "Terrance, meet me at MEND in an hour. I have something big to tell you."

"Oh, shit, of course, man!" Terrance said. "I'm all for updates on this shit."

I threw on a nicer pair of clothes and ran to my car. Terrance had no idea about the nuclear bomb I was about to drop on this whole situation. Hopefully, everything was going according to plan. I called up Grant.

"On my way, driving to Mantiss right now, man!"

"Wait, you're actually showing up to their office?"

"I wasn't kidding, man. This is the biggest case I have. I'm going to hand-deliver this shit straight to their doors."

I burst out laughing. "Holy shit! Show-offing much?"

"Hey! Hey. Don't even get me started on the amount of show-offing you've done." He said. I nodded, even though he couldn't see me.

Grant continued over my car speakers. "I'll text you when the deed is done, alright? Have a good rest of your day, sayonara." And he hung up. I knew it would be a small event, probably just a trip to reception or to HR, but I could only think about the look on the rest of the tech executive's faces when they finally got the hard-copy subpoena slipped across their desks. I was sure the entire office would be thrown into chaos once everyone knew.

MEND was empty once again, maybe three or four others, but it was a weekday. I knew Terrance was on lunch, so I needed to be quick with conversation. He was perched on a barstool, scrolling on his phone. I took the seat right next to him.

"So," I said. "We're serving Mantiss a subpoena."

Terrance looked dumbfounded, unsurprisingly. "What the fuck? That's a fucking way to start a conversation."

"Yeah. My lawyer's on his way to the office right now."

"I don't believe you. That's it, and I just don't believe you."

"I mean, it's happening in the next ten minutes, so I guess it doesn't matter if you believe me."

Terrance looked at me again. "That's ballsy if it's true. Dragging the whole corporate office into this case."

"I talked about it with my lawyer yesterday. If Thomas and Cary and Laurie and everybody are going to treat me like this, I'm

"Yeah, Thomas. He's not been happy with you recently."

"Well, tell him the same. Doesn't seem like he could tell me anything to my face."

"Yeah, well, this whole case is mostly his project. All the information's going to him."

"Well, he knows it's bullshit, right?"

"Your case? Oh, yeah. I think he knows what Laurie's trying to do."

"I'm starting to think that even if Laurie hadn't told Thomas and Cary about this, Thomas wouldn't have spoken to me anyway."

"I'm sure he wanted to."

I waved my hand and showed off my middle finger. "Yeah, fucking whatever. He's always talking about how we shouldn't be messing around with each other, but honestly, he's done a pretty bad job of stopping it from happening if that's true.

"Yeah. He doesn't actually care, or else he wouldn't have said it like that, right? 'Don't fuck the help.' He's just trying to fix everything after it already happens so they don't get sued. Or, honestly, maybe it was just wishful thinking. Maybe he thought he could just change the culture over time."

"Couldn't even fucking bother to tell me he was going to go silent. I think he'd rather throw me off a cliff than admit that all this stuff is Mantiss' fault."

"Fucking jackass. Thomas was my friend. He couldn't help me, and he couldn't stop this whole situation from happening. Genuine cunt."

"Whoa, what the fuck?" Terrance said, looking around the bar. "Out in the open like that? You're just gonna say that?"

I grinned through my anger. "Tell anyone who complains that I'm English."

Grant buzzed my phone. I picked it up. It was a text and an image message. *"Don't worry, I've got your back on this one, mate."* The image was a picture of the Mantiss office and the subpoena, signed and on the desk of the receptionist. Holy fuck. He'd done it.

"It's done," I told Terrance. I showed him the text. He leaned back in his chair and his eyes widened. He ran his hand over his hair. "God damn. Signed and everything."

"We're not fucking around."

"You know the board is in town, right? I think the meeting's today."

"Today? Holy shit!" I burst out laughing.

"Yeah, no delays on *this* train station, I guess."

"Fucking, all in the board room, papers flying everyone, they're all sweating and they start yelling at each other… 'what fucker would do this?' and 'this is going to cost us our shares!' and all that. Serves them right."

"Best of luck, man. I do have to go. Can't wait to return to work today with a shit show on our hands."

"Hey, all I can say is I'm doing things my way. Fred Durst style."

"Mantiss is going to fight back. And Laurie is going to as well."

"Well, I can't talk to any of them. But if you want to send Thomas a message, tell him that Mantiss is the one who's under attack. And that I'm not going to let up."

Terrance just chuckled. He slid off his barstool and walked out, leaving me with empty seats all the way down the bar. I just sat alone for a second. I hadn't even ordered a drink. There were just the random sounds of the bartender pacing back and forth, suffering from the boredom of a slow day at an empty restaurant.

I looked back at the subpoena on my phone. My work at Mantiss had been done. Now, it was time to reveal their horrible mess to the world. Laurie, Thomas, Cary, Elliot, everyone… Those fuckers all thought that I'd just keel over. They didn't know about Grant, they didn't know about Dan, and they didn't know about me. The subpoena was just the beginning. They didn't know what I had in store for them.

"I love the smell of Napalm in the morning."

- *Lt. Kilgore*

www.ingramcontent.com/pod-product-compliance
Lightning Source LLC
Chambersburg PA
CBHW070404310726
48977CB00003B/549